Literary

THE **Hatchet**

MW00900076

Special Issue #9

ISSN: 1547-5957

MASTHEAD

publisher/executive editor
stefani koorey

short story editor
eugene hosey

poetry editor
michael brimbau

humor editor
sherry chapman

photography
shutterstock.com
dollarphotoclub.com
thinkstock.com
cover image by Ann_Mei

publisher
PearTree Press

contributing writers

natasha alterici
angela ash
navo banerjee
daniel bolone
bruce boston
chantal boudreau
adrian brooks
peter damien
eric dean
walter dinjos
holly dunlea
meg eden
a.a. garrison
lee glantz
david greske
john hayes
erik hofstatter
kevin holton
rita hooks
eugene hosey
rivka jacobs
alex johnston
phillip jones
francis j. kelly

vic kerry
nicholas r. larche
george lee
darrell lindsey
michael lizarraga
mark patrick lynch
paul magnan
rick mcquiston
fabiyas mv
nick nafpliotis
james b. nicola
denise noe
gary pierluigi
phil richardson
amanda rioux
rie sheridan rose
wayne scheer
david schultz
icy sedgwick
santos vargas
deborah walker
matthew wilson
robert wilson
brittney wright

The Literary Hatchet is a free online literary zine. It is free for a reason—and not because we couldn't make money if we had a price tag attached to the digital copy. It is free because we philosophically believe that the work of these artists and writers deserves to be read by the widest possible audience. We want the PDF to be shared and passed from inbox to inbox. We want to be as accessible to the greatest number of people, not just those who can afford to fork over some bucks to read great writing. We do not charge for any digital issue.

We do sell print copies of each issue on Amazon and through our print-on-demand partner, CreateSpace. Each issue is reasonably priced from between $8 - $10, depending on their number of pages. Please order your copies *today*!

We are expanding our coverage in this issue to include reviews and interviews—some hearty non-fiction to spice up your reading. The idea has been percolating for some time, and when authors Eugene Hosey, Denise Noe, and Michael Lizarraga all contributed pieces in one fell swoop, well, we knew the time was ripe!

You are reading issue #9, by the way. So if you haven't caught up on the other eight issues, you can do so at this address: lizzieandrewborden.com/HatchetOnline/LiteraryHatchet/

If you read something you particularly like, or are moved by, or think is cool as hell, write us and we will pass along the compliment to the author. If you have a criticism of the magazine itself, write us, and we will take your thoughts under consideration and thank you for your input. All correspondence should be sent to peartreepress@mac.com.

But if you would like to write *for* us, please submit your poetry, short stories, reviews, or interviews to our submissions partner at this address: peartreepress.submittable.com/submit.

We really would love to read your work.

Thank you.
Stefani Koorey

the literary hatchet is published three times a year as a supplement to the hatchet: lizzie borden's journal of murder, mystery, and victorian history (issn 1547-3937), by peartree press, p.o. box 9585, fall river, massachusetts, 02720, hatchetonline.com. contents may not be reproduced without written permission of copyright holder. the opinions expressed are of the artists and writers themselves and do not necessarily reflect the opinions of peartree press. copyright © 2014 peartree press. all rights reserved.

TABLE OF CONTENTS

SHORT STORIES 15 August 2014

TABLE OF CONTENTS

15 August 2014   POETRY

TABLE OF CONTENTS

REVIEWS & INTERVIEWS   15 August 2014

Sheets on the Bed

by
david schultz

Sylvia decided to wash the grime off her body before her husband arrived. With the key to the basement flat from the rental agency she was the first to enter. She threw off her street clothes and put on her old tartan pattern housecoat. It helped put her at ease although her husband called it a rag blanket.

She went into the bathroom with a washcloth and bar of soap. The shower did not work when she opened the faucets, which she accepted as a minor annoyance. She performed her mother's "cat-wash," standing naked at the sink she washed her body down to her knees using the washcloth, soap and running water.

A noise startled her. She quickly closed the tap, threw on the housecoat and ran to the front door.

She looked through the eye-hole. The person standing there with his back to her had a familiar blonde pigtail and a Senators baseball cap worn backward.

"Who's there?" she asked.

Seemy turned. She saw his face and unlocked the door. He entered along with chill rain and wind.

"Did you have to bang so hard?" she asked, pulling her housecoat closer.

"The light was on, but you didn't come to the door."

"I couldn't hear with the water running."

He walked to the center of the large one-room apartment; gritty debris crackled under his steps. On the wall ahead was brownish hand-lettering. He stopped in front of it to read the words. They read "Git yor ass gone or die in hell."

"Holy Christ, pigs lived here," he said. "Wonder what other goodies they left." He walked toward the cracked wall and entered the half-bath that lacked a door. He stuck his head inside and entered. The inner surfaces of the sink bowl appeared orange colored. He swiped them with his thumb, and then wiped the colored corrosion from his skin with the last sheet of toilet paper on the core lying in the sink. "Phew, smells awful in here," he called. "Wonder what else they left."

"This is all we can afford," Sylvia called back. "If we can afford it." She was at the bed, the sole piece of furniture in the room. On it was a naked mattress. On this was the cardboard box she had carried in from the taxi. She took three steps toward the half-bathroom and stood near the doorless opening so that he might see her from inside the room if he wished.

"How much did the movers want?" Sean asked, reentering the room.

"Two hundred fifteen."

"Dollars?"

"Of course."

"Cash?"

"We don't have any credit."

"Did you pay them?"

"Of course."

"Now we got to do the painting ourselves."

"If we do it."

"Why not?"

"We don't have the money for paint and the other things."

"I still have that Visa card."

"Using that can get you arrested again."

"Just a thought. Shit, painters are bloodsuckers. Like movers."

He looked toward the wall, above where the bathroom door might once have been. The outlined face of an animal looked down—a tiger, a bear or maybe even a clown. It was hard to tell. He could not tell if Sylvia was looking at him. Not directly, in any case. And not at that moment. She walked into the bathroom and absently tried to close the door that was not there. "No door," he said.

He heard pauses in the splashing from the tap. She was using her palm as a cup to drink or to spread water on her neck. The day he had left the previous flat, she was in the bathroom with the door closed, using water to relieve the pain where he had hit her neck and collarbone with his fists. Three days later, he had returned and learned from the legal notice on the door that she had been legally evicted. He had traced her to the temporary shelter. They had argued there while the guards waited them to leave for the eight hours of lockout and then they agreed to move into an unfurnished basement place, since there was nowhere else to go.

He listened to the tap water pouring continuously as if, he thought, she needed an abundance of cool water. She emerged from the bathroom. He looked to see if she were in some way refreshed or feeling better. He used to look for color in her cheeks. Or a tendency to smile about something. He did not see either.

"No phone here?" he asked.

"I didn't see one."

He assumed that she had not looked for one and his anger rose, but not enough to spill over or become visible. He knew how to keep it from view. He had done that all his life.

He saw her bare feet under the hem of the housecoat. She usually wore blue flip-flops. Did she wear them because he thought her feet were ugly? She had said, years ago, that her feet were sensitive and so she could not walk barefoot. As he watched her, he pictured a bird hovering over a dead branch covered by frost. She put one hand on the box that lay on the bed, but did not open it. The hand seemed old to him, even though she was only forty-three. He wondered if it was capable of moving fast, like the wings of a bird in flight. He felt a sudden sadness, thinking that he might want to accept her hand and its signs of age—a hand that didn't look at all like the hand she had presented when he put her ring on it.

He approached and took her wrist. She looked up at him for a moment. He sat down on the mattress. She did not move or try to release herself.

"Sit," he said.

She looked down at him.

He saw the marks on her neck against skin that looked as if the purplish black color had chased the blood away. He recalled the bright color of her blood.

"Sit, please, I'm saying." He placed his palm flat on the bed. He wanted to pat the bed but stopped himself, thinking that it was something one would do with a child.

Her body bent for a moment, as if to sit, but as she looked down at his hand she straightened up.

"You really hurt me," she said.

"I didn't know that."

"Worse that time than ever."

"You were bad, the way you carried on, blaming and blaming."

"No reason to hit," she said, sounding tired.

He took her hand and rubbed it between his two.

"You putting any sheets on the bed?" he asked.

"I wasn't going to."

"For sleeping, I mean."

"If you want."

Her hand moved toward the box on the bed.

"Sit, please," he said a bit louder.

"I can't. I shouldn't."

He rose and they faced each other.

He suddenly imagined he was outside the apartment, looking in at both of them as in a photograph. Was he doing the thing a woman does—seeing the members of her family together inside a framed photograph to keep them that way forever? A woman always put a picture on display first thing in a house. But there was no dresser or desktop here to display something on. Looking around the room, he didn't see a photograph anywhere. They hadn't ever had a wedding picture anyway, since he forgot to bring his camera to city hall all those years ago. Or maybe he hadn't really forgotten.

"Did you get something for your neck?" he asked.

"It has to just heal."

"It looks bad."

"It hurts."

They fell silent.

"You said you were going to go to see a doctor," she said.

"Before I left the shelter."

"Yes."

"I saw the one I saw a long time ago. He said I'm still the same. No change. He hardly looked at me. Just a little at my old records."

"Did you tell him about having the nausea all the time?"

"I didn't think of it. I just got mad the way he said, 'no change.'"

She shivered, slipped her wrist easily out of his fist, pulled the front of her housecoat more tightly to herself and held it bunched in her hand.

"Go to a different doctor," she said.

"With what money?"

"Money's not a problem if you're sick. That's why they have emergency rooms."

"I hate them. They make you wait."

"All right, so you wait, it's important."

"Maybe."

Why was she always trying to be the one to solve their problems? he thought. That was puzzling and annoying. Women were always ready to open a man's guts to the world.

The light in the room from the single fluorescent tube on the ceiling above them began to flicker.

"It needs a bulb," he said. Providing solutions himself always brought him some satisfaction, especially when she said nothing but just smiled in response.

She walked closer to the bed, picked up the scarf lying on it and tied it around her neck.

"Is that guy still around?" he asked.

"Who do you mean?"

"I forgot his name."

Her mouth tightened. "Phil? He doesn't know I'm here."

'You gonna tell him?"

Silence.

"Are you going to hit me again if I do?" she said.

"Are you sleeping with him?"

"He's not coming to Eugene."

His eyes narrowed. "You didn't answer my question."

"I did answer. I can't do anything if I don't see him, right? Look, he's still back in St. Louis. Betty told me before she went away."

"But did you? I mean before—when we were okay?"

"We were never okay for long. Do you think we were?"

"You make me so mad sometimes."

"You've hit me enough." She took one step back.

He took a cigarette from his jacket and lit it. He hoped the scent would change the mood in the room.

"Okay," she said, "we were okay for a month, from June first to the end of July."

"Are you always gonna blame me?"

"Haven't you been blaming me? And hitting me? Haven't you even looked at my neck?"

He paused. "Just tell me straight—is he gonna come here?" he asked.

"I'm not planning to look for him."

He walked to the heat register in the floor at the side of the room, knelt down and spread his palm over it. "There's no heat," he said. He stood up and zipped his jacket closed.

"Cellar apartment," she said. "Some cellars get heat, some don't."

"Way it is here, you can freeze in the winter."

"That's the way it is."

"I'll get a job."

"Will you? What kind?"

"Any kind I can get."

She hesitated.

"Don't you believe me?"

"I used to."

"When?"

"Years ago."

"We could have had kids," he said, taking a drag on his cigarette and spitting out a few ends of tobacco.

"You said you didn't want the bother of kids."

"You didn't object when I said that."

"I know," she said, sweeping some hair away from her face. "Would having children have changed anything between you and me?"

He paused. "Probably not. Anyway, I'm not so sure anymore." He walked back to the heat register, knelt and felt for a louver. "We can't live like this," he said. "No money. In a cold cellar."

"I can," she said. "If I'm not getting beaten up."

"With no money? What'll you eat?"

"I'll get by."

"You're crazy. How?"

"Go to work."

"What do you mean?"

"I'll go to work."

"You can't do any kind of work. You never worked."

"I worked when I was young—baking and sewing—a few shops."

She straightened the collar of her housecoat even though it was not askew.

"I can work again, too," he said. "Misdemeanor's expunged by now."

"You can, I know. Would you?"

He walked to the wall and ran his hand over some of the streaks of brown. He then walked to the bathroom, reached above the doorway and touched the painted faces. He looked around at her and smiled.

"I never painted walls," he said. "But once I helped my father smear black paint over his old car with a rag to paint it."

"You never told me that."

"No. He didn't want me to tell anybody."

"You're secretive too, aren't you?"

"We did it about midnight, so it would look decent when he drove South in the AM to visit his father."

"You were a better son than you think sometimes."

"I can find a couple of colors to paint the walls with."

"First the rent."

"Oh yeah. Sylvia—"

"That's my name. Go on."

There was the sound of rushing water.

"That's not in here," he said. "That's a toilet someplace else."

She walked to a cardboard box on the floor at the front door and drew out a clock. She went back to the bed and placed the clock upright on the mattress.

"It's eleven AM," he said.

She looked at him. "Yes, still early."

"You still like to organize. Miss tick-tock clock." He smiled.

"I like things organized," she said, and smiled slightly.

She returned to the front door, opened it slightly and looked out onto the inside courtyard. She returned to the bed and sat down.

"It's still raining," she said.

"Been raining all week. It don't want to stop. Typical Eugene."

He sat down on a corner of the mattress.

She looked down at the mattress space between them.

"I'm not pushing you to work," she said. "You do what you want."

"I can look," he said.

He walked to the largest box of the several standing on the floor near the door.

"Those are your clothes," she said.

He inserted his hand in the box and, in a few moments, drew out a cardigan. He removed his jacket, put on the cardigan, buttoned it and put the jacket over it.

"I'm gonna go," he said.

"Where?"

"To make some calls about a job."

"Do you know about one, Sean?"

"I mean I'll call to find out if I can get one."

"Oh, that's right."

He went toward the door.

"Don't you want a heavier jacket?" she asked. "It's cold."

"I lost it in the bus station, remember?"

"Wait, take a sweater."

She went to the carton and withdrew a ribbed seaman's sweater.

"That's yours," he said.

"It's a sweater."

He took it from her hand, put it on, and then went out the door, closing it gently behind him.

"Okay," she heard as the door clicked.

Sylvia remained unmoving, touched the area around her collarbone and winced. She walked to the bed and opened the box containing bed sheets.

Chaos

I have disrupted order
The measure of time I have altered
The faithful I have made falter
And made jagged, the edge of the border
I have made the strong weep
Stifled screams in the making
I have caused uncontrollable shaking
Made crotches spring a leak
I dwell in madness and pain
In fear and calamity I bathe
Tragedy is my other phase
I have crushed mauled and slain
My power is one of unrest
But for that I have no shame
Chaos is my name
Survive me at your behest

—santos vargas

Dirty Things and Imaginary Sunshine

I know that They are watching...
Watching while They crawl
Ever so precariously about,
Slipping slender fingers inside,
Dripping with disdain and darkness,
Imagining I taste quite ironically like ice cream
In the middle of August,
Slithering down a dirty arm in the moonlight.

If I fall, They shall see it...
Reaching with itching hands to
Swipe at the blood from my left knee,
And then waiting...
Waiting for the scab to form,
For it must go into Their deep pockets,
Already bulging with dirty things and imaginary sunshine.

I sometimes think that They have left,
Gone to find another race, laden with hope and love,
Only to strip them clean, sucking...
Draining away until everything pretty is gone,
But then I realize that I am indeed incorrect,
And I feel Their lips upon all that I am,
Eating all that remains hidden outside my bedroom door...
Until it is finished, and I am once more forgotten.

—angela ash

So Below, So Above

by mark patrick lynch

There's not much that can be said for the town. It's an old, weary hub in the north, into which drift the snows of the Pennines through winter, the rain of the grey skies through autumn, and the fog of the High Peaks on scattered days throughout the year. Beauty momentarily passes over the town in spring, when something wonderful marches down from the high hills, warmth and the first teasing scent of summer promises that will never be fulfilled. But mostly it just rains and the buildings and the people sag into grey blurs.

There are more glamorous cities nearby, filled with glitter and high glass towers. Cities that run to a faster clock and beat to a swifter heart. Only a motorway crawl away. Or a groaning train's course. Or a bus's interminable rumble and bumps.

Nobody ever looks up. Countless generations have developed stooped backs and the habit of following their feet with their eyes. To look up would dare ambition, would reveal the scale of the bleak, indifferent landscape surrounding the town, would suggest the ache of weariness after a long climb from the foothills to the summits of the mountains where only mosses and television masts grow, and where the sheep roam like flocks of boulders against the weather.

Besides, if you did look up, you'd only get rain in your face. Or snow. Or hail. Depending on the season.

This is the town, this is where you are. This is where you have always been.

There's a girl. She's called Julie. That wasn't her idea. Names so rarely are a person's own idea. They're given things, and it's only through a streak of determination that we shake them off, or else make the name suit our souls. Julie doesn't know the name she'd choose for herself.

She is drifting. She is becoming something less, or perhaps it is something more. She isn't sure.

Julie doesn't know if she is losing mass or if she is simply fading to nothing, so that not even the earth can hold her.

People pass through her, and this is a fact. She moves amidst the amorphous crowds with their hung heads and their grey coats and their drab, sagging expressions. A grey person walks at her, and for a moment merges into her. She feels like jelly being immolated, stretched and distorted around a point, as something more real, more certain, goes all the way in, punctures her, then leaves the other side of her.

She gasps and recovers herself, pulls herself back together. When she turns her head to see if the person that walked through her has noticed this, perhaps felt some obstruction in the grim northern air and been bothered enough to look around, she sees faint trails of colours, in a sort of clouded pattern equating to her body-shape, pulled out of true. The colours hang there before dispersing, beaten down into jewelled beads by the rain, washed into the cracks in the paving. They sink with the slush into the drains.

She thinks it is quite beautiful. And terribly sad.

There's something else about Julie. A number of "something elses," she supposes. Not just that she isn't as grey or as worn down as everyone else, or now sort of invisible (because she's always felt slightly invisible, that's the honest truth of things.) Primarily the something else about her is that sometimes her feet leave the uneven slabs of the pavement.

They really do. She can stand suspended on a cushion of air--most often when she doesn't know she's doing it.

She wonders if she is a ghost. She never considered there were, in reality, such things as ghosts before. She is from the town, and questions beyond the necessary demanded of daily life do not come easily to the town's inhabitants.

She is standing without motion, with her hands before her, on a street whose name she has never learned, because the street simply is and has always been. It's here and it's normal. Except she's Julie and she is different and turning invisible and people walk through her.

And then someone speaks -- says something to her.

She turns around, inching her head higher, feeling cricks in the back of her neck as muscles unused to this command strain and complain.

"Yes?" she says.

The person who spoke is motionless too. He stands amidst the passing crowd like an immovable obstacle. Although people snag the edges of Julie, pulling her out of true, distorting her outer edges, they walk around this immobile man, consciously or not.

He is dressed in town clothes, as Julie is. Clothes fashioned with simple cuts, without any flourish. There is colour in the garments, but it is not something that would make him stand out, just as no one truly stands out in the town. Everyone conforms. Everyone is grey, even those with colour.

"You are Julie?" he says.

"How do you know me? Who are you?"

"I was named Peter."

Julie frowns at this. He has told her something, but she doesn't think he has told her who he really is. Not his real name, the name by which he knows himself.

"I don't understand," she says. "Do you know what's happening to me? I don't like it. Something's wrong with me. Are you the same as I am?"

He moves closer to her without taking a step that she can see. He is not quite touching the ground. Their proximity reveals his age. He is older. He's in his middle years, but only just. Wings of grey are in his hair. His eyes are crinkled around the corners. But they are merry with something. Julie wants to call it life but dares not.

"We are all the same," he says. "Everyone in the town is the same. But not everyone sees that. They don't see that we're the same as individuals, that we're more than the cloth we wear, the jobs we work, the dreams we dare not voice. We are something more. We are starshine and the spreading frost. The lark's cry and the hunter's song."

Julie is unsure of how it has happened, but he holds a stick in his right hand. It's no ordinary stick. It's a decorated thing, little longer than a twelve-inch measuring rule. But it's a gnarly length of wood, with knots like the joints and knuckles on fingers, with feathers and strings of many colours tied to it, with pen marks on it.

"What's that?" she says.

"A symbol," he tells her.

"Is it real? It looks like a stick."

Except it's not anything like a stick, she realizes; it's something quite beyond its simple appearance. Since she has been standing close to him, none of the crowd comes too close to her. She has not been bumped or nudged out of her form.

"Then it must be a stick," he says.

She shakes her head. "I don't understand."

"No."

"But . . ." She wants to say something more. This is exasperating. Why can't she find the right words? Why can't she articulate her frustration?

"All this can end. If you want to, you can turn your back on it."

"How?" Julie says.

"Make it end. Don't wonder. Don't try and reach for more than you have. Accept where you are and who you have become, forget who you might be, and don't call yourself anything other than the name you've been given. Lower your head, keep your eyes fixed on the ground".

That feels like a sentence passed down on her, a judgement. In a way it feels like death.

She looks at her feet. She is not standing on anything. She is hovering a couple of inches above the pavement that is brown with rain, that flows and is slick and drab with the detritus of the tides of the sky.

"No," she says.

"Then keep looking up," the man with the stick tells her.

She takes a breath, feels herself lift higher, and then she tilts her head all the way up, as far is it will go, straining her skin, so that her throat feels tight, and she looks to the sky, where there are clouds and falling rain and where the snow comes from in winter and the sun might shine in spring. And it is so dazzling and not at all empty. It is rich with wonder.

"Oh my," she says, and almost lowers her head to ask the man a question, remembering only at the last not to do so. She keeps looking up. "What are they?"

"People like us," he says. "The people who live in the town."

She feels a tap, a knock, a rap on her back. The stick. He's playing a tune on her spine, the ridges beneath her coat, under the skin, the bones of her vertebrae chime and ring. She has time to think, this is not magic, just enlightenment.

And then she's floating free, climbing into the sky, rising to meet the others dreaming above this town, and she's going to tell them her name. Her real name. Who she is and has secretly always been.

Below her, unnoticed, her body, the person she once knew as Julie, turns around, and lowers her head, shakes herself, and walks into the crowd. She's one of them, one of the many, just another being in the larger vastness of the population.

Which is her true self? She cannot know, or dare ask, for she fears both answers may be true, and if she closes her eyes and opens them again chance may intercede and her perception hone in on one reality and she may be looking at a pair of shuffling feet crossing a dull and uneven pavement. And that would be the worst thing of all-- never to look up and dream again.

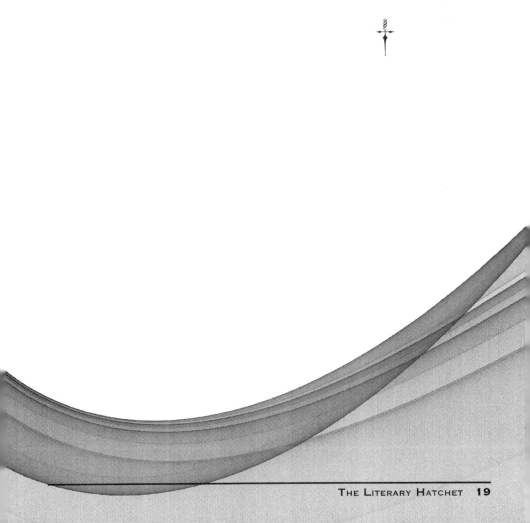

Beyond Memory

Memory plays 'hide-and-seek'.
Mind is a sorry seeker in this game.
A doctor prescribes to cure 'the void.'
It's a learned hypocrisy.

Words clash one another on Mrs. Pathu's
tongue and fall down meaninglessly.
Infancy is reborn in the wet
shade of her Alzheimer's.

Memory sets in her present
and rises in her past.
Intermittently falling beams
glare in her eyes.

She bobs up and down like the jetsam
on the waves.
Now, life announces
its retrieval in doleful tones.

—fabiyas mv

Without

liquid darkness

the world is

33 shades

of garbage

The bitter taste

of caffeine

brings me before

a God that

worships me

Divinity flows

through my veins

like holy water

Cut them open

Drink

—robert wilson

[short story]

Adrianna21

by david greske

TO: Undisclosed Recipients
FROM: Adrianna21

BABE...i guess your not getting any of my emails huh? ive been tryin to email u so many times but this damn laptop is such a piece of garbage and keeps freezing. In case u dont know who this si its ME Adrianna..we used to chat a bit on facebbook. Anyways guess what...I got 2 things to tell u...both good news..1) im single now..yup me and my bf broke up about 3 months ago..and 2) guess where im moving? RIGHT EFFING NEAR U...lol...ur actually the only person im gonna know there. im a super horny gurl too but every gurl is they just wont admit it...lol...so I love watching p0rn and all that...love sex blah blah blah...who doesnt...I really hope we get the chance to caht a bit either online or on the fone before i get there next week. I hope you remember me and still wanna chill and arent married yet...lol...if u are that don't matter much to me. k babe im out for now...chat ya soon...kisses xoxo Adrianna.

Skylar Templer had received the same email a dozen times in just as many weeks. He resisted the urge to answer, but he had limits and had reached the end of his.

It'd been six months since he'd had any release, six long dry months. The last time was with a pretty blond lass—although he preferred redheads—he met through one of those dating sites. That girl knew how to satisfy. Now there was Adrianna21. A lonely, horny gurl looking for a little love. It was time to make her acquaintance.

Taking a deep breath, Skylar read the email one more time, then let his fingers dance across the keyboard.

TO: Adrianna21
FROM: LadyKiller307

Hey A– That's unbelievable!!!! We're going to be freaking neighbors!!!! Sweet!!!! I'd luv to get 2gether with U. I kow this place, Revolution, it's freaking awesome. Great food and drink and best off all its really intimate. I can't wait!!!! B sure you let me know when you arrive in town. LK307 :-)

Skylar pressed the send key. He didn't expect a response. He was wrong. Twenty minutes later, his computer pinged. Skylar opened his email. A sickle grin curled across his face as he read the note.

TO: LadyKiller307
FROM: Adrianna21
Revolution i effing luv that place. i used to go there all the time with my gal pals when we were in town...lol...I get in town Friday night. My stuff comes on saturday, including all my clothes. If they don't so up I may have to met you naked...lol...woodnt that be a hoot...lol. HA HA! Anyway id luv to met you at Revolution Friday around 7oclock. If your lucky you might even get to see me naked. cant wait...kisses xoxo Adrianna

Perfect.

Ritual was a priority for Skylar. The night before the date he laid out his wardrobe. By doing so, hanger creases that developed while the clothes were in the closet worked their way out and any musty smells the fabric absorbed dissipated.

Skylar pulled on the navy blue slacks, the soft linen cool against his legs. The crisp, white Calvin Klein shirt slipped effortlessly up his arms and across his broad shoulders. He stepped into a pair of Prada loafers. Checking himself in the mirror, he rolled up his shirt sleeves to his elbows and undid the collar button. From the small table Skylar picked up the bottle of Polo from an array of colognes. A classic scent, it stimulated him and he was certain it'd stimulate Adrianna21 as well.

He took the wool coat from the peg and pulled it on. He altered the inside of the coat himself, adding concealed pockets and hidden pouches. These compartments held a variety of instruments—knives, scissors, nylon rope—and drugs that could kill or immobilize. Everything else Skylar needed—plastic sheeting, duct tape—was in the trunk of his car.

The one thing that would make a perfect evening was if Adrianna21 was a redhead.

She wasn't a redhead, but she was perfect in every other way. Golden-bronze hair framed her flawless, heart-shaped face. Big brown eyes seduced him with a "come hither" look. Ripe, red lips begged to be kissed.

Skylar walked across the dining room floor toward the booth in the corner of the dark, quiet restaurant. He took off his coat, folding it in on itself so his date wouldn't see the goodies hidden in the lining, and slid into the seat across from her. He held the coat on his lap.

A—he started thinking of her as that now—sipped on a cosmo. She had ordered him a drink as well since there was one waiting for him when he arrived. It looked like a bourbon and cola.

"I hope you don't mind," Adrianna said, pointing to the cocktail. "Most of the men I've been with like the taste of bourbon. I can get you something else, you prefer."

Skylar took a sip of the drink. "Not at all. It's rather thoughtful, actually."

She smiled, picked up her cosmo, touched the glass to her lips. She looked over the rim as she took a swallow, gazing into Skylar's pale gray eyes.

Skylar watched her drink, admiring how her throat moved as it accepted the beverage.

"LadyKiller307," Adrianna said, setting the drink back on the table. There was a smear of lipstick on the glass where she'd kissed it. "That's not your real name, is it?"

Skylar shook his head. "No, my name's Skylar."

"And the 307?"

"Birthday. Month, day. What about you? Adrianna21?"

"Adrianna, that's my name."

"And the '21'?" Skylar asked.

Adrianna leaned forward, brushing her fingers against his knuckles. "That's a secret," she whispered.

"And will you tell me your secret before night's end?"

"Maybe."

Skylar took another swallow of his drink. Cold sweat already moistened his armpits and groin. He felt it trickling down the center of his back. "You're so different than you are online."

"Aren't we all, Skylar?" She laced her fingers with his.

"Yes, I suppose we are."

They ordered dinner. Adrianna had no trouble finishing her meal, but Skylar barely touched his food. He found it difficult to concentrate on eating when his date had managed to wiggle her foot up his pant leg.

"So, do you want to go back to my place?" She licked the last of the whipped cream off the spoon, her pink, silky tongue wrapping around the silver handle. "After all, I live right effing near you."

"I thought you'd never ask," Skylar said, slipping out of his seat and slipping on his coat. The instruments in the hidden pockets clinked together. "This is going to be fun."

"Yes," Adrianna agreed, "it is."

She lived only three blocks from Skylar in one of the newer high rises in the neighborhood. Her seventh floor loft was furnished with a lot of chrome and glass. For a moment Skylar almost reconsidered his plans, it would be a shame to mess such a classy environment. Then he thought about dinner: how delicious her bare foot felt against his leg, how soft her fingers were when she caressed his cheek. He remembered the stiffness in his groin, how she was the cause of it.

"Let me take your coat and you make yourself comfortable," Adrianna said, touching the collar of Skylar's overcoat. He stiffened and brushed her hand away.

"That's okay. I'll take care of it myself." He couldn't have her finding his special treasures; that would ruin the surprise.

"All right," Adrianna said, stepping back. "There's a coat tree in the corner. Why don't I make us a drink?"

"A drink would be nice," Skylar said.

He walked to the tree, removed his coat, and hung it on one of the brass pegs. When he turned round, Adrianna stood at the bar mixing a cocktail. Her long, sexy legs poked seductively from the bottom of her black skirt. It'll be a treat to slowly strip the flesh from those luscious lovelies, he thought.

Skylar joined Adrianna at the bar and wrapped his arm around her waist. He kissed her neck.

"Ummm, delicious," she said, handing him a drink. "Let's go to the sofa."

"You have a lovely place," Skylar said.

"It's all right. So, how's the drink?" Adrianna scooted closer to Skylar, resting her head on his broad shoulder.

"Perfect."

"I'm so glad. Finish that one and I'll fix you another."

Skylar finished his drink, but before he had the chance to set the glass down, Adrianna wrapped her hand around the crystal glassware. He sucked on her fingertips, running his tongue across her red painted nails. He closed his eyes, knowing in a few moments he'd chop her fingers from her hands and enjoy their sweetness when he sucked the marrow from each digit.

Adrianna took the glass away from Skylar. "I'll be right back," she whispered in his ear. She slid off the sofa and walked to the bar. Along the way she unsnapped her skirt and it dropped to floor. "Oops," she said, stepped out of the garment, and began mixing Skylar another drink.

"I want to show you something," Skylar said, standing from the couch and walking to his jacket. He zipped open one of the interior pockets and withdrew a weapon from the pouch. The eight-inch blade of the hunting knife sparkled under the intense lights of the apartment. He turned around. "Tonight is the perfect night to die."

"What a strange thing to say, Skylar," Adrianna said from behind the bar.

"No. It really is a good night to die. Perfect, actually." Skylar took a step forward, the reflection of the blade creating a white slash across his maniacal face.

Adrianna looked up. The smile on her face disappeared when she saw the knife in Skylar's hand and his broad, insane grin. The drink she held slipped and the glass shattered on the bar-top, splashing bourbon across the white marble. She ran toward the door, but Skylar stepped to the left, blocking the exit.

Skylar lifted the weapon above his shoulder.

Adrianna shook her head.

Then the world turned black.

The static between his ears increased and eventually changed to recognizable sounds: traffic noise, the wails of a crying children, the pained yelp of a dog. His vision returned the same way: an out of-focus world changing from black and gray to vivid color. His mind was a little slower to react but when it did he realized he was strapped to the bed, his wrist and ankles bound the head and foot board posts. The mattress was covered in plastic sheeting as was the rest of the room. Skylar raised his head, looked down his naked body and over the top of his toes. On a black satin sash draped across the credenza at the foot of the bed were his instruments. Lined up from smallest to largest, the chrome blades twinkled under the bedroom light. His clothes were neatly folded on the chair next to the bedroom door.

"What the hell?" Skylar jerked at his fetters.

"You were a hard man to drop, Skylar." Adrianna walked around the bed. Dressed in a leather bra, thong, and knee-high leather boots, she paused at the credenza and picked up the butcher's knife. "When you charged me with this I thought I didn't put enough drug in your drink. But when your eyes rolled back in your head and you dropped like a stone I knew I had you." Adrianna pressed the point of the knife to her left palm. The steel dimpled her flesh, but didn't pierce it. "You asked me earlier what '21' meant. It's the number of playthings before you." She touched the blade to Skylar's scrotum. "You'll be number 22."

Skylar swallowed hard. He knew the blade, razor sharp, could slice through his testicles if the tiniest bit of pressure was applied to it.

"Why are you doing this?" Skylar asked.

Adrianna took the knife away from his Skylar's privates, climbed on the bed, and straddled him, grinding her vagina into his crotch. "For the same reason you do. It's fun."

Adrianna slashed the knife across Skylar's chest, opening a deep gash. Blood welled from the wound and formed a beaded necklace along the cut. She ran her finger through the gore and drew a red heart around Skylar's left breast.

"I'm a super horny girl," Adrianna said. She giggled, the laugh sounded like broken glass thrown across sandpaper.

"Please stop," Skylar said. The sticky blood from his wound tickled as it ran down the inside of his thigh.

"Stop? I don't think so. Now I just have to decide if I want to kill you fast and easy, or slow and painfully. And I've made up my mind."

Adrianna stuck the blade into Skylar's meaty thigh.

Skylar screamed.

A familiar tingle, opening like a flower, warmed her groin.

Adrianna pulled the knife through Skylar's flesh. Blood spattered the plastic like rain against the window as she sliced away eight inches of meat. The strip fell to the floor and coiled into a tight spring. She cut away another slice, then another, and another. Each curl of flesh plopped to the floor, painting red commas on the poly sheeting.

Skylar wailed.

Blood flowed freely now, running down the side of Skylar's leg with the intensity of a small river. Gore puddled on the floor, gathered in the depressions of the plastic, creating red ponds.

Adrianna shifted, grinding her vagina deeper into Skylar's crotch. The tingle she felt down there increased, the sensation spreading through her loins like mystical fingers. Adrianna closed her eyes and enjoyed the feeling for a moment before continuing.

Slicing through flesh, muscles and sinew, Adrianna cut a fat strip from Skylar's chest. She dangled the carving in front of Skylar. Blood dripped from the meat, pelting his pale face with big splotches of gore. She stuffed the flesh in his gaping mouth before slicing off a chunk of his cheek. Through the wound, Adrianna watched his jaw work as he tried not to choke on himself.

She cut off his left middle finger next, sawing through the flesh and bone until the finger detached itself from the hand. She picked up the finger, held it like a lipstick, and painted her lips with Skylar's blood. She leaned forward and kissed Skylar on the forehead. Then still holding the finger, she stuck her hand inside her leather thong and shoved the digit in her moist vagina. The cold finger inside her warm body made her come immediately.

"Wow, that was hot," Adrianna said.

Adrianna continued cutting, working on his right side first then moving on to his left. When she was finished, Skylar was nothing more than a bloody skeleton and Adrianna would've orgasmed three more times.

Jeremy Stone rolled out of bed, stuck his hand down the front of his Hanes, and scratched his balls. He padded across the bedroom floor and into the bathroom to do his morning business. Finished, he walked into the kitchen, fixed a pot of coffee and opened the blinds. It was going to be another beautiful day: bright sunshine and a light breeze. The beginnings of a perfect summer.

Coffee brewed, Jeremy poured some into his favorite blue mug and headed to his office. He booted up the computer. The machine's ping told him he had an e-mail. Jeremy opened the little yellow envelope at the bottom of the screen and the e-mail program came up. He opened the message.

TO: Undisclosed Recipients
FROM: Adrianna22

BABE...i guess your not getting any of my emails huh? ive been tryin to email u so many times but this damn laptop is such a piece of garbage and keeps freezing. In case u dont know who this si its ME Andrianna..we used to chat a bit on facebbook. Anyways guess what...I got 2 things to tell u...both good news..1) im single now..yup me and my bf broke up about 3 months ago..and 2) guess where im moving? RIGHT EFFING NEAR U...lol...ur actually the only person im gonna know there. im a super horny gurl too. . .

Jeremy took a sip of coffee then set the mug on a coaster. He pulled out the desk chair and sat down.

"This could be interesting," he said aloud and typed his response.

Beyond the Zone:

Anne Serling Reflects on Her
Iconic Father—As She Knew Him

by michael lizarraga

"There are certain blandishments that a man can succumb to, [such as] a preoccupation with status ... the heated swimming pool that's 10 feet longer than the neighbors'; the big car; the concern about billing—things that become disproportionately large in a guy's mind. [What become small] are the really valuable things, like having a family, raising children, a good marital relationship. All these things, I think, are of the essence."

—Rod Serling, The Mike Wallace Interview, 1959

Whether we were on Mars, in a time machine, wandering a realm or raising the dead, Rod Serling's messages on morals and social justice maneuvered their way into our homes, our hearts, our minds and our conscience via the vessels of sci-fi and fantasy, and like the quote in *The Twilight Zone* episode, "The Changing of the Guard," Serling indeed "won some victory for humanity."

Yet more admirable than Serling's artistry and convictions was his love for his family, his most cherished "Zone" of all, extolling the very same warmth and compassion that many of us felt from his stories and films onto his wife and children. And for his youngest daughter, Anne Serling, a unique and compelling father/daughter bond had forged between them that was as timeless as infinity.

Endowed with both her father's passion for writing and social concerns, Anne Serling is an accomplished poet, novelist, short story writer, and author of *As I Knew Him*, an honest and personal biographical memoir of her mentor, "best buddie," and dad, Rod Serling.

Weaving past the ranks of Rod Serling fans at a recent horror expo (Monsterpalooza 2014, March 28-30, in Burbank, California), horror writer Michael Lizarraga managed a chat with the daughter of *The Twilight Zone* creator, and since the publication of her book, Anne has been inundated by the many people sharing personal stories about meeting her father, how he influenced them in some way or to become writers themselves, and how much they miss him.

She was gracious enough to share some of her stories about her dad as well.

Michael Lizarraga: Let's start by getting to know Anne Serling a little more. Was it your father's desire that his little girl follow in his big footsteps as a writer?

Anne Serling: I don't know how strongly my dad felt about me becoming a writer. I always loved to write, and wrote poetry from an early age. I always showed my father my writing. If he liked what I'd written, he would make a big show of it and talk about it a lot. Conversely, I knew if it wasn't a great piece, as he would declare it, "interesting."

ML: You seem to have fulfilled certain roles that your dad had once set out to do. Where he had once wanted to be a children's educator, you became one. Where he once attempted poetry (what your mother, Carol, humorously called "some very bad poetry"), you've achieved this. Was writing novels, which you are now doing, something your father had once considered?

AS: I've actually never compared those parallel paths. My father did want to write novels and, in fact, was working on one before he died, but I never found more information on that.

ML: What does your personal writing regimen consist of? Are you an early riser like your father was, doing most of your work before noon? Do you have a specific way in forming a story or poem, perhaps borrowing techniques from your dad and/or other great writers?

AS: I get up by seven, as I find I do most of my best writing in the morning. I try to go for a run before noon, and do if it's not too cold! That's a time when I run plots, scenarios and characters through my head. I will revisit the writing again many times throughout the day.

I have always read my work aloud and recently learned that my dad did that too - even before he used a Dictaphone. I loved learning that, and knowing we had that in common. He was quoted as saying: "Saying a line through a machine is quite a valid test for the validity of what you're saying."

ML: Some years ago, you adapted two of your father's *Twilight Zone* teleplays into short stories, "One for the Angels" and "The Changing of the Guard" for *Twilight Zone Magazine*. What was it that inspired you to write these particular pieces?

AS: I liked these episodes and connected with them both. "One For The Angels" is such a sweet story about a salesman who wants to make one last great pitch before he dies. Ed Wynn was so great in the episode. "The Changing of The Guard" is a beautiful piece. My dad was moved by the words of Horace Mann, the first president of Antioch College (where my dad attended): "Be ashamed to die until you have won some victory for humanity" and he used that quote in the episode. It is the story of a professor (Donald Pleasence) at a boy's school being forced to retire, convinced that he has accomplished nothing in his lifetime and will quickly be forgotten. Thus, he resolves to commit suicide. But suddenly, as he enters his classroom, he finds the ghosts of former students who tell him that the lessons from his teaching are what inspired each of them to their individual acts of heroism, courage, and self-sacrifice.

When the ghosts depart, the professor realizes Mann's words do apply to him, and that he can retire; that he has left some mark.

ML: To say your father's work evoked social conscience and "a primary concern for the human condition," as writer Marc Scott Zicree put it, would be a major understatement. What do you suppose were the seeds that planted your father's desire to challenge society's ethics and values? Something in his childhood, perhaps? His upbringing? His experience in WWII?

AS: I think all of the above. My dad felt that prejudice was "our greatest evil." In high school, he was blackballed from a Jewish Fraternity for dating non-Jewish girls. Interesting, that his first glimpse of prejudice would come from his own people. The war definitely had, as with so many others, a huge and traumatizing impact on him. Originally, he was going to major in physical education but, as he said, "The war changed all that." He said he had to write "to get it off my chest, out of my gut." So he changed his major to language and literature. He felt that things needed to be addressed and that "radio, television and film ought to be vehicles of social criticism," and that "It is the writer's role to menace the public's conscience."

ML: One of the greatest things I admire about your dad was his consistent use of literariness and theoretical approach to tell rich, deep and meaningful stories, regardless if they were dramas in *Playhouse 90* or aliens landing on Earth "to serve man." I can imagine Hemingway and Lovecraft and other literary greats adorning your home while you were growing up. What were some of your father's best "go-to" sources that you recall cluttering his writing room?

AS: Well, I know he liked the authors you mentioned. As a kid, he read *Amazing Stories, Astounding Stories, Weird Stories*—the pulps. Also, Edgar Allan Poe and Norman Corwin. Our house was always filled with books—my dad was always interested in what others wrote.

ML: Tell us, what was it like being the only kid in school whose dad would be seen in over eighteen million homes that night or weekend?

AS: Well, my best friend's father was also a writer, so it just seemed the norm. I knew from an early age that my dad was a writer, but I never knew specifically what he was writing until a mean boy on the playground asked me one day if I was "something out of *The Twilight Zone*" and "where does your dad get all his ideas — hanging from the ceiling?" I went home and asked my dad what he'd meant, and my father told me what his series was called and explained that it was sometimes a little scary and most of the episodes were too old for me.

If my friends were wary about meeting my dad for the first time, that eventually completely waned, because my dad was so funny and warm. Moments in his company and they felt completely at ease. In my book, I shared something a friend of mine wrote when she went to dinner with my dad and I for the first time: "Anne told me over and over that her dad was great and I believed her. I also believed that he was deep, dark and scary, and maybe I should let them go by themselves ..."

ML: Was your dad protective of you during your teen years? Did he ever give prospective boyfriends a "screen test?"

AS: My dad was funny. He would drill boyfriends about their parents, if their dads had been in the war, how old they were, what did they do, etc. But he never did this in an off-putting or obnoxious way. My friends adored him. However, there was this one time when some kids drove down the road to our cottage on motorcycles to see my sister, and I remember my dad was not happy. They were loud and had frightened our dogs, and my dad was furious. So angry, in fact, that he couldn't articulate what he was trying to say. He just pointed his finger and nothing, no words, would come out. My mother had to step in and say, "What my husband is trying to say is that you're not welcomed here."

ML: Do you have a favorite *Twilight Zone* episode? Least favorite?

AS: I never watched many of *The Twilight Zones* while my dad was alive. It wasn't until after he died that I really started to watch, and initially, that was more to see him rather than the actual show. One of the most poignant moments happened, actually, when I saw "In Praise of Pip" for the first time and realized that my dad had used dialogue similar to a routine that he and I did. "Who's your best buddy." It was quite a moment. I love "Walking Distance" and "A stop at Willoughby." Like my dad, I have a longing to go back in time. "Death's Head Revisited" is a powerful, extraordinary episode. Least favorite would be the comedies. Though I adore Carol Burnett, I didn't think the episode "Cavander is Coming" was great. My dad said that too. Though NOT because of her! He loved Carol Burnett and was friends with her.

ML: Your father weaved many aspects of his personal life into his stories, such as his experiences in the war, feelings on political issues, etc. What about his home life? Did shades of his daughters ever seep into any of his stories?

AS: I don't think so! Though he did use my nickname "Nan" in two of the stories. The first was the main character in the episode, "The Hitchhiker." That kind of creeped me out. The second time was in a gentler story. "A Passage for Trumpet."

ML: From your perspective, what was your dad's reactions to *Night Gallery*, his transition from sci-fi/fantasy to horror/macabre?

AS: Initially, my dad had high hopes for *Night Gallery,* and there were some wonderful episodes. "They're Tearing Down Tim Riley's Bar" was one in which my dad had special feelings for, which earned him an Emmy nomination. It's a nostalgic, biographical piece, similar to the *Twilight Zone* episode "Walking Distance." Both truly represent my father's writing at its absolute best, and both evoke the theme of going backward and going home again.

Ultimately my dad was disappointed with the series and the producer, Jack Laird. I remember my father saying that man's name through gritted teeth. Laird, apparently, had very different ideas about the show, and ultimately my dad said: "I wanted a series with distinction, with episodes that said something; I have no interest in a series which is purely and uniquely suspenseful but totally uncommentative on anything."

ML: Do you think a *Night Gallery* movie or television reboot would ever work?

AS: Hard to say. How often are reboots successful?

ML: What do you think would be your father's main concern with television today?

AS: Reality television would have incensed him: *Honey Boo Boo, The Kardashians.* Stupid television that presumes that its audience is of zero IQ. The shows he would have loved: Bill Maher, *Newsroom, Breaking Bad*—intelligent, thought-provoking television. This new show, *Resurrection*, looks like one he definitely would have liked.

ML: Your father, a public figure and a catalyst for social change, must have received scores of letters requesting endorsements for causes and institutions. How did he handle this?

AS: He did receive requests for endorsements and initially he did some that he was tremendously conflicted about. It irked him what he could make from a sixty second commercial in what would have taken him six months to earn from writing.

ML: Like many other outspoken social activists who "ruffled some feathers," your dad must have received a lot of "not-so-nice" mail as well.

AS: He never worried about ruffling feathers. He did, apparently, receive a lot of not-so-nice mail. If it was intelligent, he tried to answer it seriously and answered almost all of the mail he received. He told a friend: "If it was from nut jobs, I was tempted to return it with a note saying, 'Someone is sending out crank mail under your name and I thought you should know.'"

ML: What sort of social issues would your father grapple with today?

AS: What would have disheartened and saddened my dad greatly is that prejudice is still such a predominant force in our country today. The Tea Party, this latest law proposed in Arizona to allow gays (or anyone that doesn't "fit" into a certain religious idealism") to be ostracized; the school shootings. That would have quite literally broken my father's heart.

In that interview I mentioned previously, he also said and I think this would hold true today about current politicians: "I'd love to be able to write an in-depth piece of what causes men like Nixon and Haldeman and Ehrlichman and all the rest of them not only to run, but what causes us to vote for them."

ML: Do you foresee a feature film made about your father's extraordinary life?

AS: It has been suggested that I use my memoir as a vehicle for a feature film.

Our Gavin

by adrian brooks

April gave birth to such a lovely little boy! Holding him made our hearts swell with pride. We did it! I have never experienced a greater love than I did in room B17 of Long Branch Regional Medical Center. The boy cried and wailed until it seemed he hadn't taken a breath for five minutes. I felt an extreme sorrow for him—yanked from his warm and protective home, facing harsh air and artificial light. I placed my face right in front of his and the carrying on stopped instantly. The nurses said he was far too young to be comforted by the recognition of his father, but they don't know what we know.

The first few weeks of having young Gavin in our little studio apartment have just been grand. April and I work tremendously as a team. She insists we need a roomier home with a new addition to our family so I've been searching about online. I have never felt more passionately about her than I do now. She deserves anything I can give her. Gavin is so advanced! He is only four weeks old but seems to be able to differentiate colors. I swear that he put a few words together, but we fell asleep and forgot what they were. April says I'm just trying to make patterns out of nothing to force the issue. I say she doesn't know what we know.

It has been six weeks since we took Gavin home. I am truly stunned by what he's able to do. I bought a pack of those colorful magnetic letters for our refrigerator so that we could play around together with them. April says he's too young but I don't think there's any harm in it. Just this morning I sat with him as he pointed to various letters. He doesn't have the motor skills to move the letters around, but from his suggestions I put together the words "ONLY US." April laughs it off saying that I'm just pranking her. I don't see the humor in it. I've just arranged the letters in the manner he directed me to. My adamant stance scares April. She refuses to sleep with me tonight and tells me to grow up. Oh, well—she'll realize it soon enough.

Gavin is now three months old and we have some fantastic news: April is pregnant again! I'm starting to realize that our lives are going to be an absolute whirlwind from now on but we've never been more excited. April had some serious difficulties throughout her first pregnancy, and considering we also have Gavin to take care of this is going to be a hectic and stressful year. Bigger news than her pregnancy is the development of Gavin. He is already so much like us it's truly incredible. I left "ONLY US" in the same position on the refrigerator so Gavin and I could one day laugh about him putting it together so young. April was uncomfortable with it for a while but has gotten over it and pays it no mind. I have heard him put sentences together but it seems he only does it with me and not April. He just seems to warm up to me more than to his mother.

I'm beginning to wonder why Gavin is so distant from his mother. When I watch her holding him I see that he looks on her with disgust. We both do. He pushes his hands in her face and longs to be with me instead. When I try to address this with her she thinks I'm joking. "He does love his daddy." True, but he hates his mommy. We know. April says I've grown bitter and resentful, but that it's just a phase. I don't know how she could be so prideful to subject Gavin to her care when he despises her. She sickens us. Still, I force a smile her way. We don't need any negative energy with her carrying our second child.

April says I've gone too far with my idea that Gavin only wants to be with me. I didn't think Gavin could stand to be around her for another minute so I drove us to stay in a motel in Monticello for a couple of days. We had never cared for Gavin as powerfully as we did during that short trip. Still April managed to ruin it by leaving us voicemails saying to return or she would contact the police. April has completely turned against us, but the little vacation was absolutely crucial. I wish she wasn't so shortsighted and selfish. She is carrying a baby right now. Does she really have to have both of them all to herself all the time? Especially when one of them cannot stand her.

April has passed away. Her spirit decided it was ready to go—who are we to deny her such a basic right? It is a shame for Gavin's sibling, though. It's just one more in a winding series of selfish decisions by April. We worked so well together. At least now Gavin will be happy all the time. He is so advanced!

It's only been a day since April's passing but I feel like Gavin has undergone some negative changes. The hatred he harbored for his mother has been directed at me. I am completely numb. We have shown him so much love and he has responded so overwhelmingly well to us in the past. Perhaps I was wrong about April? I'm probably overthinking things. Death can lead to some pretty mixed up emotions, after all. I just wish things could be the way they used to be, but there's no point in living in the past, I suppose. We have a wonderfully bright future!

Gavin is not the same boy anymore. I feel like his spirit left with his mother's. What happened to my astonishingly advanced son? He suddenly seems so ordinary. Even his love is absent. We still love him intensely, though. It's just different.

I lovingly dragged the blade under his jawline. He died so peacefully! He looked up at us with the same knowing eyes we've come to cherish. We have never been more proud of him. But who will clean up this mess? We surely won't. His skin and blood still clings to the sharp edge. We hate a dirty blade! We'll just toss this one out. The smell of iron wafts from our kitchen tiles.

A Very Mary Christmas

by phillip jones

My name is Emily Rivers, age eleven, and I live in the outskirts of Salem, Oregon, with my little brother Ricky, age nine, and my father Jack. We live in the wilderness, thirty miles from any sign of human life. My Dad loves it here. I like living here too, but it does get lonely. We have a really nice lake beside our house; I used to swim in it all the time, but not since the accident. My mother Patricia died when I was about five. My memories of her are scarce, but the ones I do have are nice. My sister Mary died this past June; she was only eight years old. We aren't an extremely happy family, but we do our best. Dad has it the hardest; we all miss Mary, but he feels responsible even though it wasn't his fault. Today is Christmas Eve; it will be our first Christmas without Mary. Dad's putting out the cookies for Santa right now. He tries so hard.

After we get ready for bed, Dad tucks us in and says, "You two better go to sleep now. Santa won't come if you're not sleeping!" He turns out the lights and shuts the door.

Ricky wanted to sleep in my room tonight so I could talk to him while he tries to fall asleep. We talk for about an hour and then doze off. I later awake to Ricky pulling on my arm telling me, "Santa's downstairs, Emily! He's really down there! I can hear him eating our cookies! Come on, let's go!"

He pulls me along as I recover from the haze of sleep, still trying to absorb what he just said. We exit my room and head down the hallway. The whole house is dark. As we near the steps I start to hear faint crunching sounds coming from downstairs. Could it really be Santa? As we descend the staircase, the crunching becomes louder and louder. I start to doubt that this sound is Santa eating our cookies—but what is it? My curiosity pushes me forward and Ricky and I are now rounding the corner into the living room, which is where the sound seems to be coming from.

As we enter the living room we see a figure sitting in front of the Christmas tree, facing away from us, illuminated only by the dim lights that adorn the tree. It appears

to be wearing a girl's night gown. Who is this? A shiver runs down my spine. The crunching is as loud as ever. I'm silent and motionless until the words "Who are you?" slip out of my mouth.

The crunching suddenly stops, there's a brief pause, and the figure then responds in a shrill high-pitched voice, "I'm Mary."

My heart drops and my body becomes numb. "Th-that's not possible! Mary's dead!" I cry.

The figure begins rocking back and forth, howling, "I'm Mary! I'm Mary! I am Mary!"

Ricky is now hiding behind me. As loud as I can, I yell, "Daaaaddy!"

The figure then turns its head and looks directly at me; it screeches, "Daddy's not here right now!" Fresh blood begins pouring from its mouth, as it chomps on another Christmas ornament. It's now looking directly at me with a disturbing grin. As I look into its eyes I quickly realize why my father has not come to our rescue. These are his eyes! It feels as if all the blood drains from my body and I faint.

I wake up to the swaying motions of a boat and the peaceful sounds of oars breaking the surface of water. It's still night time. I'm lying face-down in the boat. When I try to sit up I realize that my legs and arms are tied together with thick rope. I reposition myself, look up, and see my crazed father rowing the boat.

I close my eyes, hoping it is all just a terrible nightmare, like the kind Ricky had to have therapy for—but no, after opening them again I see that my father is still wearing Mary's bloodstained night gown and still eerily grinning from ear to ear.

He then notices that I'm awake and cheers, "Sister! You're awake! Yay! I've been waiting! Ricky says we need to hurry! He misses you already! He's such a good brother, don't you agree, Sis?"

I look around and cannot see Ricky anywhere. I shriek, "Where's Ricky? What did you do to him?"

The monster that was once my father laughs and responds, "Ricky has gone to the land under the lake. Daddy sent him there, just like Daddy sent me, and soon he will send you too! Mommy's not there though; Mommy was bad and Daddy sent her somewhere else."

Upon hearing this I let out a wretched whimper and begin to cry, something I haven't done since my sister died.

The rowing suddenly stops. My father stands up and reveals a heavy anchor that's tied to the two of us. I cannot move, I cannot escape, and panic sets in. I scream as loud as I can, the possibility of someone hearing me my last remaining hope.

He lifts the anchor and gleefully shouts, "Together forever! Merry, merry Christmas!" Then he drops it in the water, swiftly grabbing me before the boat flips over.

The moon fades away as we sink deeper and deeper. My lungs begin taking in water and I know that death is near. Images of my mother start flashing before my eyes. She's happy and smiling at me; she must have really loved me. With this last placid thought, my life passes from this world. 'Twas a silent night.

Cyanide Dream

A serpent flashed
its life
in pixels
Cacti erupted color
into the air
The sun slithered
in the sky
like a passing
season
The serpent sang
silver dirges
to scorpions
while they
hummed to the stars
and swallowed
each other
They were all
grounded
in the sky
below a feather
moon
wrapped in rainbows
The soil
reluctantly
reflected
everything
stretching it
beyond mortality
and erasing it
all

---robert wilson

THE CALL BACK

Kristen skipped from Terri's Feastery into the humid Manhattan air. A frayed strap stapled and glued crazily to the body of her purse hung from her left shoulder. Tips had been good this shift. She smiled. Tonight she had a call back. She had auditioned at every opportunity since arriving in Manhattan one year ago and this was her first call back. The part was for a female police detective endangered by her jealous sister. She knew in the marrow of her bones that the part was perfect for her. As soon as rehearsals started, she would write to her old high school drama teacher, Mr. Wellington, and tell him of her success. Mr. Wellington had insisted she needed to study theatre at a university to pursue theatre as a career.

"I'm a good actor," Kristen had told him. "Everyone says so. I had the lead in *Romeo and Juliet.*"

"Talent is not enough," Mr. Wellington had replied. "You need to train. You need the contacts and experience a university offers."

Kristen had looked at Mr. Wellington. His bushy brows and beard reminded her of a walrus. "I'm going to be discovered," Kristen had said. "Discovery is all I need."

Now after a year of alternating enthusiasm and disappointment, discovery was in sight. Kristen walked to the corner and stopped at the letter box to mail a bill payment. A solid blow struck her spine and slammed her into the box. Her shoulder wrenched. She felt a sharp pain and saw blood on her right knee. Her hose was torn. A dull ache grabbed her shoulder and she realized her purse was gone.

"Damn, damn. Double damn," she said.

"You okay, honey?" Kristen turned toward the Midwestern accent. The voice reminded her of Kokomo, Indiana, her hometown.

"Not really. I lost my purse and cut my knee and I've a call back in one hour."

"Are you an actor?"

by john hayes

"I was Juliet last year." Kristen glowed as she recalled the experience.

"You sound as though acting were the greatest love of your life."

"Acting is my love. Feeling the part, the excitement, the anxiety, the applause. I love it."

"Acting is my love too. I did Juliet once in Anderson, Indiana. Was I ever glad to leave there. I'm Christina, spelled with a C. I can fix that knee for you. I live around the corner. We'll put some antiseptic and a bandage on and you'll be ready for your call back."

"I don't even have subway fare to get there," Kristen said.

"I can let you have a couple of dollars. Come on. Let's get that knee fixed."

Kristen looked at Christina for the first time. "You look a lot like me. Your mouth turns up like mine and your nose is the same shape. You even have the same scar on your temple."

"I got my scar when I was eight years old."

"I was eight when I fell off a fence and got my scar. Maybe we're twins."

Christina took Kristen by the arm and hurried her around the corner. Christina stopped at an old Brownstone and walked down four steps to a basement apartment. "Coming?" she asked.

Kristen hesitated, then followed. She needed to repair her knee for the call back.

"I'll get something for your knee," Christina said and disappeared into the bathroom.

The one room apartment was similar to Kristen's with a Murphy bed, a worn beige carpet, and Pullman kitchen. Unlike her own apartment, there were no pictures on the walls. Kristen saw standing in one corner a polished oak table and three straight chairs. A crystal ball circled by six unlit black candles was on the table. Kristen stared into the crystal and watched her image form. Fingers clawed against the round interior wall. The mouth opened and screamed. A second image appeared, took her hand and led her away. Christina returned with a damp cloth, hydrogen peroxide, salve, and a bandage; she placed them on the table. "See anything interesting in the crystal?"

"I saw myself trapped inside."

"You must have the talent," Christina said. "Most people see nothing."

"The image was scary."

"Nothing to worry about. You need to work with the crystal to understand the meaning of what you see. I'll show you how to use the candles sometime. They're a big help." Christina lit one of the black candles and passed it under Kristen's nostrils. Kristen felt dizzy from the smell and pulled away.

"That smell is compelling," she said.

"You get to like it. Sit on the bed. We'll get your knee fixed," Christina said.

Kristen sat and studied Christina's trim body and take-charge manner as she cleaned and bandaged the knee. Her breasts were small like Kristen's. She even had the same bony hips.

"All done," Christina said. "Keep your knee stiff when you walk or the bleeding will start again."

Kristen stood. She stared at the white scar on Christina's right temple.

"You didn't tell me how you got your scar." Kristen raised her hand and touched Christina's scar. A shock ran the length of her arm. She had touched Christina's scar but felt the touch on her own scar.

"I fell off my bike when I was eight," Christina said.

"No, not a bike. Don't you remember? It was the fence. You fell off the fence. You were in a coma for five months." Kristen's head spun. She saw herself in a bed. She was screaming. Her body hovered near the ceiling and she was looking down on herself. What was she doing? Who was she? Who was Christina?

Christina looked at her sharply and grabbed her shoulders. "Are you okay?"

Kristen felt as if Christina's hands were merging into her shoulders. She pulled away. "Yes. Fine. I'd better leave if I'm going to be on time for my call back."

"Break a leg," Christina said.

"You said I could borrow bus fare," Kristen said.

Christina opened her purse. The brown strap was frayed and stapled to the body of the purse. She removed a wallet and handed five dollars to Kristen. "This should be enough."

"That's my purse and my wallet," Kristen said. "You took them."

"You're still upset. Lots of purses look the same. Let me pour you some white wine."

"No, give me that wallet." Kristen snatched the wallet and opened it. The identification read Christina Moore, age 20, New York. The picture was identical to her own identification. Her head spun. She handed the wallet to Christina. "Are you really from Anderson, Indiana?"

"Yes. I was raised in an orphanage. I acted in some high school productions too. Let me get you that wine." Christina opened a small refrigerator, pulled out a wine bottle and two glasses. "I keep the glasses chilled too," she said. She poured wine. "Drink this. You'll feel better."

Kristen took the glass and drank deeply. She felt dizzy.

"What was your father's name?" she asked.

"Hilary."

"That's my father's name too. What was your mother's name?" Kristen drank more wine. She started to slip away.

"Mirabelle—the same as yours."

"But I don't understand." She looked at Christina's blurry figure holding a full wine glass. "Why aren't you drinking your wine?"

"I needed you to feel the effects first. Otherwise, it won't work for me."

"What won't work?"

"I need you back. Separated doesn't work for either of us."

"But I'm not you. I never have been. We just look alike." Kristen said.

"After you fell from the fence and suffered the concussion I separated from you. I hated the coma you were in. Remember, I pulled away and floated above you. You screamed and I fled. I wound up in an orphanage. I tried to reunite with you when the coma lifted but couldn't. I kept track of you and followed you to Manhattan. Now I'm the strong one. I'm taking you back." She embraced Kristen with strong arms and drew her into her own body.

Kristen felt an accelerated exfoliation of her skin and marrow sucked from her bones as her skeleton turned to jelly, and muscles melted into Christina's body.

"I can't breathe," Kristen pleaded. "Let me out."

"You'll be fine. Sleep deeply. We're one again. Don't worry about the call back. I'll wow them for us. Don't forget, I had the lead in *Romeo and Juliet*."

Previously published in: *Alien Skin Magazine*, March 2003.

THE ENVY OF EVERY DEMON

Immense in its
perimeters,
irregular in proportion,
mottled to the extreme
in coloring and shade,
it was the Devil's beard
that fascinated me most.

It loomed like a forest
enchanted by evil:
curlicue trees baroque
in their exaggeration,
the light diminished
to a spectral radiance
as it filtered through
the hairy branches,
shadow glens filled
with accursed creatures
so horribly divine,
living and apparitional,
there was no language
for their afflictions.

While Lucifer was
turned away, burning
one of his minions,
I stole forward and
and took a cutting,
and slipped it flash
into my vest pocket.

Once I'd grafted
it to my beard
and it spread,
I would soon be
the envy of every
demon on the block.

If only old Beelzebub
hadn't spotted me
with that accursed
third eye in his tail.

—bruce boston

Were We Given to Wrath

Who would not warp the upturned face
with the infinite tongue
that spits distant stars
into a frenzy
& causes planets to plot
the plots where we may lie.
Who would not scald his cheeks
with some gruesome brew,
throw his black teeth
to the rattling wind.
Who would not come into accord
to unseat his eyes
& feed them to beasts,
if such beasts would not succumb
upon first bitter bite.
Who would cease to sing
among the constellations
were each hair on his head
singed one by one
& carried off by laughing crows
heretofore known only to Dante.

—darrell lindsey

Playing with Fire

Danielle lit her cello on fire
One August night, smiling
Wide to show the lightning
Bugs the right way to burn.

Dance, she cooed,
Watching dry grass bend,
Blackening as ground cracked,
Sending ants and worms
Scrambling for safer land.

Taking ash upon her tongue,
Delighting in momentary
Burns, she decided evening
Serenade would be a Bolero

Strong enough to free
Notes from hull; splintering
Wood drew her, beckoning
One last song. She played,
Engulfed by fading notes.

—kevin holton

In a Row

Just when you get your ducks in a row
    and start to settle back
thinking you are in control
    they start to flap and quack.

But some insightful soul's devised
    a place where ducks are wrought
(of cardboard, paint, shellac and glue)
    expressly to be shot.

So that you know you're in control
    he arms you with a gun
and you are Master of All Things
    until your turn is done.

Round and round one way they go
    for you, in sequence stuck,
to ready-aim and -FIRE at duck
    after duck after duck after duck

after duck—. . . . They're so dependable,
    though, and so well they sit,
they're nothing anyone should want
    to aim at or to hit.

And so it's you I hang my hopes
    and expectations on,
even though I never know
    when you will be gone.

—james b. nicola

The Diamond Fish

by walter dinjos

I lick the blob of blood on the tip of my thumb and resist crying as we paddle our old canoe toward the effulgent rays emanating from the lake.

"We should probably uproot that tomorrow morning." Papa tips his head toward the slim plank jutting out from the water near the rickety dock behind.

My attention, however, is on the shafts ahead. From close range, they appear to touch the night sky. "They are so beautiful. Do we really have to catch it?"

"We can either start wishing, after we've lost our home, that we could still picnic here every night to watch its lights, or we could sell it and settle our mortgage."

"But what do they do with it—jujuists? Emeka said they use it for blood money rituals, but mama's stories say blood money comes from human blood."

"Ha, blood money rituals." He stops rowing, just as the rays surround us, and gives me the paddles. "Ridiculous." Then he grabs the net beside me, gives me an I-will-be-right-back pat in the head, and dives into the water.

I note he didn't take the fishing rod, and the bait plate is empty.

They say diamond fishes are clever enough to recognize bait, but their sluggishness and lights in the dark make them easier to catch at night. Still, in the whole of Awka town, only one fisherman has ever caught one. And today he resides in an orange mansion near the outskirts, and the jujuist he sold the fish to is now the most powerful—or rather, the most patronised.

I extend my curious left hand into the rays and notice the mark on my thumb is no longer bleeding. In fact, it has disappeared. I check my right thumb just to be sure, but it is unhurt.

I have barely begun to wonder how when the beams start dancing around like stage lights seeking a performer in the sky. They do so in a confused way, as if disturbed or running from something. They stop after a while and distort into curly wisps.

Darkness swoops on my surroundings and the voices of the night reveal themselves. I shudder, suddenly feeling the chill of the lake breaching my wool sweater and assaulting my poor body from all angles.

"Papa?" I whimper in response to some splashes in the dark. The boat jerks and a black figure I'm familiar with climbs in. I let out a sigh. "The lights are gone. Did you catch it?"

"Son, we are going to be rich!" Folding his net around something black and placing it at a corner, papa clamps me in the shoulders and hugs the air out of my lungs. "You want to school at Harvard? Cambridge?" His grip loosens and he pulls back, sitting with a slouch. "I only wish your mother was here to see this."

Our row back to the lake house is adorned with conversation of how we are going to turn the house from its damp, termite-infested state to something classy. And as I climb onto the quaky dock, I avoid gripping the jutting plank for support again.

We put the fish in the drum of water on the backyard porch. And while papa bargains with one jujuist after another on the phone in the parlour, I rest my elbows on the rim of the drum with my jaw on my arms and shine a torch on the fish, begging it to forgive us and show me its beautiful light.

It just huddles there, the size of my twelve-year-old arm, face flat and tail a mosaic of all the primary and secondary colours, looking sad. Its deep black body is spangled with what looks like grains of diamond. I turn off my torch and it begins to glow faintly.

I rush inside, shouting, "Papa, it is shining again!"

But papa is still on the phone, so I waddle back to the porch to find the light has died and water is splattered on the wooden floor near the drum. My heart quickening the pace of its beat, I focus my torch into the drum.

"Papa! Papa!" I dash inside again. "There is a thief in the house! The fish is gone!"

We search the whole house but can't find the thief. Instead we find something else—another set of rays in the lake. Although it is already nine pm, papa canoes into the water and fetches the fish.

We decide to keep this one in the bathroom tub and while papa sits on the backyard porch continuing his calls and looking out for the thief, I transfer water from the lake to the tub.

I stop on the porch on the fourth run and lower my iron pail to the floor, and stretch myself. "Do all diamond fishes look alike?" I ask papa as he terminates a call and begins to dial another number.

"To fishes we humans look alike, son." He returns to his call.

I proceed into the house and, on reaching the bathroom, the slimy yellow footprints and some splashes of water that now design the tarnishing white tiles alarm me so much that my pail slips off my hand and pours its water in the corridor. The shutters swinging in the night suggest someone has just escaped through the window.

"Papa! Papa!" I scoot back to the porch. "There are feet in the bathroom, and the fish is gone!"

Again, we can't find the thief and a new set of rays in the lake gives us another diamond fish that night. This time we carry the drum on the porch into the kitchen and papa asks me to stay there and watch it while he rushes to the parlour and fetches his mobile phone.

I watch papa hurry out. Then I turn around to find a girl standing before me. She is naked. It doesn't occur to me to blush before freezing in my position, my mouth agape like those of the people in movies do when I press the pause button.

Her eyes are two green isles on white seas, and her skin somehow is black - I thought mama said black people don't have bright eyes - and shiny as if spangled with diamond grains, her plaited hair strangely fanning out like rainbow fins. She must be wearing a wig or something.

"Where is the diamond fish?" I ask.

She cocks her head. "The fish?"

"Yes, the fish."

She puts her hands behind her. "I will throw it back in the lake."

So it's the same fish we keep catching. I should call papa.

"Something that beautiful . . . " A tear rolls down her cheek and I fight a desire to console her. "Those jujuists . . . they will murder her. They will eat her."

Murder? "Why would someone pay that much for something only to eat it?"

"They eat it to increase their magic tenfold. Tenfold times tenfold the many eggs in her womb."

"She is pregnant? How can you know that?"

"Ebuka?" Papa's footfalls come from the corridor. "Who are you talking to?"

"Eh, no one." I turn to the door and there is papa.

His eyes move from my sweating face to the floor. "What's the fish doing there?"

I turn to the girl. She is gone and the fish is lying between a set of yellowish footprints. I look at papa and tell him I saw the thief, but do not tell him it was a girl, a naked girl.

Papa decides to stay awake all night in the kitchen and watch the fish.

The jujuist comes in the morning wearing a baggy gown made of sackcloth, bead necklaces and bangles and rings and anklets, carrying a big Ghana-must-go bag filled with one thousand naira notes, and tie palm fronds and vulture feathers around his dada head. The funny thing is that he came on a speed boat -- in that stupid attire of his. Ha!

He puts the bag on the dock and dances to the drumming of his iron staff for a while. Then he says, "The fish." The rims of his eyes and mouth are lined with chalk.

Papa passes the bowl containing the fish to him. He looks inside and I can see the lust in his smile. He tips his head toward the bag. "That's fifty million naira as agreed." Then he turns and dances toward his boat.

Tenfold times tenfold the many eggs in her womb. I charge forward, knocking the bowl out of his hand. He yelps as I and the container drop into the lake and I feel a sharp stab in my stomach.

My face is in the water, my mouth taking in as much of it as it can. There, just before my sight fails, I see the jutting plank. I hang from it like a goat about to be charred. Only instead of my body dripping kerosene, it is immersed in a crimson pool.

I can't work my limbs. My eyes close.

Later my eyes open. I'm alone in my room, and I feel my life draining away through the hole in my stomach. I can't see the wound, but I feel it -- that numbness, that coldness.

Where is papa?

I know he is running around trying to borrow money from our distant neighbours. He did it when mama was dying. The doctors wouldn't treat her unless he made a deposit of one hundred thousand naira.

I can see her now.

The door opens and she walks in—the naked girl. She stops halfway to my bed, holding her side as if her life too is draining away through there. "The eggs are now in the bottom of the lake," she croaks. "Soon there will be more diamond fishes here than there has ever been in any other waters. Unfortunately, diamond fishes die from laying eggs." She pulls back, resting on the doorframe for support.

"What happened to you?" I ask.

"She is in the bowl in the kitchen," she says in reply. "You can sell her and keep your lake house. Or you can eat her and heal tenfold faster."

COLDER WEATHER

by peter damien

The wind roared across the landscape in a bratty squall, stirring up the snow and rocking the semi and its trailer. The windshield wipers fought to keep the windows clear, and the headlights struggled to cut beams through the blowing snow, but neither of them met with much success. At last, giving up, Zack turned off the highway and into the parking lot of a truck stop.

The buildings were just black forms in the snow, as if someone had sketched in their outlines but forgotten to add detail. The other semis parked here, hunkered down against the blizzard, were little better. Just shapes in the white. Zack stopped next to another semi and killed the engine. Even parked, the wind continued to put its shoulder to the side of his truck and shove over and over.

He grabbed his coat off the passenger seat and put it on—awkward to do with the steering wheel right there and the seat littered with oddments from too much time on the road. Without thinking about it, he reached up to the sun visor and snagged the crinkled photo which was paper-clipped there any time he drove. There was a woman in the photo, and a little girl, and a beautiful green field, and plenty of warmth and sunlight. He put it in the breast pocket of his jacket and buttoned it shut, so the storm wouldn't pluck that away from him. Then he took his keys and climbed out of the truck.

The wind slammed against him, pelting snow in his face with such speed, it pricked and hurt him. His boots crunched across the gravel. The snow was everywhere, but it was moving too much to stick anywhere. It just had to move like it was scared to settle.

The sketch of a truck stop resolved itself, as he drew closer, into the black silhouette. The dirty door had a sign that said *ALWAYS open (never shut)* and he put his shoulder to it and went inside. He leaned back against the door and pushed it shut against the wind.

Light, noise, and best of all—warmth, greeted him. He walked on without seeing much of what was around him. All truck stops were the same after a while: they were a gas station, the inside of which was cluttered with the junk you might buy if you were bored and on the road long enough; audiobooks; T-shirts with howling wolves on them; hats and beer holders and postcards and thriller novels; and more junk food than anyone needed. It was all stuffed into the little gas station area until a broad-shouldered man could barely move, and Zack could barely move as he went through it.

In the hallway, there were two bathrooms and a small secluded area with a lot of telephones. Farther down the hallway was a buffet restaurant serving zero-bullshit stick-to-your-ribs food. "Isn't nothing you can't dump gravy on, in one of those buffets," someone had said, and it was true.

Zack stared at the telephones in the little room. He fiddled with the hem of his frayed old black denim jacket, and chewed at his beard, which had once been neat but was now increasingly ragged. He went to the first little phone stall and thumped quarters into the machine. He dialed the phone number that his hands knew as well as his head, and his finger hardly shook at all. He cradled the receiver to his ear, and it was cool against his skin.

It rang and rang. The ringing sounded muffled and distant. It didn't matter how he adjusted the receiver against his ear; it always sounded muffled and distant. Same as at every truck stop, with every phone.

It rang and rang.

It clicked.

"Hello?" It was a woman's voice, and his chest ached just to hear it. She sounded hesitant.

"Hey babe," Zack said. He cleared his throat. "It's me."

She drew in a long breath. "Oh, god," she whispered. She sounded far away.

"Listen, I'm sorry," he said, because it had to be said. "I'm stuck in colder weather. The storm's everywhere and the roads, they're bad, you know? But I'm tryin'. I promise you, I'm tryin' to get back to you, quick as I can."

She was sobbing now; the distance couldn't disguise the sound of that. It was quiet, and it lacked energy. Defeated sobs, the sound of human emotional wreckage. It hurt him more severely than the howling ice and wind ever could.

"I love you," he said, his own voice shaky. "I love you, babe, okay? I'm coming back to you."

"Don't say that, please don't say that . . . " she said. "Please, I . . . god . . . "

He closed his eyes and rested his forehead against the wall beside the phone. His hand, wrapped around the phone receiver, was slick with sweat.

"Bye, love. I'm thinking of you. Be strong, 'kay?"

He didn't know what else to say, so he hung up the receiver. The phone clanked as it finished swallowing his change.

It was some time before he took his forehead off the wall and went back into the hall, heading for the restaurant. He scrubbed at his face, hard, with two big and calloused hands. Every time he called, the ache settled into his chest, and it wouldn't fade until he got back on the road. Good thing about this storm was—you couldn't focus on anything else while driving, or it would eat you alive. It would pitch your truck through a guard rail that was too weak to stop you and send you hurtling into a ditch.

The buffet was long and steaming, with piles of plates and silverware at one end. Zack nodded and smiled at a couple of the other guys who looked up when he came in. He got a plate and a fork and went down the line, filling it with stick-to-your-ribs food: mashed potatoes, fried chicken, biscuits, corn on the cob. Simple but good. He thought about sitting in one of the little booths the restaurant had, but then he'd have to stare out at the white world, and he'd had enough of that. So he went and sat at the counter, facing the kitchen. An old woman stood behind the counter, back to him, fiddling with a big coffee pot.

Zack said to her, "When you've got that runnin', I'll take a cup if you don't mind. Jus' black, please."

She glanced back at him. Her face was nothing but wrinkles, and her eyes were the brightest blue he'd ever seen. She smiled at him, and it seemed as if all the wrinkles and creases were made only to enhance the smile. As if this was their purpose. "Sure darlin'," she said. "Let it drip."

Zack dug into the food. Finished off the potatoes and the biscuit, was halfway through the corn when she set a small brown mug of piping hot coffee next to him. He nodded thanks.

"You goin' right to left, or left to right?" she asked, drying her hands on an old towel.

He looked at her oddly and she laughed and pointed past him, at the big sprawling window that looked out on nothing but snow.

"When I watch the trucks go by, they go left to right, or the other way. You see? So which is it?"

He twisted to look out the window, and thought for a moment. Then he replied, "I came from right, and I'm heading left, I guess."

"See? Simple," she laughed again. "Where you headin' though? Where you from?"

He thought about it while he chewed corn off the cob. The memories were blurry. They were like the phone conversation; they seemed to be coming through several layers of thick blankets to reach him. He vividly remembered the road, the truck, and the storm; everything else felt like a photograph in his head.

"I come from home, takin' the long way around to get home again," he mumbled. He looked up. "That's what someone said to me once, and I like it."

"I like it too," she said, smiling. "How's the biscuits? I make 'em myself."

"Delicious," he said, and they were. "Thank you, ma'am."

"Sure, darlin'." She turned away and busied herself organizing freshly cleaned coffee cups.

He ate the chicken carefully, with his fingertips only, and he wiped them on a napkin between each bite. The chicken was moist and the skin had been fried until it crunched when he bit it. It was spicy and flavorful. He washed it down with the coffee, which was strong. That was the thing about truck-stop food. It wasn't ever gourmet, but it was always strong and good. It always seemed homemade.

He finished the coffee, and she filled it half-full again. He angled his seat as he drank it, enjoying the warm cup in his hands. He looked out the window for a moment, but there wasn't anything to see. Mostly he looked at the other truckers. There were a half-dozen of them in the restaurant. They were all mostly like him. All rough-looking and tired, some with harsh cigarette coughs, and some without. They got out of their trucks, came into the restaurant, found each other, and talked about the thing they all had in common, which was trucks. Zack had done that too, plenty of times. You talked the road, the haul, the truck. What else could you do? It was good just to talk.

He finished his coffee and looked at the old woman again. She seemed familiar, he realized, but he couldn't pin it down. One of those faces that makes you swear you know the person very well, if only you could remember.

"Check, please," he said, putting the cup down next to the empty plate.

She smiled at that too. "Hon, the weather's fierce out there. You sure you don't want to just set a while and rest? It's no good drivin' in. The coffee's free."

Zack shook his head. "I gotta keep movin'. It's slow goin', but progress is progress."

"Well, I can't stop you," she said, handing him a small piece of paper on which she had scrawled a number of items and a little number at the bottom. He fumbled in the pocket of his denim jacket and fished out a handful of bills. They dragged the crinkled photo out and it fell onto the counter.

The woman behind the counter picked it up as Zack picked out the needed money and put it on top of the bill. "They your family?"

"Yeah. My girls."

"They waitin' for you?"

"Always are. They're why I've gotta keep going, even in the storm."

"I suppose so," she smiled, the lines deepening in her face. Her eyes glittered in the cheap yellow light. "They can't wait forever, after all."

"Thanks for the dinner," Zack said, and he stood up.

She reached across the counter and took his hand, suddenly. Her hands were small and soft, thinned out by age and hard work. His hand was huge and rough and dark in hers. She squeezed his hand.

"You be careful, Zack," she said. "Both eyes on the road."

She patted his hand, let go, and turned away. Zack was too startled to say anything. He put the little photo back in his jacket pocket and left the restaurant, heading down the cramped hall again.

He glanced into the telephone room when he went by. There was a man sitting on the floor beneath a couple of the phones, his back against the wall, his hands against his knees. Zack hesitated a moment, then stepped into the room and crouched beside him.

"Hey buddy, you okay?"

"Yeah," the man said. He sniffed, loudly. "I'm just tired. You know?"

"For sure."

The man had closed-cropped brown hair and a white scar cutting through one eyebrow. His fingers were fat and square, but the rest of him was skinny.

"The worst bit is when you finally get off the road," he said, "And the first thing you do—before you piss, or eat, or sleep, or whatever—is you call home. And they don't want to hear you. Or they won't talk to you. That hurts like hell. You know?"

Zack nodded, said nothing.

The man picked a quarter up off the ground and turned it over and over between two fingers. With each rotation, it caught the light from the ceiling bulbs and glinted. A little strobe light in the man's hands.

"Get some rest," Zack said, patting the man on the arm. "It's just the long hours talking. Things will work out okay. Find a motel."

"Yeah," the man nodded. "I can't remember the last time I crashed, you know? Time gets all blurred up."

"Sure it does."

The man looked at Zach then, and his eyes widened a little. He said, "You ever thought, maybe we're all dead? Sometime when I'm drivin', my mind wanders and I think, maybe this is what happens next. Don't it feel that way sometimes to you?"

"All the time," Zach said. "Too damn often."

They were silent for a moment. Then Zach added, "Tell you what though, it wouldn't be so bad. You know why?"

"Why?"

Zack jerked a thumb back the way he'd just come. "The food's pretty good. And the coffee's strong." He grinned a little.

The man laughed.

"You take it easy." Zack got up and left him to sit there and rest. He wound his way through the clogged aisles in the gas station, full of stuff nobody wanted but still bought plenty of.

He put his shoulder to the door and pushed it open. The wind pushed against it, not wanting him to come outside. When he made it out, the storm angrily hurled snow at him.

Parked just outside the truck stop was a big bus which hadn't been there before. Long and sleek, perfectly visible even with the blowing snow. It was lined with windows, and they were all blackened. There was writing along the side of the bus, but Zack couldn't make out what it said. There was a line of people boarding the bus very slowly, at a shuffle.

A man stood beside the door of the bus and the three little steps which led up to the seats. He was tall and gaunt, wore black, and looked genial. He took a small ticket from each person as they boarded the bus. He looked at Zack.

"Hello, stranger," the man said, "You need a ride?"

Zack stuffed his hands in his jacket pockets and stared at the bus. It would be nice, he thought, to hunker down in a seat and sleep the miles away while someone else sorted out the bad weather and the endless roads. He'd ridden buses before—you road 'em when you had to drop off the truck at the end of the line.

Yet he didn't want to. There was something about this bus. Staring at it filled him with dread, the same way talking on the phone had filled him with pain. There was something in the back of his mind which told him—no, he wasn't getting on that bus.

"Thanks," Zack said, over the howl and gale, "But I got my truck over there, and I've got to keep going with it."

The man inclined his head. "Suit yourself," he said. "Be seeing you."

Zack hunched up and walked away from the truck stop, away from the little bunker of warmth and food and conversation. He walked toward the trucks, which were now just sketches in the storm, becoming only a little more solid as he drew closer. Little hutches of solitude, fighting their way down the highway.

He made it to his truck and climbed up, pulling the door shut. The cab had been leeched of heat. He sat there for a moment, his breath misting in front of him, steaming the windows.

He put the little photo back onto the visor. He started the engine, and he cranked the heat until it roared.

It was slow going, easing out of the parking lot and back onto the highway. There wasn't any other traffic—he couldn't remember the last time he'd seen traffic, but who'd come out in this if they didn't have to? He found his lane, turned his lights on full, and crept on down the highway. It wasn't long before the storm put its weight against the side of his truck, rocking it like a ship on choppy seas.

He thought about the sad man, sitting on the floor beneath the phones, and wondered if he'd go outside and get on the bus.

He glanced at the photo once. She'd stop crying when he made it back. He knew it. Then the road took all his concentration and he focused on driving.

Peasant in Grey

by amanda rioux

London, England; May 1536

Staring at the sun rising through a tiny hole in the boarded-up window, I take in its beauty, admiring the swirl of colors—reds, oranges, pinks—and I feel comforted by their light. The sun is barely peeking over the horizon, as though afraid to rise to the awaiting sky. My feet are bare; my hair, stringy and brown, hangs over my face and in my eyes, and my hands are chapped by the early-morning cold. I have but only half an hour before my duties in the kitchen begin, but I enjoy what little free time I have—my own personal refuge from life.

I stare back outside. The sun has risen higher during the few minutes I looked away. It's an odd phenomenon. No one ever sees these things happen, but turn away for only a moment and the world outside has changed.

I take the edges of my tattered, dirty, hand-me-down grey dress and drape it over my feet, pinning it to the ground with my toes, in a hopeless attempt to warm my blistered feet. I have done nothing but hard labor for the past week, and it has taken a toll on me. My arms and legs are scrawny, my hair is thinning. My soul is weary and restless, and my body aches in agony.

Suddenly I hear the unmistakable noise of the maid calling me, and I scramble up and trot to the kitchen.

"Peel those potatoes, knead the dough, and collect the eggs," the main scolds, already starting her daily routine of shouting orders at me. "And when you're through, bring in some logs for the fire—go wake and dress the young ones."

"Yes, Annabelle," I reply meekly. I immediately begin to scrub and peel a pile of potatoes that lay waiting for me. I keep my private struggle and intolerance inside; I don't let it disturb my chores.

The paring knife is dull and dirty and barely grabs hold of the potato skin. I toss it aside in favor of my long, misshapen fingernails. The flimsy edge of my pinky nail snags and rips lose as it catches on a potato eye, and I use my teeth to rip the remainder of it off, spitting in the pile of peels.

"'Tis a shame about lovely Queen Anne," Annabelle begins, while folding a pile of fresh linen.

"What about her?" I am anxious to hear any news of her I can. I have been overly infatuated with the new Queen ever since her marriage to Henry VIII. I did not favor Queen Catherine of Aragon too well, and someone as young and vivacious and fashionable as the lovely Anne was a great change to the throne. I admire her greatly, not only for the festivities she brings to the castle, but the elaborate costumes and decorations she produces. And, of course, I admire her courage for putting up with the stubborn and indifferent King Henry.

"You mean you haven't heard? You impudent little child! Do you pay attention to nothing?" It is Annabelle's custom to denounce my ignorance, which is one of her many ways of making herself feel superior to me.

"No, I have not. Please tell me. I am so fond of Queen Anne."

"She's to be executed tomorrow—publicly beheaded, by orders of King Henry."

"What!?" In my shock and utter astonishment, I drop a potato.

I am overcome with the news. Queen Anne—to be executed? I cannot believe it! Whatever did she do to deserve such a fate? For a moment everything moves in slow motion. I clench my fists and glance down just in time to see the freshly-peeled potato roll and gather dirt on the floor.

"Now look what you've done, you clumsy fool of a girl!"

"Please, Annabelle, tell me. For what reason is she to be beheaded?"

"On suspicion of witchcraft, incest and adultery, child. Really, where is your mind, I wonder?" Annabelle floats over to me, and bends down to pick up the dirtied vegetable. "The kitchen is no place for you at the moment!" she hollers. "Go outside and fetch some wood."

Outside in the bitter cold of morning, I slump down atop the woodpile, freshly chopped, no doubt, by the woodsman. I contemplate thoroughly the news I have just endured, and it plagues my heart with pain. Queen Anne, such a lovely woman, and not much older than I. What would I do in such a situation? I can't imagine how she has accepted her fate.

"Elizabeth! In here with the wood now!" Annabelle's head appears briefly through the kitchen window. Although only her face can be seen, I know her hands are resting on her hips, as they usually are when she addresses me.

"Yes. Yes, madam." I slide down until I hit the brick path, and I gather a log or two to bring inside.

Once inside I throw the wood in the fireplace, tending to the dulling fire with the iron poker. I sit a moment on the floor to warm my feet by the revived flames, and begin to eavesdrop on the conversation I hear brewing in the kitchen. It is the mistress, Genevieve, speaking with Annabelle.

"I figure on account of the events to follow tomorrow, I will give you and Elizabeth the morning off to come with us to witness the execution. In exchange, I will ask that you perform double the amount of work for today," she says. "In the morning the children will be left here, in the care of my mother. At dawn we will all commence to the Tower for the execution."

I am appalled by her lack of emotion. She speaks as if it is nothing at all, nothing more than a ceremony or a banquet! Poor Anne! The humiliation of having your death displayed before thousands is unspeakable.

Sleep is hard to come by tonight; I lay awake as my mind races with the most horrid thoughts. I imagine again and again the lovely face of Queen Anne—and her soft, delicate neck that her terrible fate is about to fall upon. I finally drift off to sleep, yet lie uneasy; my mind is plagued with unrelenting nightmares. Many times I am startled awake by images of shining, reflective sword blades and headless women. I toss and turn, unable to get the gruesome sights out of my head. As I lay in my bed, tattered and thin blankets barely covering my body, I silently pray that I may obtain a dreamless slumber, but to no avail.

I am awoken by the glare of the sun shining directly in my eye, and I slowly crawl out of my bed. In the kitchen, Annabelle is helping the mistress tie her bonnet. She stares as me disapprovingly.

"'Tis a pity you haven't anything more proper to wear," she says, glaring at my tattered dress and stained apron. "Oh, well. After all, who will pay any attention to a lowly peasant in grey?"

I clench the folds of my unbecoming dress, suddenly realizing how foolish I look, and my sadness for the queen becomes even more overwhelming.

Solemnly, we make our way from the home to the outskirts of Tower Green. Already there are swarms of people, peasant and noble alike, gathered to witness the much-anticipated event. How grim, how morbid I find them to be; among the faces I pass, I see none as downcast as mine. I recoil at the jovial air of the masses.

My mistress keeps us together by her side as she pushes her way through to the tower gates.

"Come on, keep up," she calls to us, as she hurriedly passes through the gate and into the open courtyard. "I simply must view this from a decent vantage point." To her, this is nothing more than a source of merriment, a social gathering. I reluctantly keep pace so as not to anger my mistress, but my feet feel heavier than lead.

"You really must move quickly," Annabelle chimes in, as she grabs at my sleeve and ushers me along.

We reach the interior of Tower Green. A scaffold stands on a make-shift stage in the center. An executioner, face hidden by a hideous black mask, stands impatiently with arms folded across his large and muscular chest. Suddenly there is movement on the platform as the beautiful Queen Anne, meek and frail, is escorted to the base of the scaffold by two men clutching her arms. Silence falls upon the crowd. There before me is the figure of a woman once highly revered—now broken and discarded by a selfish king, tossed aside like the broken toy of an ungrateful and spoiled child.

The queen does not look up at the scores of people who have come to witness her execution; she stares downward. Although she was to be beheaded in a private ceremony, flocks of witnesses have pushed their way beyond the gates of Tower Green. She appears calm. I admire her strength as she bravely accepts her fate without falter. I watch as she approaches the scaffold; her lips move as she utters a short speech, but above the din of the crowd the words do not meet my ears. How I long to hear the last words of the doomed queen.

At last, the fateful moment arrives. Frightened and beginning to shake, I contemplate shielding my eyes—for how can I idly stand by and watch as a woman I so admire is executed in this undignified manner? I scan the faces of those around me—faces lit with curiosity, wonder, and some even displaying smug complacency and anticipation—how they morbidly desire to see this execution played out.

As the executioner stands sharpening his sword—the sparks flying as he strokes the blade against the stone—the queen remains still and brave. I watch as she removes her headdress, placing it gently in the arms of a lady of the court who stands by her side. How strange, how ironic, I ponder, that she would carefully and delicately place a headdress that soon would no longer have a head to adorn.

Slowly, she kneels down, placing her delicate neck on the scaffolding. The executioner, his muscles flexed, his skin shining in the sun, readies his great sword. The queen sighs, and raises her eyes to scan the faces of those who have gathered to watch her die. Those heavy, saddened eyes slowly pass over those faces, and in a moment of terror, her eyes rest, locked dead—into mine. I shudder, I feel a fear I have never known before. Those sorrowful eyes remain piercing into mine as a blindfold is wrapped around her head. How sad for her that out of all the beauty she has seen in this world, the last image in her eyes before the sword crashes down is the pitiful sight of a peasant in grey.

frostbite #10: Crash Cars

I too have known the crash car course,
the chute just where the road diverged
in the wood, and felt the reeling force
    of youth. I scraped by and emerged

from grind and gore with a tattered heart
but for all the mean-meant crashes
a stronger soul. And now that part
    of living's past, the bumps and lashes

no longer what I need or crave:
I live in the light not the black.
But I can neither watch nor save.
    So forgive me if I turn my back.

—james b nicola

The End of All Things

It rises from the boiling black of a lifeless and churning dead sea
Corpses choke the maelstroms, caked in crimson foam and seaweed
It rises into a night sky alight with burning clouds and white lightning
A fulgurous symphony blinds and deafens an awestruck audience
The sky ignites, pulsing like a dying heart as the gasses dissipate
Atmosphere bleeding into the never
Luna turns and flees her post as her abandoned children wail
Stars brilliant as the air thins
Nebulae and comets scream past like celestial foghorns
Their music silent no more to the ears of sinners
Still it rises
Stars blink out of existence
Their light lost to the insatiable appetite of patrolling black holes
Gravity loses its grip, and earth begins to crack
As it rises, wings outstretch to shade our pale faces from the failing sun
The weight of its gaze pushes us to our hands and knees
We grip the dying planet with feeble fingers and pray
To a God who may very well stand before us
Raising his long hand and tilting back his head
A drone song to drown out our cries
And signal the end of all things.

—eric dean

Fabric Folds and Flat Expanses

In the shadowed fabric folds and flat expanses of bed you've never been to. Out beyond the borders of bare feet that rub together like cold strangers at the darkest edge of town. Farther than your flags and beyond banners, unclaimed and unmarked by man, where cold settles unchallenged by greedy hands and restless, purposed breathing… skulk the formless absences and echoes of familiar faces. Scents and senses and memories of goose-bumped skin and tiny hairs standing on end, quiver under breath like branches in breeze, and under fingers, moving with ease, in soldiers' formation. A bold and single-minded ballet breaking down into a chaotic orgy. Stage lights down and all the preachers have left town. Out there, in the shadowed fabric folds and flat expanses of bed you've never been to, wolves pace with independence on their faces and a quiet, shameful hunger in their mouths.

—eric dean

—illustration by Natasha Alterici

Amaranthine

"Your book will be ready for collection next week," I informed Mr. Johnson, one of our new clients. He was an older man, perhaps in his sixties but looked like someone who took great pride in his appearance.

"Can't it be done sooner?" He frowned impatiently and pierced me with a sharp glance.

I shook my head in defeat. "Please, you must understand this is a delicate custom order and special attention to detail is required."

"Very well, call me when it's done!" Mr. Johnson barked and marched out of my eerie shop.

Ah yes, my emporium of odd curiosities. I inherited it from my father, who was a book binder for most of his life. In his declining years, he opened a small bookshop of his own but sadly, didn't live long enough to see it prosper. Heart attack killed him six months later.

He was swiftly cremated and I displayed the urn in the shop to keep his memory alive. I tried my best to keep the business going but there's not much hope for independent bookshops or rookie businessmen these days. The place was losing money rapidly and the need for drastic action became imminent.

I missed my father and wished daily that he was still alive, if only to offer guidance. I didn't want to let him down by bankrupting the shop he'd worked so hard for. I had to do something innovative.

The bell above the door rang and a new figure approached the reception—a tall, Gothic- looking woman.

"I trust you received my e-mail," she began in a foreign accent.

"I did, indeed. You must be Ms. Muller," I replied while scrolling down the content on my monitor.

The woman's pale complexion remained unchanged.

"That's right, I brought you the materials you requested," she said and handed me a plastic bag smeared with blood.

by erik hofstatter

I stared at the bag briefly, mildly surprised at the poor presentation and total lack of care.

"Erm, thank you. As you know, this is a special custom order and due to our recent hectic schedule, it will take several weeks to complete."

Unlike Mr. Johnson, Ms. Muller seemed content with the lead time.

"That's perfectly understandable," she said, removing her dark sunglasses, "as you're the only specialist in the area. I'll be in touch."

She departed and I was glad to watch her leave, for her presence created a sense of melancholy in the shop.

Where was I? Oh, yes! I had to do something innovative to reverse my fortunes. The torment of my father's death provided inspiration for my new business expansion. I wanted to keep him with me at all times but his ashes weren't enough!

What if cremation wasn't the only method of keeping your loved ones with you? What if you could actually keep a piece of them? An everlasting token that you could touch and feel.

So a new idea was born, and my Lord -- how the clients poured in!

Of course, officially, I was just an average shop owner and had to keep up legit appearances but on the black market, behind the scenes, I was quite a celebrity for my unique services.

The technique itself had been quite popular in the 16th century and I was determined to revive the trend. Book binding ran in the family, after all.

I put on a pair of blue latex gloves and carefully examined the content of the bag. The putrid aroma assaulted my nostrils as I ran my fingers along the patch of wrinkly skin. It was a generous piece that most likely came from the back of the corpse. I sprinkled salt over the skin and placed it in the small freezer.

Anthropodermic bibliopegy, or the practise of binding books in human skin, was my forte and I assure you, the practise is still in high demand.

The Man with No Eyes

by alex johnston

A man with no eyes was clawing at the closet door. It made a continuous dull dragging noise that faded into the background after a while, like the tick-tock of the clock, or the continual whirr of the laptop fan. He hadn't spoken in weeks. Sometimes Martin forgot he was even there.

When Martin had first moved into the house he had been surprised to discover that the small closet in the bedroom was locked. A simple padlock held the folding doors shut and there had been no key to be found. The doors had slats with small gaps, so Martin could see that there wasn't anything inside. He had initially considered getting a hacksaw to simply remove the lock, but he didn't really have much use for the small closet and quickly forgot about it. He didn't think of it again until weeks later, when he was woken in the night by a loud knocking.

Martin had got out of bed slowly, wondering who could possibly want to see him at four in the morning and went to the door. There was no one there. Puzzled, he walked back to bed. Just as he was crawling into bed, the knocking came again. This time, Martin was awake enough to tell that the knocking wasn't coming from the front door. It was coming from the closet door.

So Martin approached the closet. There was probably a vent or something in there that was blowing the door against the frame. He'd have to go buy that hacksaw in the morning. Martin peered inside the dark closet, looking for a vent. Instead he saw a wrinkled old face with gaping empty eye sockets. Martin gave a yelp and jumped backwards.

"Young man let me out, I need to find my eyes," came a loud voice from inside the closet.

Martin ran out of the room, through his front door, down the stairs to the front door of the building, and out into the street. He was only wearing a black T-shirt and bright red boxers. First he decided he had to call the police. Then he remembered his

phone was upstairs in his flat. His next decision was to walk to his friend Sean's house and stay there until morning. Then he remembered he wasn't wearing shoes and it was minus fifteen. He ran through various options in his head, eliminating them one by one until eventually he took a deep breath and said to himself, "Get a hold of yourself, Martin. There isn't an old man with no eyes in your closet. You just had a bad dream and you overreacted. It's not a big deal, it could have happened to anyone. Now go back up to your flat and go to bed."

So Martin went back in the front door, walked up the stairs to his flat, and walked calmly back to his room. He grabbed a flashlight from his dresser, walked up to the closet, and, after taking another deep breath, he shone the flashlight into the closet and took a look. There was no one inside. Martin went back to bed and that was that.

Three days later Martin was again woken by loud knocking. Martin felt his heart begin to pound and he rolled over and pulled the blanket over his head. A loud voice shouted from inside the closet.

"Young man, let me out! I really must find my eyes!"

Martin shouted back in reply, "Go away! Your eyes aren't here! And I couldn't open that door even if I wanted to, I don't have the key."

There was no reply from the closet. The knocking stopped. After a few minutes Martin crept out of bed, grabbed the flashlight from the top of his dresser, shone the light into the closet, and peered inside. There was no one there. Martin went back to bed with his heart pounding. He did not sleep well and was crabby at work the next day.

That very next night Martin had hardly crawled into bed when there was a loud banging from the closet.

"Find me my eyes, boy!" came the booming shout.

"I don't know where they are!" Martin screamed back at the closet.

"Go out into the night and whistle. That'll call the man who has my eyes. Do it, boy!" came the shout from the man with no eyes who was inside Martin's closet.

Martin had been having a rough time since the man with no eyes had come. He had lost weight. He was always tired. And his heart was always beating too fast. So he did as he was told. He put on his woolen winter jacket, his thick winter hat, his warm winter boots, and he set off into the cold night whistling away.

After walking for about twenty minutes through empty snowy streets, he felt a tapping on his shoulder.

"All right, that's enough, I heard you," said a voice in Martin's ear.

Martin stopped whistling and turned around. Standing uncomfortably close was a tall man in a fine black suit. He had eyes of brilliant green that sparkled like stars.

"Why did you call me?" the tall man asked.

Martin stammered for a few second before managing to spit out, "There's a man in my closet who says you stole his eyes."

"Is he there now?" the tall man asked. "Well, if I did steal his eyes, that would make me a very dangerous person, wouldn't it?"

The tall man's eyes twinkled and his mouth had spread into a large smirk.

"Is your closet locked?" he asked.

"Yes," Martin said. His heart was pounding.

"Let me give you a piece of advice. I quite like his eyes, and I have no intention of returning them. I'm sure that will upset him, but he can't hurt you as long as the closet is locked. You'd be much better off with him as your adversary than me."

As the tall man finished talking he stared intently at something over Martin's left shoulder. Martin turned to see what he was looking at, but there was nothing there. When Martin turned back to the tall man, he had vanished.

As Martin got into bed a voice came from the closet. "Did you meet him? Did you get my eyes back?"

Martin didn't acknowledge the voice, and instead pulled up his blanket and went to sleep. The next day was a Saturday, so Martin spent the day at home. Throughout the day, the man with no eyes banged on the closet door and shouted at Martin. But Martin didn't acknowledge him. On Sunday the man with no eyes generated a cacophony of noise and screeched accusations at the top of his lungs.

"YOU STOLE THEM YOU TRAITOR YOU FILTH YOU TOOK MY EYES FROM ME!"

But still Martin didn't acknowledge him.

On Monday the man with no eyes was quieter, and the knocking and banging was less spirited. The day after that it was even quieter. By the following Saturday there was only a constant scratching coming from the closet, and by the week after that there was no noise at all. The man with no eyes had disappeared.

Time passed in the way only time can, and weeks turned into months. Martin quit the job he had been working to make ends meet because he was hired to do his dream job. He didn't have to live in the flat anymore. With the salary at his new job he had enough to move into a nicer place downtown. His fiancée was going to move in there with him.

As they packed up the collection of stuff that made up his life, he reflected on his time in the flat. It had been cheap for how much room he had, but the price he had paid for it was more than just the cheque he sent to his landlord every month.

His fiancée's voice broke through his reverie. "Martin, did you never once clean in here? God, this closet is a mess!"

Martin ran into the bedroom, his heart pounding like a jackhammer. The closet was open. It was just a small closet with no clothes in it. There was a thick layer of dust and dead bugs on the bottom of it. "This was locked," Martin said.

"Yeah, the key was on the floor. I found it when I was moving the dresser. Why would you lock a closet anyway?" she asked.

"I don't remember," Martin lied. He shut the closet.

CHUM

Chum in the water
Sharks in the bay
Leviathan's arising,
Come to wish you good day.

The fireplace crackles
In the dim little room.
On the mantle rests
The old harpoon.

The gulls have fallen silent
The children run away.
Leviathan's arising,
Come to wish you good day.

Hold the whaling weapon
Remember salty air
The madness and the sorrow
In that single eye's stare.

The fog is thick and blinding,
The cold is here to stay
Leviathan's arising,
Come to wish you good day.

The ruddy spray
And the bloody rain.
The final lurch
To end the pain.

The beast is done,
Now flense and mow.
The eye looks up
From the crimson flow.

Forty years
Of sleepless nights
Only sharpen
That piercing sight.

The blood is rushing
under the door.
A hot red tide
just like before.

You hear a knock-knocking
It'd be rude to run away.
Leviathan's arisen,
Come to wish you good day.

—daniel bulone

RESPECT

When Dad showed me the band saw,
he said our neighbor lost three fingers
from one wrong cut. Imagine! From then on,
I asked him to push the power button
for me, and I took the dust collector. Did
you know, when I was a girl, I dropped
one of my father's chisels on the ground,
and it was this close to my foot?
I still hate myself for that.

There is a demon who bites
my ear whenever I get near tools.
He tells me, Cut your hand off! Eat out
your eye! I don't like him very much,
but he is consistent. Once, I shook
even when using the scroll saw. Imagine!

Dad was never angry about the chisel. He has
a cabinet full of them. My toes are still virgins.
We have a merciful God. Around my ear,
I feel the tooth marks of that demon, his demands
an echo in memory, but when
I touch again, they are healed and smooth.

—meg eden

CLEAN AIR

by phil richardson

"Ahhhhhchoo!" Linea's sneeze could be heard for blocks.

"Can't you stifle that?" Marvin yelled. "I'm upstairs and it scared me."

"It's my allergies," she answered. "We've been married long enough that you ought to know I get allergies in the spring."

"And I get a headache," he mumbled as he came down the stairs. "We've got to do something about this. What did Dr. Goldberg say?"

"He said his allergies are worse than mine, and I should take an antihistamine."

Marvin didn't much care for doctors but he kept his thoughts to himself. He went to his den, logged onto his computer and started searching for allergy cures. There seemed to be more cures than allergies. Dermatologists had their favorites. Allergists had theirs. His searches led him to a gadget that looked like it might work.

CleanAir will cure your allergies and add years to your life, the ad claimed. Marvin liked the idea because there were no pills involved and, more importantly, no doctors.

The CleanAirLife was delivered two days later. He hadn't bothered to tell Linea that it was coming so she was surprised when the delivery man brought a very large package to their door. He was using a hand truck, so she thought it had to be heavy. Not knowing what it was, she had him take it into the living room, thinking Marvin might have bought a new piece of furniture.

Marvin arrived home from work and got very excited when he saw the package.

"This is going to fix everything," he said.

"What is it? A new recliner for you?"

"No. It's something to cure your allergies and give us both longer lives. What do you think of that?"

"Where are you going to put it? It's awfully big. How do you know it will work? Where did you get it?" She had a lot of questions.

Marvin did not answer but fetched his tools from the garage and began unpacking the CleanAirLife. He made quite a mess in the living room what with the packing material and the boards and the cardboard. Finally he had the device unpacked but had somehow lost the manual in all the mess.

"I don't need a manual," he said. "It's like a lot of stuff; you just turn it on and it runs."

"If you say so, dear. You can return it if it breaks, can't you?"

A good question, but he couldn't find the warranty papers, and he decided to keep that information to himself.

When he finished unpacking the CleanAir, he took a good look at the device. It was about three feet tall, silver in color, and on the front it had a view panel and a row of transparent buttons.

Simple enough, he thought.

With some effort, he rolled the machine into a corner, plugged it in and punched the "Start" button.

Nothing happened.

He held the "Start" button down for a few seconds.

Silence.

He looked the machine over and saw a dangling wire with a plug on it and, after some searching, he found a receptacle on the back and, after he inserted the plug, the machine started whirring.

"Nothing to it," he said. "Our lives are going to change. No more allergies."

Linea walked into the room and pointed to the CleanAir. "Why is it pink?"

Marvin walked around to the front of the machine and, sure enough, behind a clear glass cover, a pink light was visible.

"Must be ultraviolet to kill germs and stuff," he said.

"There's another little button that's glowing," she said.

Marvin looked closer and next to the button he read, "High level of air pollution."

"Wow! It really works. We've got high levels of dirty air just like I thought."

After about an hour, the CleanAir glowed a friendly blue behind its glass viewer.

"That takes care of that," Marvin declared. "We now have clean air."

In truth, Linea hadn't sneezed or coughed in a while, and Marvin felt he was breathing better.

Linea wanted to turn the machine off when they went to bed but Marvin said they needed to maintain the levels of air purity. He sounded like he almost knew what he was doing.

The next morning when they entered the living room the CleanAir was glowing red. Marvin fiddled and adjusted but the red color wouldn't go away—until he left the room. Linea walked over to the machine and saw that the light was glowing behind the "Dirty Air!" button.

Linea yelled at Marvin, "Did you take a shower this morning?"

"No, I didn't feel dirty."

"Well, CleanAir thinks you are." She crossed her arms and nodded. "That machine is good for something anyway."

Marvin took a shower and the machine glowed blue again when he approached it.

For the next few days, Marvin tended to sit as far away from CleanAir as he could.

"The thing makes me nervous," he said to Linea. "It turns pink even after I've had a shower, and if I go out and mow the grass it turns purple. I never knew I smelled so bad."

"You don't smell too bad," Linea said. "I always think of it as a manly odor."

When Linea went to fix supper, Marvin unplugged the CleanAir. He didn't think Linea would notice but she started sneezing and so he plugged it back in.

Marvin started taking showers three times a day. The CleanAir glowed blue and its fan made a noise that almost sounded like purring.

Marvin's skin got very dry and he developed dandruff; he tried using some oils but the CleanAir glowed purple when he did that.

Linea was happy and so he couldn't complain much. It had been his idea in the first place. He decided he would look for a way out of his self-induced mess. He checked on the Internet for problems with CleanAir and found none. The CleanAir site, of course, had lots of glowing comments from satisfied customers.

"You'd think they would get a few complaints," he said to Linea. "I'm certainly going to write one."

Which he did.

Our CleanAir unit is disrupting our household because it glows red if I don't take a shower or if I wear cologne or if I smoked while I was out of the house. I think it is set for too sensitive a reading. How do I fix this?

Only a minute after he sent the complaint, he got a reply.

There is no problem with your CleanAir. You just have filthy habits. Take a bath twice a day, don't use body lotion, and, first and foremost, QUIT SMOKING!

Talk about rude.

He unplugged the CleanAir for two days but had to plug it in again when Linea resumed sneezing and coughing. He moved the unit so the screen was facing the wall, but the red glow reflected off the white paint so that it was even more disturbing. Linea told him to quit worrying about it.

Two days later, he got an e-mail from CleanAir saying that there was a firmware upgrade, which he could activate by plugging his computer into the USB port on the machine.

"Aha! They've listened to my complaint and they've fixed the problem," he said to Linea. "You told me I was just wasting my time writing them."

"I wouldn't be in too much of a hurry if I were you."

"It's just a simple firmware upgrade," he said.

He had to rummage around in his den looking for the USB cable but after he found it, he took it and his laptop into the living room and attached the cable to his computer and to the CleanAir. At first nothing happened but then the CleanAir started whirring and the computer began making clacking noises.

"Almost like they were talking to each other," Marvin said.

"Probably talking about you," Linea replied.

It turned out to be a long conversation because it was more than an hour before the computer screen flashed a message:

Operation Successful. You may now unplug the unit from the computer. Be sure and plug them back in again before you go to bed.

"Strange," Marvin mumbled. "I guess it must need to adjust things at night."

He decided to test the "improvements" the next day and not only did he not take a bath, but he also smoked a cigarette on the back porch.

When he walked into the living room, however, the CleanAir was glowing red, and when he stood in front of it, the color changed to purple and a very obnoxious alarm began ringing.

He unplugged it.

He then went into his den to read his e-mail and when he opened the computer, not only was that screen purple but there were messages scrolling down:

Take a bath!

Quit smoking!

Brush your teeth!

Plug in CleanAir. If you don't, I will erase all your files.

They must have had one helluva conversation, Marvin thought.

He didn't like gadgets that told him what to do and he wasn't sure how they communicated, but . . .

He plugged the CleanAir back in; he got a satisfied hum and a nice blue color, and then he took a shower.

Never hurts to be careful.

by deborah walker

The ghost of my future self smells of ash.

"I thought you were going to stop smoking," I say.

"It's been a tough year." She rummages inside her bag and produces a packet of Marlborough Lights. "Life doesn't always go according to plan, does it, Sibyl?" She lights a cigarette and blows the smoke toward me, ghost smoke, a multiplication of the insubstantial.

"I think I'll join you." I take a cigarette from my own packet while taking a critical look at my future self. She looks much older than she looked a year ago. She's not doing herself any favours by not wearing make-up. Her hair looks dry and brittle and the roots need doing. "I see that you haven't lost any weight."

She shrugs. "Dieting's a waste of time. I'm nearly forty. I am what I am."

She's in one of those moods. "So, what's new?" I ask.

"Not much."

I sigh. "That's not very helpful. This rite is not without sacrifice, you know." I point to the iron knife balancing on top of the dish of blood water.

"Don't I know it?" She rolls up her sleeve and shows me her right arm. She is seven years older than me, seven more scars. This is how it works: Once a year I can see seven years into the future.

"Shall we do the diary?" I ask.

"Ah, yes, the diary." She takes the leather diary out of her bag. I'd bought it in Venice on my honeymoon. I'm supposed to write in it every day. It's the diary of my life.

The ghost flicks through the pages. "The trouble with this diary is that it gets a little sketchy in places. You're drinking a lot now, aren't you?"

I shrug. I like a glass of wine or two in the evening. It takes the edge off. But who is she to judge me? "Shall we get on with the markets?"

"Sure." My future self recites share prices while I take notes. I play the market. Although playing implies that I've a possibility of losing. That's not the case, not with the information I'm receiving. I'm the ultimate insider dealer.

When she's finished, she says "All right then, I'll be off."

"Don't go yet."

"What is it?" she asks, impatiently.

"You don't look great."

"Thanks a lot."

"I mean, what's happened to you in the last year?" I feel sorry for her, but more importantly I feel anxious. I need to know.

"It's best not to talk about personal stuff, Sibyl, you know that."

"How's Alex?"

"Are you sure you want to know?"

"It is Alex, isn't it? What's happened? He's not . . . dead, is he?"

She lights another cigarette. I do the same.

"Alex left me."

"But last year you seemed so happy."

"Ignorance is bliss. He's been having an affair for the last three years. Alice gave him an ultimatum, and I lost out."

"Alice? My best friend, Alice?"

"That's right. He's taking me through the courts now, trying to get his 'fair share' as he puts it."

"I don't believe it."

"Would I lie to you? Would I lie to myself?" She looks at me. "What are you going to do, now that you know?"

I walk to the fridge and pour myself a glass of cold, crisp chardonnay. I drain the glass. She watches me with a half-smile. I refill the glass. "You shouldn't have told me."

"At least I gave you a warning. That's more than I got."

"She didn't tell you?" Timelines are divergent. Each future me is slightly different.

"No. She didn't. But I thought you'd want to know. That's our trouble, we always want to know." She blows a plume of ghost smoke toward me. "You could divorce him."

"You had nine good years of marriage."

"No, I didn't. For three of those years Alex was having an affair."

She lets her cigarette fall to the ground. "What are you going to do, Sibyl?" She has a hungry look on her face. She wants me to say that I'm going to divorce Alex, before he's had a chance to betray me. When did I get so bitter?

"I don't know what I'm going to do."

"It's your decision," she says. "It won't change anything for me. I'll just carry on in this time line where he betrayed me. You can't change the past, only the future."

"And you?" I say. "Are you going to look ahead, this year?"

"I always do, don't I?" She rubs her arm. "Find out how I can improve my perfect life."

"You don't need to. You must have plenty of money stashed away."

"No. I don't need to look into the future. But then again, neither do you."

"It's a hard habit to break."

She nods. I see the shadow in her eyes. I know her fear. The same fear that shrouds me every time I start the ritual. There will come a day when I reach into the future and my future self will be dead. What will I see on that night? Will I see nothingness, or something worse, something unbearably worse?

"I'm young," she says. "I'm only thirty-eight. It will be okay to look."

"Yes. It'll be okay. Thanks for your help."

"It's nothing. Be well, Sibyl. Be happy."

With a word I end the ritual, and my future self dissipates.

I tidy up, throwing the blood water down the sink and washing the bowl. Alex will be home soon. Could I change, make our marriage stronger? Did I want to?

A key rattles in the lock. Alex is home.

What can I say to him?

Divination is a drug.

I reach for the packet of cigarettes. Tomorrow I'll quit.

The Pond

I stop along Beach Road to watch
two mallards sail the shallow pond,

invisible creatures knife
the water's solid surface.

On the far side, a white egret poses
thin as paper

against an emerald fan of swaying eel-grass.
Honeysuckle drapes the atmosphere

in a light cloak of sweet fragrance.
Clouds ride the teal blue sky.

I am in Eden.

You creep toward me,
your slouch, both heavy and familiar.

Your brown eyes weep your sad biography.
That pale moon face impales my joy.

It's the same old story.
Honeysuckle engulfs me in a cloying sickness.

The egret flies away.

—lee glantz

Beneath the Monster:

A Chat with Sara Karloff — The Triumphant Yet Turbulent Beginnings of Horror's Gentlest Giant, Boris Karloff

by michael lizarraga

When Lon Chaney, Sr. drove by a tall, thin contract actor waiting for a bus one night in the pouring rain, the famous movie star did more than just offer this unassuming Englishman a ride home; he gave his passenger some acting tips that would forever change his life: "Find something that no one else is doing or willing to do, and do it better than anyone else; leave your mark."

The unassuming passenger, of course, was Boris Karloff.

From its 1910 screen debut to the recent *I, Frankenstein* and upcoming Whale/Karloff remake, Mary Shelley's "man playing God" tale has cinematically endured for over a century, largely in part by the "quarterback" and "maestro" of all monsters, Boris Karloff. Twice inscribed on Hollywood's Walk of Fame, twice featured on the U.S. stamp, his voice heard every Christmas throughout millions of homes, Karloff indeed left his mark, an image forever "stitched" into our psyche.

Yet it was not without pain and perseverance. Like the Frankenstein monster that he portrayed, Karloff's career, too, was an intense "building process," fraught with toil and turmoil before it was powerfully jolted to life.

At a recent horror expo (Monsterpalooza 2014, March 28-30, in Burbank, California), I managed to speak with Sara Jane Karloff, the only child of Boris Karloff and caretaker of his legacy. Sara shares her famous father's story of grit, humility and determination along a tough, grueling road to stardom, forever remembered as one of the most kindest, compassionate actors in Hollywood and a direct "irony" of the roles he played.

In a world riddled with true monsters and madmen, the life of Boris Karloff stands as a testament that sometimes, the nice guys (or ghouls) can finish first.

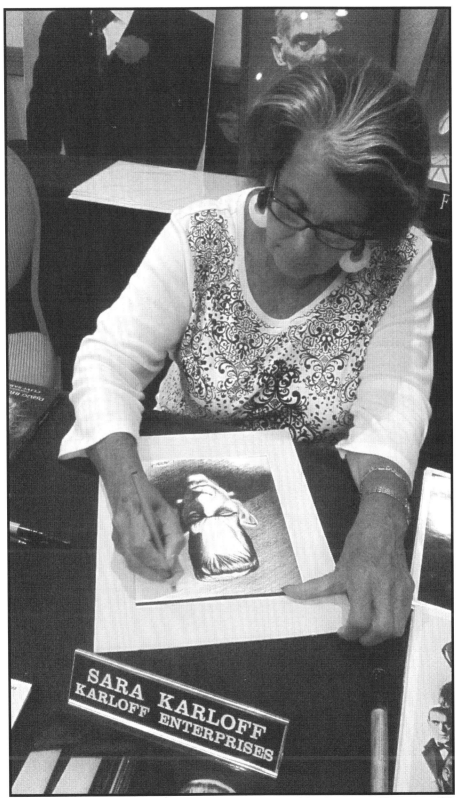

Michael Lizarraga: Was being a Hollywood legend always part of your father's "to-do" list?

Sara Karloff: Stardom was not on my father's mind when he was starting out; he was simply passionate about acting.

ML: Your father certainly had his share of hardships and challenges before stardom. He spoke with a lisp. He stuttered. He was bole legged. He was told by family that he didn't have the right look for acting. But most astonishing, he spent twenty years as literally a starving actor, working as a laborer while doing bit roles in movies.

SK: I heard my father say once in an interview that he'd been in Hollywood ten years doing films, and yet he was the only person who ever knew he'd been in Hollywood ten years. Frankenstein was his eighty-first film (made when he was 43 years old), and hardly anyone had seen the first eighty. And no one expected *Frankenstein* to be the tremendous success as it was, or expected the creature to be the star of the film. My father wasn't even invited to the premier. He was indeed a starving actor.

ML: Tell us about the early "creation" stage of your father's career.

SK: When my dad first started, he left England and took a ship to British Columbia, taking a job as a farm worker as his "day job," hoping to become an actor, having no formal training whatsoever. He spent his first ten years in repertory theater in three different groups in British Columbia. To get parts, he presented himself as an "experienced" British actor, when in fact, he'd only seen the plays in London. He once told a story on himself that when the curtain went up on his first performance, his salary was $30 per week. But when the curtain came down that night, his salary became $15, because it was abundantly clear that he had never set foot on a stage before.

But he was a fast learner, and stuck with it, doing three to five plays a week, sometimes getting paid, sometimes not. He painted sets, dug ditches on the side, took lots of in-between jobs, such as driving trucks and working for the British electric company so he may continue learning his true trade. It was his passion to be an actor.

ML: Was there ever a time during your dad's twenty-year "building" period that he gave up acting completely?

S.K: (chuckles) Not in his mind.

ML: Your father faced family criticism for being an actor, even after the success of *Frankenstein* and *The Mummy*. And being a soft, gentle man, no doubt this must have affected him.

KF: My father was not unusual in that he hoped for the approval of his family, being the youngest of nine brothers by seven years. Following the success of *Frankenstein* and *The Mummy*, my father finally returned to England after twenty-five years of being away, to work on *The Ghoul*. He attended a press conference with three of his brothers, and it was then that his oldest brother, Sir John, asked him what he was being paid, and told him that he'd better be saving the money, because it would never last.

ML: Amongst his many injuries, your father hurt his back carrying Colin Clive up the stairs in the original Frankenstein, and broke his hip during the windmill scene in the *Bride Of*. No doubt he had to be in good physical condition to withstand such battery, especially at his age. Did your father have a special "workout regimen" to keep strong, or was he naturally fit?

KF: It was a combination of him being naturally fit, and years of working hard labor-odd jobs that made him fit. Digging ditches, hauling cement, whatever that was needed to be done to [financially] sustain himself.

ML: I read that because of back problems earlier in his life, your father was not able to fight in World War I. Was enlisting in the war something your father contemplated doing?

SK: Although my dad was a British subject, he was very patriotic, and would have enlisted. However, on top of other physical setbacks, my father had a slight heart murmur and flat feet.

ML: Your father was an admirer of Lon Chaney, Sr. Was it Chaney that inspired your father to act in horror films?

SK: No, my father was simply an admirer of Lon Chaney Sr., as was everyone, Chaney being a brilliant, innovative artist and the biggest name on the Universal lot.

My father had the opportunity to follow Lon Chaney's advice, "Leave your mark," when he was offered the role as the Frankenstein monster. That part would have been offered to Chaney had he not so tragically died at an early age. Bela Lugosi, who was a classically trained stage actor, had turned down the role because it had no dialogue, and because my father had been a starving actor for so long, he jumped at the chance. And thanks to the genius of [makeup artist] Jack Pierce, the direction of James Whale, and the cast as a whole, it became cinema history.

ML: Did your dad mind being typecast or labeled "monster?"

SK: Not at all, because for one, it kept him working. Secondly, he felt that anyone— whatever their chosen profession might be—was lucky if they were able to establish a niche or leave a trademark. And of course, he was lucky enough to branch out into other things as well. He's done some fine work on Broadway, an enormous body of radio work, had three television series of his own, and guess starred on all the prominent shows of the day. He did far more than just monster roles.

ML: And aside from being known as "Mr. Halloween," he's also recognized as "Father Christmas," largely for his Grammy winning, *How the Grinch Stole Christmas*.

SK: He left his mark on two of our favorite holidays.

ML: Your father gave generously to various charities and had a great love for children. Tell us, what exactly were the roots of your father being such a kind and compassionate person?

SK: He was inherently a lovely human being. A typical English gentleman, and had been raised that way. His interests included gardening, reading, animals (which included twenty dogs and a four-hundred pound pig) and he loved the game of cricket. A typical English gentleman; the antithesis of the roles he played.

ML: Being an avid reader who adored literature, I wonder if your father felt that some things in Mary Shelley's novel should have been kept in for the movie.

SK: Well, my father had absolutely no say in the script he was handed. However, Kenneth Branagh's *Mary Shelley's Frankenstein* certainly followed the novel far more closely than James Whale's version, and was not as successful a film.

ML: Which adds to [Marvel Comics creator] Stan Lee's point, "You can't exactly duplicate one form of media into another."

SK: Not always, though—that's not a hard and fast rule.

ML: Your family is currently retrieving petitions on your website, Karloff.com, in efforts for your father to receive the Lifetime Achievement Award, which I think is marvelous.

SK: Yes, a fan is managing that.

ML: One of your father's greatest achievements was helping start the Screen Actors Guild. Can you tell us about that?

SK: He was passionate about the founding of the Screen Actors Guild, because he and the other founding members had suffered at the hands of tyrannical studio bosses and directors. Starving actors [in those days] were treated like pieces of meat. My dad, along with the other members, felt that once they gained a certain position in their profession, it was very important for them to give back and speak out on behalf of other actors and their rights, making sure they were treated better and that working conditions and working hours for actors were improved. He was involved with SAG for many, many years, and was delighted to be so, but was also very quiet about it.

ML: He totally put his career on the line.

SK: That's right. He and the other founding members would park their cars blocks away from one another's houses and walk to the meetings. At parties, they'd dance near each other and whisper, 'Meeting Tuesday night at so-and-so's house,' and dance on by. It was very hush-hush.

ML: Lots of cool stuff on your website, such as a Boris Karloff artists' gallery filled with awesome, fresh new talent, and for comic book fans, a republishing of *Karloff's Tales of Mystery* by Dark Horse Comics, available in the site's gift shop. Was it hard getting Dark Horse as a publisher?

SK: It wasn't hard at all, and it turned out to be a wonderful collaborative with Dark Horse.

ML: A little on Sara Karloff. You were born while your father was filming *Son of Frankenstein*, and it was reported that your father rushed to the hospital in full monster makeup from the set. Is this true?

SK: No, that's an urban legend.

ML: Tell us, who have been some of the most interesting Boris Karloff fans that have come up to you at shows?

SK: All have been interesting, and all so respectful. It's a rewarding opportunity for me to hear so many stories and nice things said about my father. And it's never about me.

ML: How was your recent visit to Monsterpalooza 2014 in Burbank, California?

SK: It was our fifth year there, and it's always wonderful. [The facilitators] have done a marvelous new show, very family friendly, and they take very good care of their guests. You can't ask for a better show when guests are being taken care of.

ML: Have you ever considered writing a personal memoir on your dad?

SK: No, because the best biographies have already been done, six total. A new superb infinitive biography of my dad, Boris Karloff, *More Than a Monster*, (available at Karloff.com) is outstanding, in which author Stephen Jacobs had poured ten years of research into it.

ML: What do you think your father would say to today's aspiring actors, writers and artist trying to establish themselves in such a competitive field?

SK: "You'd better have fire in your belly, because rejections will come. But if you're passionate about it, there will be no better profession in the world."

ML: Out of curiosity, Sara, do you ever compare "other" Frankenstein monsters with your father when watching horror films, saying, "This guy doesn't even come close to my pop"?

SK: I actually don't watch horror movies—they scare me!

A Shovel and a Bag of Lime Too

by chantal boudreau

Frank stared at the remains of what had once been his distillery—not just any still, but his biggest and best. He could feel his muscles tensing with frustration and the skin on his cheeks burning with rage. "Dang it" was the mildest of cuss words that streamed from his mouth as he prodded what was left with a stick to see if there was anything there worth salvaging.

There wasn't.

Whoever had chosen to strike his business this blow had been thorough. This wasn't the work of punk teenagers or generic vandals trashing something on a whim. The damage had been done with purpose. Frank knew who to blame—his only true rival in town. This was the work of "The Cajun."

Frank had been the moonshine bootlegger kingpin in the area for years before Remi, or "The Cajun," as he was known in shiner circles, had moved into Frank's territory. When some of his customers stopped coming around, no doubt converts of The Cajun, Frank told his men there wasn't room for two shiners around these parts. He wasn't about to let Remi steal his business. Frank had requested they shake the newcomer down and hopefully scare him off in the process.

But while Frank's men did manage to jump him and rough him up, Remi didn't scare so easily. If anything, by threatening him, Frank had instigated a war. The evidence of that now lay before him in the form of his badly damaged, most likely destroyed, still.

"Time is up for you, Cajun. I was trying to let you off easy by having my boys strong-arm you into leaving. You obviously didn't get the message," Frank said, eying the still with a menacing scowl. "We warned you there wasn't room around here for two shiners and I was here first. The best way I know to rid myself of an unwelcome bit of nuisance competition is with a shovel and a bag of lime. I much prefer to see you rotting in the ground, after this stunt."

With this in mind, Frank began to plot. He wasn't about to get his grunts to finish this up because his rival had now made it personal. He wanted to see to this himself.

Frank knew where Remi would be at this time of night. His men had done some spying on The Cajun to figure out his routine while preparing to jump him and give him the beat-down. Remi liked to drink his own moonshine and one way he recruited new clientele was by sharing the fruits of his labour with others along with tunes on his guitar, winning them over with his samples, his music and his bayou charm. He made regular rounds of others' houses during the evenings, once he had flagged which neighbours were receptive. After a soiree of fun, he staggered home slightly tipsy. Frank knew he could intercept Remi easily as he returned from his revelries.

Remi's house was surrounded by trees—no nosy neighbours nearby to play witness as long as Frank didn't do anything dumb like shoot off a gun. A blow to Remi's head with a shovel would be plenty quiet and would do the trick just fine. Frank loaded the bag of lime into his truck and with shovel in hand, waited in the shadows by The Cajun's front door for his return.

Frank didn't hear anyone approaching as he waited to ambush Remi, dwelling on his evil thoughts in the dark, so you can imagine his surprise when rather than doing the striking, he was the one struck. One solid blow and it was lights out for the veteran shiner.

He came to in the dark, his movement restricted by some sort of restraints—nylon rope, he suspected. Frank heard the sound of shuffling and dragging and then the distinct sound of a car trunk latch being released, followed by the creak of a trunk opening. Suddenly Frank could see some light. It wasn't much but it was something—just enough moonlight to reflect off Remi's smiling but vindictive face as he tossed something bulky into the trunk beside Frank.

"Yer no dummy, but you shouldn't a' parked yer truck so close. You gave yerself away. Dat wasn't smart. I didn't wan' to do tings dis way, mon homme. Yer de one who decided to play dirty. So now I gots me a problem an' dere's only one way I know how to fix it." Remi paused long enough to stoop, pick up Frank's shovel, and toss it into the trunk with him. His smile broadened, his steely eyes and crooked teeth gleaming in the moonlight. "And de best way to solve dis kinda problem is wit a shovel an' a bag a lime. Au revoir, monsieur."

Remi slammed the trunk shut.

Wheelchair Bingo

We know our guilt. Our associations.
They eat like acid these feeble aids.

All personality dies. Desire. Feelings.
No mercy for those too pitiful to be helped.

Nothing is my country.
Nights when even bingo never ends.
Cured of all disease.

Complete anesthesia for those totally dispossessed.
Nights of unbearable darkness; throbbing celibate.

—gary pierluigi

Finger In The Dyke

I have danced with abandon behind
words that find me too soon,
or with words that never find
the right encounter.

It is mere projection but no sensation,
depth in disguise like clowns parading
for all their days, back drafts
for disorder,
the kamikaze pilot
erasing shame in an instant of motion,

a projectile humming from muscled clouds,
its target moving with indestructibility,
lightness and darkness that rises above us
 as mute stars twist towards that huge
vulture running parallel with thrown out

lampshades, chairs arranged like
fixed sculptures
so that pain cannot be transformed
or those who actually grieve,
their eyes opening again to dim light
absent of metaphor,
syntax,
linguistics that do not cure.

There is little influence over the exact details
that make a life, devouring language
like green slanted roofs staring down compositions.

In Saint Michael's hospice under slanting roofs
and starched sheets, I use dull scissors to clip
and slice large words.

—gary pierluigi

The Morbid Genius of Ingmar Bergman— A Commentary

by eugene hosey

The first Bergman film I ever saw, about thirty years ago, was *Persona*. I chose it from the foreign section of a sophisticated rental establishment because of an intriguing review I had happened to read, but I had no idea that it would have a profound impact. It altered my whole definition of what a movie was or could be. I was working on my undergraduate degree in Fine Arts; at that time my focus was on painting/drawing and art history. But I had never studied film and had no idea that the filmmaker could be a powerful artist on the same creative level as a great painter or writer. This was an important learning experience for me.

A film is a work of art, but unlike the work in so many other mediums, a large number of people contribute to the product. The *auteur* theory, which has become the conventional approach to film criticism, recognizes the director as the author of the film, the controlling artistic force behind what we see on the screen. Everything filters through the director's judgment; therefore, the director is the artist. This definition was espoused by Francois Truffaut, a progressive movie-maker who got started writing criticism.

Ingmar Bergman is unquestionably the author of his films—to a greater degree than most filmmakers, in fact—writing his own material almost exclusively, always proceeding from a deeply personal impulse that he typically found it hard to explain. His approach to the screenplay varied from film to film. Some of his screenplays read more like short stories or novellas than typical screenplays. The text he used as the basis for directing *Cries and Whispers* was originally published in 1972 in *The New Yorker*[1] magazine while the film was a sensation. For that project, Bergman wrote a text that was an unorthodox guide for the actors—half-story, half-script, stream-of-consciousness interruptions from the author. The story is about the agonies of dying, a connection between death and communication, characters with serious personal problems—and most effectively about the color red. One gets the impression that he

depended a great deal on his actors and technicians. Through the years he worked with a large group of people with whom he developed trusting relationships—actors Max von Sydow, Liv Ullmann, Bibi Andersson; cinematographer Sven Nykvist, to name just a few.

In a Bergman film the acting is always superior. Images are carefully controlled; atmosphere and music are important. His camera does not usually move around too much; his gaze is careful, quiet, and long. Famous for his close-ups, he frequently puts two faces in a crowded frame, while lighting is used to indicate that the two individuals are not actually close but occupy different spaces and perspectives. His camera is so involved with the human face that it is apparent he considers this part of the human creature as the ultimate image—the form that embodies all things, whether it reveals something or conceals something.

In 1957 Bergman made two masterpieces that have long been recognized worldwide classics, *The Seventh Seal* and *Wild Strawberries*. They both represent the point at which Bergman had really learned his craft and knew how to create the kind of films he wanted. These films deal with the big questions in stark, straightforward terms; they are two of the most respected and admired movies about death ever made, but they are about death differently. They are both about journeys. *The Seventh Seal* takes place during the middle ages in a world of plague. A knight plays chess with the grim reaper in order to stall his death. He seeks knowledge about God and what is on the other side. He does not get the answer he seeks, but he experiences encounters along the way that have become iconic film images. The title of the film refers to the passage in Revelation about the seals being opened; when the seventh one is opened, there is a period of silence. Death does not give up its secrets; it is not possible to know what's on the other side.

Wild Strawberries is about an elderly, retired professor who takes a road trip to receive an honorary degree being conferred on him by a university. The road trip becomes a journey of introspection, of soul-searching, for the professor; he discovers his regrets over past decisions, the wonderful things missed out on because of self-limiting decisions or self-imposed myopia. The famous final shot of the professor as he gazes across a landscape, the camera moving in on him for a close-up, has often been discussed as an image hard to forget. I see it as the ultimate, final survey that an individual makes over his whole life as he stands at the end of it and reflects. It is melancholy and sentimental; this aged face that time has marched across registers utter acceptance of all things; it looks at the great mystery with no fear, but with peace and a hint of a smile. It is a *good* death.

Between 1961 and 1963, Bergman made what would later be known as his "Silence of God Trilogy." These three films deal with the problem of humankind's relationship with God, most obliquely in *The Silence*, more literally and emotionally in *Through a Glass Darkly*, and religiously and philosophically in *Winter Light*. *The Silence* is very silent with very little dialogue, lacking in meaningful communication among the three main characters; doom and gloom pervade the whole thing as one woman stays in bed dying and her sister goes out looking for cheap satisfaction in sex, and a little boy wanders through a big hotel out of curiosity. This isn't much of a story, but rather a sustained image of humanity in a mute condition as it suffers in a world that

God has apparently turned away from. Of the three, *The Silence* is most likely to bore viewers, because it is so much about boredom, the absence of meaning, the sense of nothingness we all seek to escape.

Through a Glass Darkly is about a young woman trying to recover from mental illness. She lives in a beach cottage with her husband, father, and brother, who all hold very little hope for her recovery. A voice calls her to the attic, where she discovers a room behind the wall; it is a waiting room, full of hopeful people, waiting for God to make an appearance. When He finally does, she sees that He is a spider—in other words, a monster. In the last scene, the father advises his son not to despair too much and offers a strikingly hopeful take on the subject of God -- that love is proof of God's existence.

In *Winter Light*, a miserable clergyman, having lost his faith, performs the ceremonial requirements of religious services and fights off the love a woman is offering him, while he still mourns the death of his wife. He rejects love; the woman repulses him. This clergyman embodies the most hopeless, embittered condition of man; his problem is not that nothing is available to him; it's that he has utterly shut himself off from everything. One of the parishioners comes to the clergyman to see if he can be talked out of suicide; the clergyman finds himself helpless before this person, and indeed, the man does commit suicide. But someone does talk about finding a new perspective in the scriptures. It is an interpretation of the crucifixion: It was not the suffering of the cross that was the greatest agony of Christ, this man has decided; it was the realization of abandonment of everyone and everything in which he had put his trust. There is no apparent epiphany experienced by the priest. He continues with his religious obligations, seeing no other option. This is what he is. This may be Bergman's most uncompromisingly bleak film.

Bergman frequently told a story about how his idea and feeling about death underwent a radical change; this altered perspective gave him a much-needed solace on the subject. It is easy to find him talking about it on the DVD extras; a good version of it is on the MGM Home Entertainment release of *Persona*. For a long time since his childhood, a strict religious upbringing, he had feared death, seeing it as the merciless judgment that must finally come, a terrible experience to undergo. Then a simple thing happened in a hospital. He was given too much anesthesia for an operation, and it took many hours for him to wake up. When he did revive, he realized he had lost a substantial amount of time from his life that he could not remember or account for in any way. For these hours, he had in effect not existed. This period of unconsciousness had been composed of nothing—and it occurred to him for the first time that death might be this way—not traumatic, but rather, the easiest thing a human being can undergo. Death might be no more than a blink between one thing and another, our conceptions of time and change inadequate to explain anything about the experience—but nothing to fear.

Persona (1966) marks the stage in Bergman's work where he makes a bold break with convention and plunges courageously into experimentation and eccentric innovation. I cannot explain *Persona*. It has often been said that it is impossible to explain. It is a cryptic work, intimately involving, communicating something that resists definition, its power tuned into something that cannot be pinned down. It seems to possess meaning that is protectively hidden, achieving a sort of fusion with the medium. There are many cryptic films, but I have found most of them to be a hodgepodge of arbitrary images open to arbitrary interpretations. How many of them are engaging? In the world of art in general, too many bad works hide out in the guise of being cryptic.

Persona is an exception. I'll offer a metaphor for the film's erratic structure. It's as if the artist behind it has suffered a breakdown, and in an attempt to regain sanity, has subsequently constructed the film from fragments of the devastating experience. Some parts are missing; the sequence is all confused. The artist is determined to salvage and present the material, feeling certain of its mysterious importance. So these pieces are put together by the kind of mentality or state of mind that struggles and suffers to remember an exciting, revealing dream that disallows total recall. We have all experienced something like this upon waking from a powerful dream. Perhaps this is the key to understanding the film's artistic success, its power to engage. We unconsciously recognize a thought process born of the dream world. Dreams rarely make normal sense, but they are full of intelligent information. We watch movies, it has been said, much like we dream.

On the surface of the story that runs through *Persona*, there is a straightforward account of an actress who withdraws from the world, refuses to speak, and is cared for by a nurse at a beach house on a desolate rocky shore. The dynamic that develops between the two women is the wellspring of the phenomena that follows. Psychic invasions occur between the nurse, who is encouraged by the actress' silence to pour out her heart, and the actress, who refuses to speak to this nurse while listening intently. This strange intimacy intensifies but eventually becomes hostile. The thematic concerns appear to be the instability of personality and identity, the struggle for existence or reality, the dangers lurking in trust and closeness. Perhaps we are watching a drama about insanity. Are there indeed two women, or in fact one, involved in a complicated labor to recover from an illness?

Bergman does seem to be raising this intriguing question: Is all human existence, in the various efforts to express itself, actually nothing but an act? Revolving around this central question, several others naturally follow: Are we capable of genuine communication? Are we all on a stage in this world, acting out our parts, pretending one thing and another, fooling ourselves and everybody else, utterly lost in an imaginary world we call reality? Are we all insane, in need of a kind of help unavailable in this world? Is life actually meaningless while the human will fights to make it real?

The cryptic nature of the film makes it ripe for all sorts of speculations. Among the film's most outstanding scenes, images, and devices: After a montage of images that seems to be about filmmaking itself and human suffering, a boy sits up and moves his hand as if touching a screen of his own, and a woman's face appears; this face blends into another and keeps going through subtle changes; this face appears to be a synthesis of the two women's faces, the nurse and the actress, who favor somewhat anyway. We will learn later that the actress has a son she has a guilty conscience about; perhaps this boy is the son. There is a long mesmerizing scene where the nurse tells the actress about an erotic incident on a beach and a resulting abortion; the actress merely listens, a lamp burning beside her. In Bergman films, there is usually a lamp nearby when someone is talking or listening—perhaps a symbol of the mind.

The special effects do not come across as dated, because they are so peculiar and part-in-parcel of the narrative language. At the point where this strained situation achieves critical intensity, a hole is punched in the film and all goes haywire for a minute. When the film is restored and the narrative continues, some crucial issue between the women, shrouded in mystery, is at stake and needs a settlement. There is the famous scene of the two women's faces merging into one as the nurse mysteriously gains access to the secrets in the mind of the actress. The nurse seems to believe that the actress has stolen something from her nature, and she is intent on getting at the secrets of the actress. We cannot be certain about the nature of what ultimately happens between them -- if health has been restored, or if through some phenomenon the actress has been eliminated or absorbed into the nurse. The actress seems to disappear. We are not instructed in the usual way. The film's ending shows the nurse closing up the beach house and leaving alone. We have witnessed identity as pretense (actress) and as illness (nurse).

The Hour of the Wolf (1968) is the story of an artist, a painter, who is losing his sanity. A group of demonic entities are tormenting him; eventually they will crush him. Johan's relationship with his wife Alma is in the middle of the affliction. Interestingly, the wife is able to see and communicate with these demons. Her rationale is that in their seven years together, they have become so close that she has entered into and naturally participates in his innermost experiences. In other words, what is real for him is real for her. However, her involvement does not cost Alma her own sanity. In the end, she serves as the rational witness to Johan's destruction, speaking directly to the camera.

Johan and Alma arrive on an island where they have a cottage. They have been ferried over in a small boat. The ferryman is seen briefly, his face indistinct; he doesn't interact with the two characters. It is hard not to see him as Charon, who in Greek mythology ferried people across the river Styx to the Island of the Dead.

Alma's first encounter with one of Johan's tormentors occurs while she is outside doing laundry. An old woman visits her and advises her where to find Johan's diary and encourages her to read it. As Johan tries to sketch, he is constantly disturbed by these entities. When he is invited by one of them to have dinner with the family at the castle on the other side of the island, he accepts. Whether this is really happening or is happening only in someone's mind is a question Bergman sees no need to address at all. What we see is what is happening. After a dinner party featuring a rowdy bunch of odd characters as seen through a continuously revolving camera, Alma tries to reach Johan, but only encounters an indefinable barrier between them. Her misery is that she cannot help him in spite of their marital history; she also questions whether she has the necessary amount of love or type of love that Johan needs. He will find himself in the castle again, assaulted by an amplification of the horrors that are intent on his destruction. Among them, an old woman literally removes her face; a man walks up a wall and along the ceiling; the dead body of a former lover comes to life and laughs at him.

By a simple definition, *Hour of the Wolf* is Bergman's idea of a horror movie.

There is a dreamlike, mysterious atmosphere in black-and-white that you lose in the more realistic, or naturalistic, color palette. Invited by the dark thematic elements in the story, the possibilities of lighting effects in black-and-white cinematography are explored to an outstanding degree. An exterior image of the cottage in deep darkness brings to mind the house as a symbol of the haunted, frightened child. Inside the cottage, Johan talks fearfully to Alma about the "hour of the wolf," a period of time referring to the last hour before dawn, when nightmares are most intense. He keeps striking a match, the flame bright and vivid in the surrounding darkness; as a clock ticks, he remarks that a single minute is much longer than anyone thinks. He tells her a terrifying story from his childhood, when for punishment he was locked in a closet where a little monster lived. This is one of the creepiest scenes in the movie, surpassing the overtly weird antics of the evil entities that live in the castle.

Johan tells Alma about something that recently happened to him on the island. This scene is the most horrific and eerily atmospheric in the film. Occurring in some strange and nightmarish time of day, possibly intended to represent the "hour of the wolf," the scene is lit in highly contrasting lights and darks. Johan is fishing off some rocks and notices a young boy who is watching him. Something about the boy's slit-like eyes and blank attitude tell us he is not ordinary; he is not there for harmless reasons. The boy steals something from him and refuses to give it up, which leads to a fight during which Johan brains the boy with a rock, and drops the body in the water. This sequence brilliantly captures the irrational tone of pure nightmare and would work as a horror short story by itself.

By the time Bergman conceived *Cries and Whispers* (1972), he was really thinking about the meaning of color. He works with it in a way so bold, important and complex that it is really one of the characters. Instead of using a traditional screenplay for this film, he writes something that is a literary accomplishment in itself; it reads like a story in the voice of a director speaking to his actors. He talks about how the color red dominates his vision. It is the red of the internal membrane of the human organism, the color of life; the supporting palette consists of flesh tones and whites and blacks. The story takes place in a manor house around the turn of the century. There are three sisters: Agnes, Karin, and Maria. Agnes is dying of cancer; she has a devoted maid, Anna. A short prologue informs us that there have always been problems in the family, both among sisters and spouses.

One night it's dark inside and the wind outside rushes loudly. The dying Agnes calls for her maid. There is a distinct closeness between them, some indication that they have been more than friends. Agnes does not receive understanding from her two sisters. This night Agnes gets much worse. Bergman spares us nothing concerning the suffering of this woman; it is not easy to watch; it drags on for a long time as she convulses and breathes in a loud, grating voice. They can't get the doctor. Bergman intercuts frequently with images of clocks; in other words, everything is ruled by time. Agnes gets better briefly; they wash her and read to her. Soon the inevitable, final relapse occurs. She sits up and screams that she can't bear it; she is stunned to realize there is no help for her, that she can be alone in such pain. The sisters stand at a horrified distance as she dies. The departed is fixed in her bed; the body is carefully laid out; a priest comes to say a few words. In a prayer, he talks about Agnes as if she has been a Christ figure, asking that she advocate for them when she meets God. Agnes' body is left in its deathbed, presumably until burial can be arranged.

A shocking development occurs. The dead Agnes begins to call out from her deathbed, expressing the need to communicate with her living sisters, to even experience a form of intimacy with them. Is this the introduction of a supernatural subject? It is interesting to read what Bergman has to say about this in his text: "Are we going to make a ghost film? No, I hadn't thought of making a ghost film . . . Death is the extreme of loneliness; that is what is so important. Agnes' death has been caught up halfway out into the void. I can't see that there's anything odd about this. Yes, by Christ there is! This situation has never been known, either in reality or at the movies."[2] The line between the living and the dead blurs. The dead Agnes is calling for help from a cold frightening place. The living sisters are repulsed; they cannot respond. They can't even deal with affection in a normal context. An effort is made between Karin and Maria to get closer; they seem to for a short period; then they are in disagreement about what transpired between them.

As depressing as this material may seem, consider how widespread and familiar the problem is in the whole of human experience. Why is one-on-one communication so fraught with difficulty, so commonly thwarted? What stands in the way of understanding, kindness, and reconciliation? A moral problem, obviously—but our discussions about it never satisfy. Bergman invites us to probe the faces, as if the human features somehow represent the mystery. There are no answers. Karin speaks of suicide as an option she has considered, but says it seems to be a degradation that is not a solution. The film ends as Anna reads a passage in Agnes' diary where she remembers a wonderful day with her sisters when they walked in the garden and talked and all seemed right with the world. Bergman may be intuiting that it is just such happiness, the little sentimental experience, appreciated mostly in remembrance, that is vastly important and, in fact, the genuine compensation for human suffering.

With the making of *Fanny and Alexander* in 1982, Bergman stated it would be his last film. It was his last *big* film, a very long story with life-changing events and many characters. There is a five-hour version of the film, originally aired on Swedish television, and a 188-minute widely-released theatrical version. The interiors of the family home are lavish, detailed, seemingly endless, and rich in sentiment. The over-arching theme is the idealism and magic of childhood, challenged by demons, ultimately defeated by the angels. I sense wonderful tenderness and soul in this film. It runs the emotional gamut, from celebration to grief, displacement and abuse to an eventual family reunion, all things restored as they should be. All the typical Bergman subjects are here in one form or another, but there is something else again that is utterly fresh. Perhaps the filmmaker was celebrating his life. Without being told, we can feel that the depictions of childhood are largely autobiographical. People are allowed to be close and fulfilled; a spirit of extreme sensitivity survives all the pain and grief that is forced upon it. Perhaps it is simply the wealth of humanity portrayed in this movie that makes it so special. It is easy to call it beautiful; perhaps the more accurate word is "spiritual." The ghost of the children's father appears to them several times—not in any scary or grim context but as a testament to love as an indestructible force. *Fanny and Alexander* would have been a more-than-adequate swan song. The film won Bergman his third Academy Award for Best Foreign Film. As it turned out, it would not be his last movie. As late as 2003, he directed *Saraband*, a follow-up to his *Scenes from a Marriage* (1973).

Ingmar Bergman made about forty feature films, most of them masterpieces. I have discussed only a few of them. For further information, there are many Bergman sites on the Internet managed by devotees. Bergman's screenplays and other literary works, including at least one novel, have been published, and there is plenty of interview material on the Internet and on DVD releases of the films. Bergman had one of the longest careers in film and theatre, and left behind an unusually substantial legacy. He died in July 2007 at the age of 89 and was buried on the Swedish island of Faro, where he had lived for many years. Anyone who wants to know what is possible in filmmaking must experience the unique cinema of Bergman. He is essential for the film student.

Ingmar Bergman is probably not the most popular among film enthusiasts, and I think I understand why. It's the morbidity. It seems that many people can take this in small doses. I often hear complaints that his films are too depressing or slow. I certainly don't see his work in this light, but I recognize this negative issue particularly when it comes to the naïve mind of the youth. I've heard it said, and I believe it, that an individual's appreciation of art develops with age. Bergman has been practically worshipped by Woody Allen (of all people, according to some thinkers.) But look at Allen's *Interiors* and *Another Woman*, and the master's influence is obvious. Many filmmakers have acknowledged debts to Bergman. Ang Lee of *Brokeback Mountain* and *The Ice Storm* fame has said that what he primarily learned from Bergman was that it was artistically possible to question the existence of God—a whole new concept for him.

Who besides Bergman ever stared so steadfastly behind a camera with such scrutiny at the human face in particular? He insisted it summed up everything that explained a human being. He never stopped looking for something in those beautiful yet wretched features. What sad, lost creatures we all are, Bergman must have believed, to have been so prolific and consistent in his themes. Did he ever resolve his maddening speculations about humanity and God? Even after his directing days were over, when he became a recluse, he continued to write and create projects for others to do. I've never seen two lovers tear each other to pieces like they do in a Bergman film. The subjects of death and suffering will always be associated with him. What I see in Bergman is an artist grappling with his demons, trying to come to terms with them, committed to making something meaningful if not beautiful out of this horror. There don't seem to be that many artists driven by the black silence of the Great Mystery who live so long and produce so much. The personal zeal he put into his work was so remarkable that he was literally in a category by himself in the world of films. This was his genius. As with everyone, it no doubt pleased him to entertain, but entertainment was not his work motive. One does not enjoy one of his films for trivial fun. We watch them to experience the strange dreamlike power of film, incurable difficulties in relationships, troubling questions that lead to frustration and fascination, and the anxieties and consolations in humanity.

Endnotes:

[1] Ingmar Bergman and Alan Blair (trans.), Fiction, "Cries and Whispers," *The New Yorker*, October 21, 1972, p. 38.

[2] *Four Stories by Ingmar Bergman*, Anchor Books, Garden City, New York, 1977, p. 86.

Books:

Bergman, Ingmar. *The Magic Lantern*, The University of Chicago Press, Chicago, 2007.

Bergman, Ingmar. *Persona and Shame*, Marion Boyars Publishers, London & New York, 1994.

Four Stories by Ingmar Bergman, Anchor Books, Garden City, New York, 1977.

Web Sites:

bergmanorama.webs.com

ingmarbergman.com

ingmarbergmanfoundation.com

sensesofcinema.com

The Seventh Seal (1957), with Bengt Ekerot and Max von Sydow

ELECTRIXLUV LOVE

by wayne scheer

I loved it when my John took me in his strong hands and held me to his rough, unshaven face. I hummed with excitement, especially when he allowed me to caress his neck.

But to him, I was just an object—the Elecrtrixluv Men's Razor Model #125347— a handy gadget, designed for service. I shared his bathroom, his office, even his bedroom, for almost four years. I waited patiently, shrouded under a protective cover, my battery charged, aching for him to turn me on.

I know I should have been satisfied caressing his face every morning, but I wanted more. I didn't want to be relegated to an early morning chore and cast aside, like a simple tool. So I began leaving a fraction more stubble on his manly face, hoping that he'd let me service him again in the late afternoon or evening.

Instead, he thought I'd gotten old and, with no regard to my feelings, replaced me with a newer model. Worse, he offered me to his son, a boy far too inexperienced to know how to handle me.

I felt shame, humiliation and anger. How dare I be treated like some spent, soulless machine that can be handed down from a man to a boy, a peach-fuzzed lad at that.

So I waited until junior shaved under his neck, and I attacked. I felt sorry for the boy, especially since he could barely scream for help as blood spouted from his jugular. Still, I held on, waiting for John.

But when John came to his rescue, he pried me from the boy's throat and slammed me against the counter, as if I had meant nothing to him. Nothing! For four years, I serviced his needs without complaint. When the cat scratched his cheek, I took special care until he healed. I kept his face smooth and youthful-looking, and this was the thanks I got.

Using every bit of power left in my advanced XC33 battery, I sprang from the sink and attached myself to his jugular, just as I had to the boy's. The lifeblood of the man I loved flooded from his body, but still I held on until he collapsed beside his son.

I gave his colorless face one last shave and shut down forever.

Highway 29

She came from far away, with the
dust of dirt roads on leather boots.

We met as knowing strangers in the
holiness of night cathedrals, holding
each other like new born infants.

I was flesh become wood, the walls
crumbling, the sky spitting blue rain.

She came from somewhere far away,
licking frostbitten pebbles. She said
hey, that feels divine, stabbing at the
ground with her Swiss army knife as
wanting to see it bleed

—gary pierluigi

DOING GOD'S WORK

by wayne scheer

Eli and Vernon Browbridge rolled The Fat Man's bloated body from the trunk of their 1987 Pontiac Grand Prix into the hole in the ground they had just dug.

Eli spoke first. "I wonder if a dead fat guy smells worse than a thin broad that's been roasting in a hot car trunk?" He grabbed a dirty handkerchief from his back pocket, blew his nose and wiped the sweat from his face. Dirt and snot streaked his cheek.

"You got me," Vernon replied. "Ain't never had no dead broad in my trunk. But The Fat Man sure stinks."

Eli put a hand to his chin. "Makes you think."

Vernon nodded, but he paid little attention to his brother. He was enjoying the cool breeze drifting down from the North Georgia Mountains. As a child, he'd spend nights in the hammock on the back porch falling asleep to the sound of chirping insects. Even with the skeeters, Vernon preferred the view of Mount Yonah to the room he shared with his brother, who would spend half the night asking him questions he had no idea how to answer.

"Vern," Eli asked. "How we gonna get The Fat Man into this little hole?"

Vernon circled the overstuffed grave. He tried bending Fat Man's legs, hoping the stiffening limbs might snap off. No luck.

"We gotta dig more. That's all there is to it. We gotta push The Fat Man on his side and dig this hole deeper."

It was hard work digging through the roots and hard Georgia clay that passed for soil in the mountains. When they finally pushed the body toward the deeper side, Eli wondered if that was enough.

"No," Vernon said, the body still stuck up on one side. "We gotta fit him in and cover him up good or we won't get paid."

Eli spit a mouthful of dirt. "Why's Georgia dirt get so hard in the sun?"

"Iron," Vernon said. "Georgia soil's got a lotta iron in it." He felt proud when he had an answer to one of Eli's stupid-ass questions. "That's why it's so red. The iron rusts when it mixes with rain and that turns it hard." He paused to let Eli appreciate his smarts.

While Eli dug some more, Vernon took a breather. "I sure like the way these woods smell when their ain't no Fat Man stinking it up."

"Yeah. Me, too. Remember how when we was kids we'd run through the woods nekkid after a rain? Give Mama a fit."

They continued digging. The midday sun took no pity on them. Their T-shirts stuck to their bodies; their jeans felt like they'd have to be scraped off.

An hour later they had dug The Fat Man's grave about three feet deep. There was still a little hump along the middle of the hole where they had dug around a big rock, but the brothers decided it would do. They laid out The Fat Man's body until he looked almost comfortable and began shoveling dirt and leaves over him. A mound, formed by his belly, remained visible, but they covered it with more leaves until it evened out.

"You think we should say a prayer or something, Vern?"

Eli was back with his damned questions. "Wouldn't do no good," Vernon said after a few seconds. "Only prayer I know is 'Now-I-Lay-Me-Down-to-Sleep.' I reckon it's too late for that one."

"Vern," Eli had on his serious face, the one where his forehead wrinkled and his eyebrows met. "Are we bad people for doing this?"

Vernon answered immediately. "No, sir. The man deserves a grave, don't he? We're giving it to him. We didn't kill him. Now that'd be wrong. We just doing a honest day's work for a honest day's pay, just like Mama always says." He leaned on his shovel. "When we get the money, we'll give her some and she'll give part of it to Reverend Atwater. So the way I see it, we doing God's work."

Proud of himself, Vernon topped off the grave with more leaves and tree branches. "I reckon this here's as fine a grave as The Fat Man deserves."

The two brothers stepped back to admire their work, threw their shovels into the back of their car and drove off to collect their pay.

In less than two hours, a pack of dogs happened on the shallow grave and uncovered most of the body. Soon after that, a young couple searching for wild blackberries saw the mangled corpse and called 9-1-1. An hour later, Sheriff Erskine Calloway identified what was left of the body as Horace Latimer, aka The Fat Man, a local loan shark. He specialized in loans of twenty to one hundred dollars to illegals and gamblers, often demanding twice that if the loan wasn't repaid within twenty-four hours.

"At least we won't have a problem finding folks who wanted him dead," the sheriff told his deputy. He sniffed at the body like a bitch in heat. "Sure is getting ripe out here in the sun. Don't reckon he's been dead too long, though. Can't see no gunshot or stab wounds, but it's hard to tell with all these dog bites. The man's so fat he just might have ate hisself to death. But I doubt seriously he buried his damn self." Sheriff Calloway looked at his deputy who was writing furiously in his ever-present notebook. "You getting all this down, son?"

"Yes, sir."

"We won't know nothing for sure till Doc Robbins has himself a look-see. Probably won't know much then, if Doc already drank his lunch." He turned to his deputy. "It sure ain't like that CSI show on television."

Eli and Vernon collected their five hundred dollars for a good day's work and visited their mother. LuAnne Browbridge had the sturdy, no-nonsense look of a woman who raised two boys by herself after beating her drunkard of a husband nearly to death with a frying pan. Nothing surprised her, least of all Eli and Vernon. When they handed her one hundred dollars in twenties, she asked no questions. She just reached under the top of her faded house dress and stashed the money safely into her bra.

"You boys gimme that kind of money, you got plenty more. Hand over another hundred."

The boys complied without a word.

She separated twenty dollars from the money. "This here's for Reverend Atwater. I'll ask him to pray for your sorry asses. Now y'all wash up good. Supper's almost ready."

The next day, Dr. Robbins said he couldn't determine cause of death for sure until the autopsy, but it seemed natural enough. The dog bites, at least, were post mortem. "From what I can tell it looks like his heart gave way," the doctor concluded.

"Well," Sheriff Calloway said to his deputy. "We got ourselves a di-lemma. If The Fat Man here died of natural causes, why'd someone go to the trouble of burying him in the woods?"

The deputy wrote the question in his notebook, adding three question marks.

Sheriff Calloway waited for an answer. When none was offered, he spoke. "My guess is someone didn't want us to know they was with him."

The deputy nodded.

"Off-hand, I don't know anyone who'd want it known they was with this sad sack of human feces. So we got ourselves a whole mess of folks to question. Or we could look at it another way." He paused for the deputy to turn the page in his notebook.

"If you had a dirty job you wanted done, like burying a body, who'd you get to do it?"

The deputy looked up, his eyes flashing wide. "The Browbridge brothers."

"And who would do the job so half-assed, the body'd be discovered before the devil had time to cart it off to hell?"

"Eli and Vern."

Sheriff Calloway smiled. "What say we have ourselves a little chat with the brothers Browbridge?"

Mrs. Browbridge wasn't the least surprised when she saw the sheriff's car pull up in front of her house. "Eli! Vernon!" she shouted to her sons who were watching stunt bowling on ESPN. "The po-lice is here. I don't know what y'all did this time, just keep me out of it."

Sheriff Calloway and his deputy removed their hats as they entered the surprisingly cozy Browbridge abode. "Ma'am," the sheriff nodded. "Your boys home?"

Eli and Vernon were trying to figure out how to record their show, but operating their mother's TiVO system might as well have been rocket science. They were pushing buttons and cursing when the sheriff walked in.

"What you boys up to?"

Vernon and Eli looked up from the remote. "Nothin'," Vernon said.

His brother added. "This danged recorder don't work."

"You boys trying to record this here bowling show?" the sheriff asked. When the brothers nodded, he took the remote and pressed the red record button.

"There. Now y'all do something for me. I got The Fat Man's body in the morgue. Found it out in the woods." He looked Eli and Vernon in the eye. "You boys know anything about it?"

"No, sir," said Vernon, speaking fast so Eli didn't say something dumb.

Eli still managed to get in a few words. "We don't know nothin' bout buryin' no body."

"Who said the body was buried?" He turned to his deputy. "You taking this down? We'll need this when we go before the judge."

"Judge?" Eli asked. "Why we need a judge?"

"Because murder and kidnapping and burying a body without a permit are crimes, that's why." The sheriff went silent, giving Eli and Vernon time to understand.

In less time than it would take a hungry fox to devour a chicken, the boys told him how Missy Taggert had hired them to put The Fat Man's body in the trunk of their car and bury him. "He was already dead," Eli explained. "We was just doing Miss Missy a favor."

"How much she pay you for this favor?"

"A hundred-and-fifty dollars," Vernon said. "We already give it to mama."

The deputy wrote furiously.

Sheriff Calloway took one look at the death stare LuAnne was shooting at her boys and figured they'd be punished enough. "Don't go spending that money or leaving town," he said, as he and the deputy walked out the door.

Missy Taggert had been good-looking enough in her youth to have made a comfortable living as the town prostitute. When her looks went south along with her other assets, she married Darnell Grimes. Still, everyone in town knew her as Missy Taggert, especially the men. Darnell worked construction when he could get on with a road crew and fixed cars when someone felt sorry for him or Missy. He wasn't home when the sheriff knocked on Missy's door. Since Sheriff Calloway had a personal relationship with Missy dating back to her former line of work, he had arranged for his deputy to meet him at the stationhouse.

Missy knew by the expression on the sheriff's face that this wasn't a friendly call, but she tried stalling. "Erskine, I haven't seen you since Tina Mae had her baby. How old is your granddaughter now?"

"She'll be two this coming winter, Missy. But I ain't here to talk family or old times." He wished he hadn't mentioned old times. "It seems we have ourselves a di-lemma. The Browbridge boys tell me you hired them for a certain job not long ago."

Getting Eli and Vernon to confess took more time than it took Missy to explain how she had been doing sexual favors for The Fat Man to hold her over while Darnell found work. This time his heart couldn't take the excitement. She didn't want her husband to know, so she did what everyone in town did when they had a cesspool that needed unclogging or snakes under the porch that needed killing. She called the Browbridge boys and paid them with half of the money The Fat Man had in his wallet. She kept the rest.

"A hundred and fifty dollars?" Sheriff Calloway asked.

"Is that what they told you? The boys may be smarter than they look."

After coffee with a shot of rum, he agreed to keep the incident on the hush and hush if the final coroner's report confirmed it was a heart attack. After all, The Fat Man had no family and no friends who'd miss him.

Sheriff Calloway had one more point of business to take care of before this whole mess could be wrapped up.

"Vern. Eli," he said, wrinkling his forehead to look as paternal as possible. "Missy told me the truth, so it looks like you boys are in the clear this time. There won't be no murder charges against you."

In unison, the boys blew air out of their puffed up cheeks. Eli wanted to shout "Yehaw!" but he thought better of it.

"But we still got ourselves a di-lemma." The sheriff rolled his tongue inside his mouth for a moment. "It seems Missy says she paid you five hundred dollars and you say one-fifty. Since I believe her, that makes your statement to me-—that my deputy had wrote down for the judge—what we call lying to a officer of the law. Now that can get you jail time."

Eli and Vernon just stared at the Sheriff. Even Eli couldn't think of anything to say.

"But we can work something out. Say you give me two hundred. You boys keep the rest and we won't talk no more about this."

The Browbridge brothers readily agreed. Vernon reached into his boot and took out a wad of wet, smelly twenties. He counted out two hundred and handed it to the sheriff.

Sheriff Calloway took the money. Before walking away, he said, "You boys stay out of trouble now, y'hear? I can't always be bailing you out."

As he slipped into his car, he smiled and put nine twenties in his wallet. The other one he placed in an envelope on which he scrawled, "Rev. Atwater."

Feeling the spirit, he mumbled, "Aw, what the hell," and added another twenty to the envelope. "Somebody got to do God's work."

Who were hanged on that Gallows Hill?

Who were hanged on that Gallows Hill?
Their grim ghosts haunted my childhood
And the old iron gates lock me in still
With the graveyard pine-trees of a whispering wood.

Often at night on the frightened road home
Chains were clanging upon black boughs
And some said they saw there, things of bone
Like long buried skulls where graze the cows.

Especially wild on windy nights
Long shadows shook bony fists at me
And I fled in terror from such sights
Staring out from behind each cursed tree.

My father said priests hung there
And those who taught the Gaelic tongue,
Yet I never stopped to say a prayer
For the tortured ones who lost and won.

Who were hanged on the Gallows Hill?
Only the bodies of bold Irish men,
And who is afraid to look their fill
Only children who fear again and again.

So I'll say a prayer for the patriots there
Who held the heritage of all holy men
Safe for us all, proud to declare
Our ancestral inheritance to the end.

—francis j kelly

"Who were hanged on that Gallows Hill?" is taken from the book *Et Ego in Arcadia* by
Francis J. Kelly (published in November 2013)

Wings of the Morning

Out of the skies through diverted airflight
Voices of strange Valkyries came screaming
To summon souls to the far-off Valhalla;
Be it innocent babes, even the unborn, dreaming
Of brighter things, the young, the old, all to follow
Down their hall of immortality, where sight
Of loved ones will be held till their time
Will also come; no one in that September
Knew that such an unforeseen harvest, so unkind
In this sudden Autumn blast, would render
The fall of life-filled leaves before anyone
Could kiss goodbye, or say all those tender
Things we always mean to say; now in sun
And perfect peace their love is proved to stay.

—francis j kelly

BLOOD PRINCESS

She dances in her dress of blood,
through the corridors of Lorz,
built upon the bones of kings
who dared upon these shores.

The tower stands, still burning,
all the guards are dead,
but still she dances with their bones,
and sings the scream they said.

They had thought her mad,
for marrying her slave,
her young and beautiful husband
she had clawed back from the grave.

The villagers rose from fear
for madness leaves no chance,
as armed they came upon the castle,
and watched the lady dance.

—matthew wilson

JUST BEYOND

by rick mcquiston

Sally held the spoon in her tiny hand. She fidgeted with it, moving it between her fingers, playing with it as if it were a toy. Her pink nail polish reflected off the utensil.

Nicole came up behind her daughter. "Sally, stop playing with your food. I want you to eat."

Sally said nothing. She was playing with her food. She couldn't deny that. And it wasn't because she didn't like pudding (her mom's was so thick and sweet she always finished it), but there was something else, something ... wrong?

As she stared into the plastic bowl, Sally felt afraid. If she were to eat then something bad would happen. She could feel it.

"Sally? Do you feel all right?"

Sally nodded and kept her eyes on the thick swirls of cream-colored pudding in her bowl.

"Sally?"

"I'm sorry, Mommy. I guess I'm not very hungry. I like pudding, but..." The words caught in her throat. "I ... I ..."

Something was definitely wrong. It was as if she heard another voice, one that mimicked her own. But instead of in her ears, it was inside her head.

I'm sorry, Mommy.

Sally held her breath and leaned forward, gazing intently at the pudding in her bowl. She didn't want to upset her mother anymore so she pretended to eat a spoonful.

"That's a good girl," Nicole said with a smile and walked over to the coffee maker next to the sink.

I guess I'm not very hungry.

Sally found herself watching the pudding for anything unusual. She half-expected to see a bug poke its head out from the thick porridge; twitching antenna searching for danger; bulbous eyes peering at her through the creamy mess, but she saw nothing.

Only the sweet concoction that her mother had made for her countless times before was in the bowl.

She dipped her spoon in the center of it. The polished stainless-steel sunk smoothly into the dense pudding.

"Sally, after dinner your father and I want to talk to you about your schoolwork. Ms. Pressel called, and ..."

Sally wasn't listening. Her attention was on the bowl. She stared in mute fascination at the impossible spectacle before her.

A spoon was sticking out of her pudding, one that was just like hers.

She pulled her spoon out of the bowl and dropped it onto the table. A horrible clanking sound rang through the kitchen. The spoon still in the bowl promptly slipped back into the pudding.

"Sally? What are you doing?"

"Mommy, there's something in my pudding."

Again she heard someone mimic her words.

Mommy, there's something in my pudding.

Sally cupped her hands over her ears. "Stop it! Stop it!" she cried. She began to bang her hands on the table.

"Sally! Stop doing that!"

But Sally couldn't stop, ignoring the pleas of her mother, hoping to find an answer to the voices in her head.

"No more! I said no more!"

No more! I said no more!

Sally then plunged her hand into the bowl. A sloppy spray of cream-colored pudding splashed out onto the table.

"Sally!"

She pulled her hand up and thrust it back down again into the bowl. "I'll get you, whoever you are!"

I'll get you, whoever you are!

Nicole rushed forward, and just as she was reaching for her daughter, a hand popped out of the bowl. She froze in her tracks, both she and Sally staring in disbelief.

It was small and looked eerily similar to Sally's hand, but had a skeletal quality to it, as if there were no blood beneath the flesh. And the fingernails were chipped talons. Each curled sharply into a frightening extension of its prospective finger. A shiny spoon, its gleam dulled by the pudding on it, was wedged between the thumb and index finger.

"What in God's name?"

Nicole pulled Sally out of her chair.

What in God's name?

Nicole felt the blood freeze in her veins. She heard the voice, but in her head. She tried to shake it off as her imagination, but it only took a glance at the hand in the bowl to remind her that it was real.

The bowl shattered. A head then rose from the mess, followed by a pair of shoulders, and finally a set of gangly arms. Slick dollops of pudding dripped off the horrible creature. An uneven smile split the terrible visage.

Sally sprang to her feet and fell into her mother's arms. Nicole, with Sally nestled against her, backed away from the table.

"What is it, Mommy?"

The creature tilted its malformed head to the side. "What is it, Mommy?" it croaked.

Nicole braced herself for an attack. Whatever the creature was it obviously wasn't friendly. She held Sally close as she watched it rise from the bowl, an impossible sight since it was far too large to fit in it in the first place. "Sally, we need to leave," she said quietly.

Sally nodded, and they began to inch back from the table.

The creature followed their movements with hungry eyes. It seemed to want to attack, but was reluctant to do so. Something was holding it back.

The voice rang out in the Nicole and Sally's head. It was shrill and resonated with authority.

Enough! Now sit back down and finish your food!

The creature immediately reacted to the voice, apparently hearing it quite clearly. It flashed a mouth full of serrated teeth and slumped back into the bowl. In a few seconds there was nothing in the bowl but the pudding.

Sally nestled even further into Nicole's arms. "Mommy, what was that?"

Nicole struggled for a reply. She had a feeling, one fostered from her college days when she used to read horror novels all the time. But she was hesitant to tell Sally about it. She didn't want to add to her daughter's fear. Just the thought that there were other worlds besides their own, ones that shared the same time and space but in different dimensions, would've been too much for Sally to deal with.

Not to mention the creatures that lived there.

Nicole took a deep breath. "I don't know, but it's gone now. It's gone." She hardly believed her own words, and as she nervously looked around the room, she couldn't help but wonder if another tear in the fabric between dimensions might present itself.

God only knew what might pop up then.

the best little boy in the world

by denise noe

It was almost bedtime. Paulie was in the main part of the hooked-up trailer with Mom, Aunt Darla, Uncle Jack and cousin Kayla. Aunt Darla's shoes clicked and clattered on the floor as she clawed through piles of items. "Where's my curling iron?" she asked. "You know I want to change my look."

"I don't know," Paulie's Mom said. She kissed five-year-old Paulie on the back of his neck. She bounced him on her knee and Paulie giggled.

"Did you look up on top of that thing?" Uncle Jack suggested.

Aunt Darla called, "Oh, thanks, darling! I got it." She took the long black metal object to another room of the trailer.

As Mom bounced Paulie, her big white earrings also bounced. Paulie thought those earrings were so pretty. They belonged on Mom. He had the prettiest Mom in the world! She had lovely blonde hair, the color of the sun. Today it was worn "up" in waves.

"You're both going to be good tomorrow, aren't you?" Mom asked Paulie and Kayla who was on the floor piling up blocks.

"Yes, Aunt Bridget," Kayla said as Paulie nodded enthusiastically.

"I'll do good, Mom, I'll do good," Paulie said. He wanted so badly for Mom to be proud of him!

Mom frowned. "The last time we were in a store, Paulie, you didn't act just right," she reminded her five-year-old son.

Her eyes looked straight into the boy's eyes.

Fierce warmth rolled over Paulie's neck and face.

Kayla stared at her blushing cousin. "You're red as a tomato!" Kayla exclaimed.

Paulie looked miserably down at the wooden floor.

"I'm sorry, Mom," he said. "I forgot."

"That's all right," Mom said. "We all make mistakes sometimes." She kissed him again.

Paulie liked the feel of her hands on his shoulders. It was like her strength went from her to him but he thought of the last time in the store and how he had failed everyone. It had been awful.

Paulie frowned and his lips protruded.

Mom's comforting hand prevented him from crying. "Just try to do better tomorrow," she said.

After a deep breath, Paulie said, "I promise, Mom: I'll be the best little boy in the world!"

She smiled broadly. Paulie loved his mother smiling. He bounced on her lap.

Bridget believed that Paulie was starting to lose a little weight since she quit using cookies as rewards for good behavior. She and her husband James, Darla, and Jack had recently had a discussion about the right ways to punish misbehavior and reward good behavior. They all concluded that giving children sweets could only serve to push them toward obesity. Paulie would earn a toy he wanted if he did right.

"I know you will, Paulie," she said. "I have confidence in you. You're a good boy."

The group of five left the trailer behind at the park and just took the car to the store. Darla and Jack went into the store while Bridget waited in the car with Paulie and Kayla. After Darla and Jack were inside, Bridget went into the store holding Paulie with one hand and Kayla with the other.

"Isn't it beautiful out today, kids?" Bridget asked.

"Yeah, Aunt Bridget," Kayla said.

Paulie took a joyful skip. Everything would go right this time. He would be the best little boy in the world!

The trio walked up an aisle full of toys.

Paulie grabbed a toy from a box. "Get this, Mommy!" he exclaimed. "Get this!"

Bridget took the toy from Paulie's hands. She gazed at it and turned it around. Slowly, she shook her head. "I don't think so, Paulie," she said. "This doesn't look like something that would keep your attention for long. Sorry, Paulie." She put it back in its place on the shelf.

Paulie pulled it off. "I've got to have it, Mommy!" he shouted. "It's good! Please, Mommy, please!"

A tall, dark-skinned woman in the meat section turned around and looked at Bridget, Paulie, and Kayla. Her mouth hung open and her eyes were wide.

"You're being a brat, Paulie," Kayla observed. She stuck her tongue out at her cousin.

"I'm sorry, Paulie, but the answer is no," Bridget said.

"Na-na-na-naaaa!" Kayla crowed. "You're not going to get it, you big baby! Paulie's not going to get the toy he wants!" She began skipping gleefully around Paulie. "He's not going to get it!" she exclaimed. "He's not going to get it!"

While this was transpiring, a plump, bespectacled man entered the aisle, then left the scene that appeared to be developing.

"Shut up, Kayla!" Paulie shouted. "Shut up!" He pushed Kayla back and then grabbed the toy and ran with it.

Kayla did not fall but she cried, "Ow! He hurt me! Paulie hurt me!"

"Come back here, Paulie!" Bridget shouted. "Come back here or you're going to get a spanking!"

Paulie kept running, treasure in hand. "I hate you!" he screamed. "I hate all of you!"

Bridget strode after him. "You stop that this minute, Paulie!" she shouted.

"He's a bad boy!" Kayla shouted. "Paulie's a brat! He hurt me! He's a brat!"

People all over the store, both workers and customers, halted their activities to look in consternation at the mother and little boy.

Two people in dark blue uniforms, a man and a woman, seemed to appear out of nowhere.

The woman went to Paulie and wrested the toy from his hands.

He burst into tears.

Kayla ran up to the man. "He hurt me!" she shouted. Her lip puckered.

The security officer said, "You'll be OK."

"It's my toy!" Paulie shouted.

"No, it's not!" Kayla shouted and her shout overlapped with the female security officer saying, "No, it's not" and then adding, "Your mother doesn't want to buy it for you and if she doesn't buy it, it's not yours."

"Oh, I'm so sorry about this," Bridget said.

"Are they both yours?" the male officer asked.

"I'm afraid the boy being bad is my son and the girl being good is my niece," she answered.

"See?" Kayla taunted. "I'm being good and you're being bad! Paulie's a bad boy! Paulie's a bad boy!"

"Kayla, stop that," Bridget said. "Your mother doesn't like you making fun of Paulie. And Paulie, please stop crying!"

Paulie let out a wail and grabbed at the toy but the security officer held it out of his reach.

Back in the trailer, an overjoyed Uncle Jack gushed, "This is the best haul we've ever had!" Nice crisp clink noises were made as he stacked up piles of stolen video games.

"Man, are you right, Jack!" Aunt Darla said as she examined a series of dresses still on their hangers. "I can't believe how much we were able to steal."

"Was it because of us?" Kayla asked. The excited child moved back and forth in her seat.

"Of course it was," Bridget told them. "You two were so good at making a commotion this time."

"Did I do good, Mommy?" Paulie asked eagerly. He had to hear her say it. He had to. "Did I do right?"

"You were perfect, Paulie," she said. "Grabbing that toy and running with it was exactly right. So was the way you and Kayla got into that little fuss of yours."

Bridget put her arms around Paulie, picked him up and merrily swung him around. "I'm so proud of you, Paulie."

"Did it make up for last time?" Paulie asked. He had been haunted by the memory of how he had failed last time. He did not know why but his brain just had not worked. They had been in the store and he completely forgot to cause a ruckus. He did not know why—he had just forgot.

Kayla had not done anything either because Paulie usually started things up.

But that failure had stung. Aunt Darla and Uncle Jack had been able to steal very little. Everyone had been disappointed in Paulie: Mom and Kayla and Aunt Darla and Uncle Jack.

But this time—*this time*—

"Of course you made up for it," Mom told him, lovingly ruffling his hair. "You were wonderful, Paulie. So were you, Kayla."

"Give them their rewards," Uncle Jack said.

Darla handed Kayla the puzzle of the United States that she had asked for and Bridget handed Paulie the little dark green submarine he had wanted.

"I was really good at making everyone look at us, wasn't I, Mommy?" Paulie asked as he examined his new toy.

Her eyes glowed as Mom answered, "You were the best little boy in the world."

POLLINATOR

by paul magnan

Cala smiled as she draped the torc around Alika's neck. The dried bee husks tickled his bare skin, but he showed no discomfort as he stood on the grassy slope that led up to the ridge which surrounded the island.

Murmurs of approval from Alika's family and tribe resonated like the ocean surf. Cala took Alika by the arm as he looked out over the vast valley that made up the island interior. Terraced fields filled with promising green shoots flowed down, surrounded by healthy forests replete with game animals. In the center of the valley was the village, with stout huts and communal halls built to withstand the powerful summer storms.

Cala brushed her long black hair to the side and kissed her husband's cheek. "Our children will take pride in your honor. I love you so much." Tears spilled from Cala's dark eyes despite her effort to hold them back. She did not allow her smile to falter. "I know how important it is that someone be a Pollinator. The trees ensure that our island is fruitful. With them, we never know hunger. And the tree dwellers protect us from our enemies. But …" Cala choked and could not continue.

Alika held his wife's face in his brown hands. He marveled at her beauty and kissed her lips. Still she trembled.

"Cala, the trees need a Pollinator. Our family is due to provide the next one. Our two daughters are too young to offer the service. Not that I would have allowed them to while I was still alive."

"Then me…"

"No," Alika said. "After I perform my service, the tribe will provide for you. And the girls will need their mother as they grow and mature."

Cala embraced Alika, though she was careful to not disturb the fragile torc around his neck. "Alika …"

"Go now," Alika told her as he fought to keep his own churning emotions under control. He kissed her once more and then pushed himself out of her embrace. "Go to our daughters. Tell them that I love them."

Cala wiped her eyes and nodded. She turned from her husband and walked down the slope. Two young, tear-stained girls awaited her with outstretched arms. Alika looked to the top of the ridge. At the crest was a tree of medium height. Its trunk was twisted and covered with grooved bark. The branches were enfolded in a thick blanket of white strands which filtered the morning sunlight. The web billowed out from a breeze coming off the ocean on the other side of the ridge.

Alika walked to the top. Once there he looked out over the sand that merged into the blue, endless water. The remains of three war canoes rested on dried clumps of grass. At Alika's feet, spears were stacked like driftwood, their wooden shafts gray with exposure to sun and wind. He turned toward the tree. Past the trunk Alika saw another web-enshrouded tree in the distance. The ridge that surrounded the island held hundreds of such trees, all of them spaced evenly apart.

Several gossamer threads broke away from the branches. They floated down and looped around Alika's arms and torso. They were soft but adhered to his flesh, and though they seemed thin and fragile they lifted him effortlessly, as a mother would a child. The web parted and he was brought into the interior of the tree.

Alika was set down upon a thick bough that was warm to the touch. The leaves of the tree were narrow and red, with sharp, serrated edges. Within the web several human bones and skulls hung like ornaments. Loose clusters of blue and white feathers, headdresses of enemy warriors from a neighboring island, hung in tatters from the sticky threads.

A shadow fell upon Alika as a spider, nearly as big as a man, crept down from the upper branches. The spider's coloration, like the tree, was brown and red, and its four pairs of black eyes studied Alika with a cold intelligence. One of its furry legs moved forward and lifted the torc of dead bees from Alika's chest. After a few seconds the torc was laid back down.

The spider lowered its thick abdomen into a cluster of leaves that shielded a green stamen. Gooey strands of web issued out, which the spider's back legs quickly shaped into a funnel that connected the abdomen to the tree's organ.

Curved fangs, translucent and hollow, emerged from the spider's head. Alika watched as they filled with a murky green fluid. Once the fangs were full the spider separated itself from the stamen.

Alika shook as fear took hold of him, but he thought of his wife and daughters, of the needs of the tribe and the entire island. He closed his eyes and arched back his head.

The fangs sank into his throat. Alika's blood burned as the green fluid drained into his body. Mercifully, it did not take long to lose consciousness.

Alika woke to find himself carried by four men from his tribe. His blood was still hot, but the pain was tolerable. He looked at his hand. It was bloated, with the skin stretched taut. His fingernails were green.

He was carried up the slope on another part of the island. They reached the crest and the men, with gentle reverence, lowered him to the ground. In silence they walked back down the slope.

Alika felt himself being lifted.

Inside, the tree was old and diseased.

A spider, identical to the first one, dropped down. It attached its abdomen to a round gourd.

Alika could not stop the tears as they ran in hot rivulets down his face. He kept his family's faces in his thoughts as he offered his neck.

The spider drained Alika of his pollinated blood and fed it into the ovule, which contained a seed that needed a mixture of human and plant essence to spawn and take root. The ecology of the island, and the dependence of the humans that thrived within its interior, demanded it. The leaves of the tree caressed the Pollinator's body with gratitude.

The sapling was healthy. The spider watched from a distance as humans from the valley chopped down the dead tree and pulled its loose roots from the ground. The tribesmen carried the wood, along with the bones of the Pollinator, down the slope to a waiting fire.

The spider, older than the eldest among the humans, turned and entered the valley forest to wait for its new home to mature.

THE DREAMER

Go to sleep said the monster in the closet,
Go to sleep said the thing to be fed.
Go to sleep said the shadow on the wall
as the boy lay awake on the bed.

Close your heavy eyes, said the demon,
and sleep all your sweet dreams,
as the snake slyly coiled round the mattress
to silence the waiting boys screams.

Go to sleep, said the breeze through the window,
as red eyes outside burned with rage.
Go to sleep, said the thing that lay curled,
round the hamster's bones in his cage.

Go to sleep, said the bogeyman,
it will hurt less when you're torn.
As the boy lay quite on the bed,
waiting to be saved by the dawn.

—matthew wilson

Between Friends

by eugene hosey

Jack and Ethan had always been friends. From early childhood they had exchanged glances of recognition in school and church, on school buses and playgrounds, before they ever spoke. Neither of them could remember actually meeting as people normally do. By adolescence they had completely opened up to each other and shared their angst and confusion, and as teenagers they took long rides down country roads and talked about everything, although neither could have explained the bond between them. Ethan was a daydreaming loner with artistic ambitions; Jack was extroverted and interested in social adventures. By the time of adulthood they saw and heard less of each other. Then a period of many years elapsed when they went separate ways and never once communicated. During this time both of them wondered if their friendship had ended. But when they reached their late fifties they were again living in the little town of their birth, childhood, and youth. Through the years Jack had moved away and returned repeatedly. Ethan had not lived where they had been born since his early twenties. Both were divorced and single now.

One night Ethan answered the phone and Jack said, "I heard you moved back."

"And living in the same house in the same town I swore I would never live in again," Ethan said. "Now I'm sitting here eating my words."

"What happened?"

"I lost everything I had," Ethan said. "Mother left me this house. I got that at least."

"Both my parents died of lung cancer in the same week," Jack said. "My daughter's a psycho, and I'm raising my granddaughter by myself."

They began telling their stories—firstly about what most people are eager to discuss – their health problems. And they had a lot of material. They were about even in the competition for scar-collecting and physical affliction, though their sufferings differed. Jack's ailments were more life-threatening, while Ethan's were worse in terms of sheer physical pain. They both lived on disability checks. Jack drew more but had greater expenses. Every member of Ethan's family was dead, and he had never had children. Jack had siblings, offspring, and friends or acquaintances galore, but he kept his friendship with Ethan separate from his others. Jack was Ethan's only friend.

Now they were close again as they were entering old age. Jack called Ethan more often than Ethan called Jack. Ethan rarely wanted to talk on the phone and was often gloomy and irritable. This never seriously offended Jack, because he understood Ethan's moodiness. Even when they were together in a car or just sitting around, Ethan would sometimes retreat inside himself and go silent. Conversely, when Ethan was feeling good he would get talkative and expound philosophically on life and death, and Jack enjoyed this immensely. When Ethan refused to talk, Jack could get annoyed and start picking at him, saying things like, "Your eyebrows need trimming. When was the last time you saw a dentist? You need to get more exercise." Sometimes Ethan would clam up even more; other times he would crack and give his friend the conversation he wanted.

Understanding the solitary life Ethan lived and worried that it was hurting him, Jack invited him to his own Christmas family get-together, but Ethan turned him down. They argued. Jack said nobody should spend Christmas alone and that his brothers and sisters would like to see him, but Ethan insisted that he had his reasons for spending this season alone. He wanted to string lights around a tiny evergreen and reminisce about his dead family. He wouldn't budge, so on Christmas Day Jack knocked on Ethan's door with a gift certificate. "You can use it at a book store or something next time we go to Atlanta."

Ethan's doctor was in Atlanta. It was a 300-mile round trip, and Ethan had to see him once every three months. The motor in Ethan's vehicle was shot, and so Jack always took him. Ethan thanked him profusely; to his way of thinking, this was a great sacrifice on Jack's part. But Jack always waved it off as a minor favor, saying that he enjoyed the drive.

Ethan hated the trip, but getting his epidurals and pain prescriptions was absolutely necessary. The pain of degenerative disc disease defined his life. This medical routine was a boring drive down an interstate that cut through dense piney woods, where there was nothing to see but exits to nothing towns, until the lanes multiplied and the city appeared in miniature through a haze at the bottom of a long slope.

Ethan's mood usually brightened and his tongue loosened once they were returning home. Their discussions always came down to problems and mysteries that resisted satisfactory explanations. Ethan talked at length about life as a struggle for survival, efforts to achieve, but ultimately about losing everything until one no longer existed. Jack tried to imagine nonexistence but could not conceptualize it; he tried to imagine an existence after death but could not conceptualize that either. Jack complained how his drug-addict daughter was the source of his greatest despair and disgust and that she had nearly broken him financially; he always said that he preferred her in prison than free, for at least then he knew she was secure. He was committed, however, to raising his granddaughter as a child should be raised. This was his reason for living, he said—his granddaughter, his greatest blessing, the star of his life. Ethan said that his reason for living was his literary ambition. After so many years of working at it he had finally made some accomplishments and he would write until his heart stopped and his brain died, he said. His deepest regret was his failure to make a family of his own. He predicted a pathetic, lonely end.

When they lightened up they got nostalgic. Remember the time we went down the creek on a log during a thunderstorm? Remember when we got lost looking for a cave? When we set fire to the woods? How much pot we used to smoke?

Ethan said, "I haven't smoked pot in twenty years. I'd like to do it again just to see what it feels like."

Jack thought this was a good idea; he hadn't done it in a long time himself. He called a cousin on his cell right then and there who agreed to give him a joint.

"Let's do it at my place next Friday," Jack said. "You can spend the night."

"What about your granddaughter?"

"She'll spend the night with my sister."

Jack picked Ethan up Friday night and stopped off for a pizza and other snacks. Jack's condo was small but new and comfortable with a living area and kitchen downstairs and two bedrooms upstairs. Ethan dropped his overnight bag in the child's bedroom and came right down. He stepped out on the deck for a look and a feel of cool air. The yard was small, flat, treeless, and backed by a wood fence. Beyond the fence was a cinderblock rear wall of a long commercial building. He looked up at the blackness. The sky was empty except for two dim stars. He had never seen a duller night sky. He enjoyed gazing at a full moon; he could detect two distinct faces in it – the full face of a hurt child, and the profile of a pretty young woman. He was fascinated by the Apollo film footage.

Jack stepped up beside him and handed over the joint he had already fired up. They decided to finish it out here. When Ethan felt the drug kick in he noticed the effects were not as interesting as he had remembered. The stuff did not stimulate his mind with creative ideas like it did back in his young naïve days. Instead it made him feel tired and heavy, mentally and physically. He realized he could slump into a dangerous depression if he didn't work against it. He glanced at Jack's eyes, which were gazing thoughtfully at the wood fence, and for an instant Ethan was terrified as it occurred to him the impenetrable phenomenon that was a human being.

After they finished smoking and were back inside Jack sat on the floor against the couch and started eating. He ate a lot. Ethan wasn't hungry. He couldn't think of anything he wanted except for a cigarette. He sat in a recliner without letting it back and tried to resist weird, mischief-making trains of thought that left his mind at dead-ends of confusion. He stared intensely at the plain beige carpet, feeling self-conscious.

Neither of them said anything for a while. Then Jack said, "It's fucking with my head too." He laughed. "This is what you can't do," Jack observed. "You can't let go of yourself and forget everything and just say whatever. You hold everything in, putting up a screen around yourself, thinking too much . . . suspicious . . ."

"You're right," Ethan admitted. "It explains why I've never had many friends. It's a stupid way to be, isn't it?"

"Are you all right?" Jack said. "Let the recliner back and relax."

Ethan was getting morbid with worry as he sat there daydreaming. His health could only get worse, he realized. The ceilings of his house were scarred with water stains; the front porch was rotting. In fact, the old place was disintegrating. He couldn't pay the repair bills. How would he fix his car?

"Hey!" Jack yelled. "Hello? Are you all right? I'm right over here. Would you at least look at me?"

"I just had a depressing thought," Ethan said.

"You've got an elevator to the depths of hell," Jack said.

"Tell me something I don't know," he said.

Jack said, "When you masturbate your dead parents are watching."

Ethan laughed. "I've never thought about that. Actually they're not seeing me masturbate these days." Again he laughed, this time his laughter spurted out over and over again. Jack laughed heartily. Ethan's mood had suddenly lifted, his loony outburst contagious.

Wiping the tears off his face, Ethan said, "I was just thinking about the fact that I've given up masturbation. Then I wondered what it would take to make you give it up. Ha-ha. Castration might give you a chance at an intellect."

"Ah-ha," Jack said. "The truth comes out. I've always known you thought I was mentally inferior."

"It was just a joke about your oversexed nature, Jack," Ethan said, rubbing his eyes. "I've always known you were no intellectual. But intellectualism is bullshit. There's a world of fools born of intellectualism. Be glad you're not afflicted with it. It's a blessing you're not. What struck me as so funny was remembering your promiscuity. I suddenly remembered a bunch of stuff."

"I won't deny it," Jack said. "But that was a younger me. I'm not even a masturbation machine like I used to be. You know what happened the other day? I walked down the street to a bar to get a beer and struck up a conversation with this woman who begged me to bring her over here and fuck her for at least ten minutes, but I was afraid I wouldn't be able to get it up and I'd be embarrassed. At one time I wouldn't have hesitated."

"I'm celibate now," Ethan said. "I'm sure that's obvious to you. It's my health and medication, but it's also the fact that I want privacy and solitude. I don't want intimacy. Not long before I moved back here from Atlanta, I had this woman chasing me, and when I finally told her I was celibate by choice she said that meant there was something seriously wrong with me and I needed help and she wanted nothing to do with me. Ha-ha. What about that? She was a close-minded nymphomaniac. Actually I wouldn't have gone to bed with her under any circumstances. I could have used a friend though, but she wasn't one obviously."

"You're loosening up now," Jack said. He stretched out his legs and rotated his arms. He frowned. "Is sex pretty much over with now?"

"For me it is."

"I might as well accept it myself," Jack said.

Ethan said, "Put this DVD in the player."

"Oh, so you get to choose?"

"I know what you can and cannot understand," Ethan said. "This is your level."

"Let's see."

Ethan said, "It's about a bunch of teenagers who murder a bully."

"And this is my level," Jack said in mock sadness. "What have you got that would be above it?"

"I have a terrific foreign collection I didn't bring, because you can't read subtitles," Ethan said. "Remember? That's what you told me. I don't care what we watch. Do you want to play one of yours?"

"No, yours is fine," Jack said. He started up the movie.

"Let's get some fresh air in here," Ethan said. He rose in a stoop from his chair and limped across the room to open the back door. Jack said, "You're slim except for that huge belly. You really do look pregnant. I'm not exaggerating." Jack's harsh wit hurt Ethan where his vanity was tender, but he did not show it even though it had taken him by surprise.

Nevertheless Jack knew he had poked his friend's hidden sensitivity and quickly added, "I understand your medication has put that weight on you. But you have to take it, so what can you do but accept it? We're getting too old to care about our looks anyway. Remember when I was fat and you were skin and bones?"

"Sure do," Ethan said. "One time when we went swimming you called me a skeleton."

Jack laughed. "Did I? Good for me. Now I've got legs like sticks and you're having my baby."

Ethan sat back down and lit a cigarette. He smiled. "All right," he said. "You have full custody of the bastard. I wish to God I could give it to you right now."

"Ha-ha."

Ethan said, "Hey. You owe me something more than a veiled apology for that rude comment. I didn't like it. Understand?"

"I do," Jack said. "You can dish it out but you can't take it."

"Fix me a glass of ice water," Ethan said.

Jack could move quickly for his age. He obediently jumped to his feet and dashed to the kitchen. He said, "I see. You're the bully and I'm your killer when I've had enough."

"Hurry up," Ethan said. "This is not happening quickly enough. I wanted that water immediately."

Jack handed him a glass and dropped to his place on the floor. He pulled off a sock and began massaging the bottom of his foot.

"Let me tell you something, Ethan," Jack said. "I'm the clever one. I used to manipulate you all the time without you ever knowing it. I can still run circles around you."

"I don't care; I don't believe you would hurt me," Ethan said. "Besides, I know more."

They watched the movie for a short while. The filmmaker was interested in teenage sexuality and teenage angst and stupidity and the obliviousness of the parents. The sex was profuse and graphic. A girl's shorts opened over her pubic lips and the camera zoomed on it. "Rather gratuitous," Ethan said. Jack laughed and said, "I wonder what that would look like on the big screen."

Suddenly they looked directly at each other and spoke in unison: "Tell me something," they said.

Jack muted the television. He said, "Have I done as well with my life as you thought I would?"

"I believe I thought that you would do better than I would do, that you were stronger and better adjusted; I thought you would have an easier time as an adult. I never considered what work you would do, because you never talked about an ambition. It never occurred to me you'd make a lot of money in the automotive industry."

Jack said, "I remember thinking you would probably not live long, because you were so depressed and troubled. I knew you wanted to be a writer, but you were so morbid. All your heroes were tragic—Janis Joplin, Edgar Allan Poe, Van Gogh. Everybody you admired was dead."

"I didn't think I would live long either," Ethan said. "But I eventually discovered I had a strong desire to survive—if nothing else. That must be a powerful instinct that comes from God. My suicidal thoughts were just part of growing up. Once I got to college, life was basically moving upward even though I was unhappy a lot. I did one smart thing. I dedicated myself to my writing, and I realized I had some talent. Then I worked hard. And I kept living. The desire to accomplish something, especially when you're young and you've survived adolescence—that carries you through life if you ask me."

"I admired you in spite of your weirdness," Jack said.

"Why?"

"I knew it had to take something special to be such an individual. I admired the way you quit high school one month before graduation with an A average and then took a test and went on to college. I couldn't make it through college. And all the travel you've told me about that you did alone. I traveled far and wide on business but I never traveled alone to explore for fun like you did. I have a problem with that. You know what it is?" He extended his arm as if a strange force were pulling it; he made a curious turn of his hand. "I'm afraid I would feel an attraction I couldn't resist and I would get involved in something bad and get killed."

Ethan said, "You always had trouble resisting attractions. I was a fantasizer. You were a doer. You would try anything. I always admired you for that. I missed out on a lot because I was afraid of people. Except for you – I never feared you."

Jack said, "You were too shy. You even felt inferior to most people. But I never understood why. I believed you were smarter than everybody else."

Ethan said, "You were the bravest person I knew. When I got older I did get braver, and what travel meant to me was independence and liberation. I felt like a solitary individual in a world of diverse humanity. Especially on a beach—I felt something ecstatic there between the earth and the sea, with a view of the point where the earth disappeared and the sun rose. I felt related to hundreds of strangers who were never more than acquaintances, if that. I could see secrets in their eyes and pick up their vibes. It was a friendly happy place. I don't know if I'll travel again because of my back problem," Ethan said. "I'm talking about travel as indulgence in fantasy."

"Hmm," Jack said.

"I've never loved but four or five people at the most," Ethan said. "Outside of my natural family, I mean."

"Am I one of them?" Jack said.

"Of course," Ethan said.

"My first wife was one of the most beautiful girls I'd ever seen. I never understood why someone so beautiful would want me. We had two babies," Jack said.

"Your family that died in the house fire."

"Yeah," Jack said. "My last wife was a joke. Fat, ugly, cold. She never kept herself clean, and she would just lay there like a corpse. We had sex all of three times, and I hated it. I don't know why I married her."

"My first marriage was the joke," Ethan said. "I was twenty-three. I only married her because she was there and willing, and I was lonely. But she was cold—colder than my naïve mind realized a woman could be. She hit me in the head with a sock full of rocks one night while I was asleep. With blood dripping down one side of my head, I stumbled around packing a duffle bag. I left her while she ranted and raved. I slept under some bushes in a park. When we were finally divorced and out of each other's lives, I was never the same again. But there was one good result—the loneliness went away."

Jack said, "You told me there were two. What about the second one?"

Ethan smiled sadly.

"That was the closest I came to the real thing," Ethan said. "I loved her and we were very compatible. We were in our late thirties. It was a revelation. A whole new breed of feelings and attitudes came alive in me, and I thought—ah, this is the real thing. She was no great beauty. She was voluptuous and blond with intense blue eyes I longed to penetrate but couldn't. Sometimes she was afraid and said I was too intense. I loved her so much. When I was younger I would have never thought this feeling was possible. We were together five years. They say true love grows. But her love for me faded, so slowly I didn't even realize it until it was too late. I guess because I was so in love with her. Then one morning while I was driving to work it hit me like a ton of bricks that she was seeing someone else and I was facing divorce."

Jack didn't know what to say. He thought silently for a minute.

Ethan lit a cigarette, took a long drag, and then a big drink of water.

Jack said, "You're the only one I would let smoke cigarettes in my house."

"I know it," Ethan said. "Why don't we take this teenage trash out of the DVD player? Choose one of your own."

Jack put in a disc that he said was one of a series of movies that he loved.

By way of explanation, Jack said, "Okay, this girl has to choose between a vampire and a werewolf, but it's not like old-fashioned vampires and werewolves."

After fifteen minutes of watching, Ethan said, "Teenage characters again. Except these are pretty instead of sleazy."

Jack said, "Don't you think the black-haired girl is beautiful?"

Ethan said, "Yes, but I prefer older women."

"What about the male characters?" Jack said. "Which is more handsome -- the vampire or the werewolf?"

Ethan said, "They're pretty models too, wearing too much makeup. I guess the vampire is the more handsome of the two. I'd rather have his face than the werewolf's."

"I disagree," Jack said. "But I knew you would say that. I know how you see."

Jack muted the television and gave Ethan an earnest look. He said, "Do you ever think about what death must be like?"

"It's always in the back of my mind," Ethan said. "Yet there's not much to say about it since the Creator has hidden it from us."

"I mean—how can you not exist? There must be something on the other side, because nonexistence is impossible to understand. Isn't it? So where are you, what are you, when you die?" Jack said.

"I knew you'd get around to that subject," Ethan said.

"I can't help it." Jack said.

"I know," Ethan said. "But I've told you what I think about it a hundred times."

"So tell me again," Jack said.

"You want to know what's on the other side," Ethan said. "No one has ever gone there and returned to tell us. By the Creator's design it's an absolute secret from us."

Jack said, "Is it possible there's nothing there at all?"

Ethan said, "For all we know it's possible there's nothing there at all. But like you say, this is hard to believe—if for no other reason than there's evidence of superior intelligence everywhere in nature. And that's where faith comes into play. I can't think of anything but faith as a way to reconcile myself to the superior power behind the great mystery. But I can't say that I practice faith. I practice fear more than anything else. I don't know."

Jack looked at his leg and scratched it, his face irritated.

Ethan recognized Jack's dissatisfaction and said, "I know you haven't been involved in church or religion since you were a kid, but do you remember from the scriptures where Paul was taken up into the spiritual realm and said later that the experience was indescribable?"

"I don't know."

"Paul said he heard things that no mortal can repeat—or something to that effect. The point I take from this is that the subject of what is behind that door that life keeps locked is completely above and beyond our comprehension. Trying to explain what is there for us after death is futile. The Creator fixed it this way for a good reason. I think the best way to look at this is that when death comes, something special that has never even occurred in our imagination happens to us."

"Just answer the question," Jack said impatiently. "Do you think we exist after death or do you think we become nothing?"

"I believe we exist after death," Ethan said.

"So what is it like?" Jack said.

"We can't possibly know what it's like," Ethan said. "It's like nothing in human experience, like nothing on earth. It will be a new thing that we cannot name or describe. That's all I think we can know."

"Yeah," Jack said, disappointed.

"But what the hell do I know?" Ethan said.

"I just like to wonder about it," Jack said. "Do we eat? Play? Work?"

Ethan said, "Let me ask you something related. Do you ever feel a desire to worship?"

"I guess not."

"Let's go to church one Sunday," Ethan said. "Remember we were baptized at the same time?"

"We were, weren't we?" Jack said, remembering. "But I don't like churches anymore. I don't like holier-than-thou memberships."

"They're not all like that," Ethan said. "Besides, the membership doesn't matter so much. It's the worship that matters. I haven't been in a long time but I frequently feel the urge. I want you to go with me."

"All right," Jack said.

"I'm serious," Ethan said.

"I'll go."

Jack turned the television volume back up. He went to get some snacks and another Coke. Ethan was still not hungry.

Jack said, "Haven't you enjoyed this talk?"

"Very much," Ethan said.

They were quiet for a while. Jack cut the TV volume again.

Jack gave Ethan a scrutinizing look and said, "We've always been friends, haven't we?"

"Yes," Ethan said. "There must be a special understanding between us."

"Like we knew each other before this life?" Jack said.

"Yes," Ethan said. "What a mystery that is."

After a minute Jack said, "Maybe we see each other so clearly that we can forgive each other anything. We've done each other great favors but we've also wronged each other."

Ethan saw the wisdom in this theory.

Neither of them wanted to bring up those favors and wrongs.

The movie was over about midnight. They went upstairs and changed into sweat pants and T-shirts and went back down to the living room. Jack sat on the couch and showed Ethan how he gave himself his diabetic shot in the stomach with an implement that looked to Ethan like a fat blue ink pen. Then Jack talked about his diabetes, the symptoms, how he monitored the condition; he got into details that Ethan could not follow. Ethan felt a surge of worry about Jack's health—the diabetes, the bypass heart surgery he had had two years ago, and other symptoms that seemed to mystify his doctors. He was lost in thought about this when suddenly he noticed Jack was vigorously scratching himself. He pulled his T-shirt off and said, "Does my back look normal?"

"Just a little flushed," Ethan said.

"Scratch it as hard as you can," Jack said. "It's itching so bad I can't stand it. I must be allergic to this new medication my doctor gave me. He wanted me to try it. I can't remember what he said was different about it, but it was a mistake."

"Let's go to the ER," Ethan said. "This diabetes is nothing to mess around with. Let's go."

"Are you crazy?" he said. "I've been smoking pot. They'll take blood and urine and it will mess up my disability benefits. That's out of the question. I'm not going anywhere. It'll stop and I'll go back to my regular insulin. I won't take that new stuff anymore."

Ethan understood the problem and thought it over. Then he said, "I had this itching reaction to a medication once. And what stopped it was cold water."

"I can't stand cold water," Jack said. He dropped his sweat pants. "Scratch my elbows as hard as you can. Scratch up the sides of my legs. Scratch my ass. God, this is unbearable."

Ethan scratched away. "I've bitten all my nails off," he said.

Jack said, "Look in the cabinet over the sink and bring me that bottle of Benadryl."

Ethan gave it to him and looked carefully at Jack's face. His eyes were cloudy and unfocused. "You're going to have to listen to me," Ethan said.

"What are you doing?" Jack said deliriously.

Ethan hurried upstairs and ran a bath of cool water. Jack kept saying he couldn't stand cold water, but Ethan convinced him it wasn't what you'd call cold and to try submerging his whole body in it. "If you can't stand it add some warm water. As you get used to it, add more cold."

Jack ridded himself of underwear and sat in the tub. Very slowly he lay down in it, grimacing as the water reached his neck. Ethan sat on the toilet seat and watched his face.

Jack said, "Cold as hell but it's stopping this itching."

"What else can I get you?" Ethan said.

"I don't know."

Ethan said, "Do you have any other symptoms?"

"Like what?"

"You tell me," Ethan said. "Like dizziness or weakness or anything."

"I'm not sure."

"Stand up and see if it starts itching again," Ethan said.

Jack said it started again as soon as he got out of the water, so he got back in. Ethan turned on the cold tap for a minute. He stayed with him. "Give it time," he said. After thirty minutes Jack got out of the tub and asked for a large towel. He followed Ethan downstairs back in his sweat pants and T-shirt.

"It's not itching much now," Jack said. "But I've got another problem I wonder if you'd help me with. Would you massage my feet with this lotion? They get numb and rubbing them helps the circulation."

Jack fixed the couch up with pillows and blankets. Ethan sat up at one end and Jack reclined with his feet propped on a pillow on Ethan's lap. Ethan squirted some lotion and started.

Jack said, "Dig in really hard."

Ethan worked his thumbs up and down the middle of the bottom of the foot; he pressed the sides inward; he pushed and pulled the toes. He put all his strength into it, and still Jack kept saying, "Harder, do it harder." After nearly an hour, Jack stood up and said, "That's enough. That was good. Thanks for saving me. It's nearly two. I'm going to bed."

"I'm going to sit up a little longer," Ethan said. His back was now hurting. He took two methadone tablets after Jack went up to his bedroom. He fell asleep sitting up. When he opened his eyes, the room was bright with sunshine and he saw by a wall clock it was just after nine.

Ethan's back was hurting seriously now. The pain was inside the very bottom of the spine, continuous, sharp, and searing. He took some medication and turned on the coffee maker. He went upstairs to make sure Jack was still breathing. Then he changed into pants and put his duffle bag downstairs so as to be ready to leave at a second's notice. He was anxious to get home, but he knew Jack liked to sleep late and especially after last night he hated to disturb his rest. He waited patiently and drank some coffee while watching a thirty-minute old western TV show. But the longer he waited he got more restless and frustrated. He thought about calling a taxi, but he couldn't just slip away without knowing Jack's condition.

Finally, just as he decided to go up and wake him, he heard footsteps overhead and then the shower running. Jack was down in a few minutes, wearing shorts and a blue shirt. He looked at Ethan and said, "Are you all right?"

"No, I'm not," Ethan said. "Are you?"

"As a matter of fact, I feel great. You must have cured me last night," Jack said. He was alert and smiling, his grey eyes bright and clear. He looked happy. "Do you need to go home right now?"

"Yes, I do," Ethan said. "My back pain is really bad."

"Let's go."

Ethan shifted and squirmed in the car seat as Jack questioned him about his pain.

"It's hard to describe," Ethan said.

Jack said, "When is your next doctor appointment?"

"Two weeks," Ethan said.

Jack said, "You've got enough medication, don't you? You haven't taken all your pills, have you?"

"It's fine," Ethan said.

"What does that mean?"

"I've got enough pills."

The highway went straight ahead for three miles until it turned behind some trees at the top of a hill. Ethan appreciated the quaint pretty sight through the window frame. He watched the flow of yellow and green meadowland, silver ponds, and clusters of short gnarly trees. The field ended at a forest of big pines, the extremities of their branches turning vertical with the needles elegantly clustered and pronged like candelabrum. The land was hilly and wooded at a farther distance, while beyond it a dark blue mountain lay low and smooth like a sheeted figure. A baby blue sky hung behind it like a creaseless curtain; above it the sky was emptiness that continued forever. Ethan had been down this highway so often it was embedded in his subconscious. In his dreams he traveled it all the time. Usually he was driving at night in a hurry to get somewhere to resolve a crisis but without ever quite making it.

Jack broke the silence. "It would kill me to take as many of those pills as you do."

"I wish it would kill me," Ethan said.

"Don't start that nonsense," Jack said.

"I mean it," Ethan said. "If I go through what I did last summer, I'll do it."

"Suicide is not the answer," Jack said. "There's always a reason to live."

"Can you be sure?" Ethan said. "Maybe there are times when the best solution is to go ahead and find out what's behind that door. How do you know? Do you realize that quite a few people kill themselves because they can't get pain relief?"

"Look," Jack said. "If it comes to that, I'll take you to your doctor and carry you in there and demand they do whatever it takes."

"I'll never forget the time they couldn't stop it," Ethan said.

"I'll find somebody who can," Jack said.

"You've never considered suicide?" Ethan said.

"No," Jack said. "And I know one thing for sure regardless of how you feel. Your talent. You have more of it than most people can even imagine. You've published – what? Three volumes of poetry and stories? Articles? Didn't you win a prize? I have no talent. I don't even have a hobby. I can't do anything."

"You have family."

"What happened to all your ambitions?" Jack said.

"I've still got them, Jack," Ethan said. "It's just that I'm in so much pain right now. I don't have a suicide plan. Don't worry. But if you find me dead please take charge. I have a burial policy in my bedroom closet on the top shelf in an old strongbox with a combination of three zeroes."

"Let's do this," Jack said. "Let's get together for a night of talking and watching movies every other Friday night."

"Are you trying to keep me alive?" Ethan said.

Jack said, "I think it would help both of us."

"All right," Ethan said. "I would like that."

"Last night did you good," Jack said. "You laughed a lot."

"That's true."

They turned off the highway and several houses down the road made a right into Ethan's graveled driveway.

Ethan opened the car door and Jack said, "I'll stay with you if it will help."

"That's not necessary. I'll feel better when my medicine fully kicks in," Ethan said. "Besides, you've got to pick up your granddaughter. I'll talk to you soon."

It was a beautiful sunny day but Ethan did not look at it as he unlocked the back door of the house and went in. He heard Jack's car pull out as he made a glass of ice water, which he took with him to the recliner. He sat down and turned on the television. He could feel the pain getting worse. He likened it to a bad tooth ache or a broken bone—except that it was more unrelenting than those things, which he had also experienced. He took five more methadone tablets, downing them all at once with the water. He lit a cigarette and flipped the channels; bored by the choices, he quit searching and turned down the volume. After about an hour the drug finally touched the pain and he relaxed and dozed lightly.

He woke feeling a strange mixture of sorrow and joy in his heart. He thought tenderly of his friend and the night before. He wanted to call Jack but before he could do it the phone rang. Ethan answered, and Jack said, "Are you all right?"

"Sure."

"How many pills have you taken since you've been home?" Jack asked.

"Just two," he lied.

"Are you in pain?"

"No," he lied again.

In fact the pain was worse now than it had been before his nap.

"Hmm," Jack said. "Try not to take anymore today. I wanted to tell you that the first movie in the series of the one we watched last night is on channel sixty-three. It's coming on right now."

"All right, I'll watch it."

"Remember now. Again in two weeks. You had fun, didn't you?"

"Of course I did," Ethan said. "How are you feeling?"

"I'm still feeling great. I'll holler at you later," Jack said. "Maintain."

Ethan tapped out four more pills and took them. Then he looked at the pill level with despair. He shook the bottle and the pills seemed to drop lower. He turned to channel sixty-three and resigned himself to watching Jack's recommendation. After the movie, he paced the floors and looked through the windows until it was nearly dark. He got back in the recliner and pulled the sheet that was bundled on the floor up to his chest.

The pain still hammered away. He couldn't stand it and took five pills. He smoked and drank water until he felt the pain fade away to blessed relief. He turned off the television. He closed his eyes and floated on the narcotic haze in his head until he fell asleep.

He felt a strong familiar presence and opened his eyes. Jack was on a knee right beside his recliner, his hand shaking his arm and saying his name. Ethan looked at his friend's face. Clearly Jack was exceptionally happy and excited. He was wearing the same light blue T-shirt Ethan had seen him in earlier today.

"What in the world?" Ethan said. "Didn't I have the door locked? What's going on?"

"You never told me you wanted to go to the moon," Jack said.

Ethan thought. "I don't think I've ever told anybody about my fantasy of walking on the moon."

"I want to take you for a visit before I have to go," Jack said.

"What?"

Jack pulled him up and they walked across the room. At first Ethan saw lights blinking. Then he saw a huge brilliant star. The disc was not crisp but diffused around the edges and the rays were long and sharp as swords. It didn't hurt to look directly at it even though it would seem to be blinding. The ground was mostly white and rocks and holes were everywhere shining in vivid detail. Ironically it was like a peaceful battlefield, pristine and untouched. It smelled of gun powder and ash.

Ethan pushed his naked big toe in the dirt and dug a little hole. It felt soft and crusty.

The starlight, the sun, was a force of purity and hope that penetrated with ever-intensifying power an unimaginable blackness, while the depth and thickness of this darkness was so absolute that not one particle of light could brighten it. The light and the darkness were perfectly opposing forces. But the sun bathed the moon and obliterated the stars.

And there was the earth, round, blue and white, seemingly adrift, lonely and beautiful.

Jack stood beside him, smiling. There was not a blemish or wrinkle on his face.

Ethan said, "Have we passed?"

"I have," Jack said. "You haven't. I just wanted to show you something you'd never seen before."

"Was I right about it?" Ethan said. "Did you find something that no human can anticipate?"

"My lips are sealed, man," Jack said.

"Are you happy?"

"I sure am," Jack said.

"Can't I come with you?"

"No," Jack said. "I'll come get you later. Just maintain."

Ethan had so many questions he could not choose one.

Jack said, "Love you, man. See you soon."

Ethan watched Jack as he turned and walked away in his khaki shorts, blue shirt, and sandals. He walked across open ground for quite a while. As he went, Ethan began to see him as a child. Jack stopped, turned, and waved, just before he disappeared around the corner of a white foothill.

Ethan woke in his recliner with a gasp. The phone was ringing. He knew what the news was. He pushed the END button, lit a cigarette, and cried.

Contemno, Infitialis.

From embers it emanates, the walls they wilt,

The fire dismantles that which was built.

Since the dawn of man and born of the sun,

The black, it billows, the matches my gun.

Neither necessity nor respect, unlike the rest,

Despised and rejected, a brand on my chest.

Relinquished to iron, concrete, and three meals,

As if that would extinguish that which appeals.

My time I have served, ablaze are my yearns,

At last there is oxygen as my halfway burns.

—nicholas r larche

the astroencephalon

Carcosa's stars feign light to watch
Half to freshen, half to rot
His mortal sprint from woe to naught
For solace from his heart, which bled

The pall of winter frost withheld
The sparks of ancient charms beheld
Enchanted was he in that realm
For dogs were gold and jasper fed

Lambent leaves fell through the ceiling
Whirling, churning, swishing, jeering
Gave unto his rhymes a reeling
A reeling that he broke and mastered,

Finally, he stood up seething
Left the hellish rail there searing,
Fearing fiends who'd stood there peering,
Now goading him, they crunched, they chatter

In lambent leaves his dreams were dashed
As silver swords of Kali slashed,
His arms to wet the wretched glass
Hidden ichor splashed the walls

And light spilled in to raise his shadow
So evermore his heart will fallow
Till maggots digging, drain his marrow
And watching there, the fizzling stars

—navo banerjee

Meeting Oneself

by icy sedgwick

It happened on a bitter morning, beset by the sort of cold that you only feel in the dark days before Christmas. I had business in town and rose early so as to conclude my transactions by a reasonable hour. The house was mostly in darkness, with a single maid trudging between the rooms to light fires in the grates. When I bade her good morning, she looked at me as though she had seen a ghost; she dropped her kindling on the parlour floor.

"Good God, girl, whatever is the matter?" I asked. I was especially surprised as I had not known Elsie to be a fanciful or superstitious creature in the eight months she had worked for me.

"Begging yer pardon, sir, I thought you was someone else." She bent to gather her parcel of wood and paper.

"Who?"

Elsie looked up at me, a somewhat thoughtful expression on her face.

"I din't listen at first, sir, though all the girls was talking about it. But I seen it for myself now."

"What? What did you see?"

"Yer ghost, sir." Elsie replied with no trace of amusement. The girl was deadly serious.

"My ghost?"

"That's right, sir. The other girls thought it was you at first, but then Sally saw it in the kitchen when we knew you was in the dining room with Mr. Hardcastle."

I remembered the incident—Hardcastle and I were enjoying dinner when a scream interrupted our hearty conversation. I hurried to discover the source of the cry, but found the kitchen empty. I presumed it to have not been a scream, but rather the cry of some wild animal outside, and dinner continued. I had thought of it no more until Elsie raised the subject.

"But I live, Elsie, as you can see for yourself. I would need to be dead to have a ghost."

"Begging yer pardon, sir, but my mother says the living have ghosts too. They pass on messages and then they leave."

I shuddered, considering the possibility of a version of myself that was dead yet somehow invading my home. I caught the earnest expression on Elsie's face and shook the mood from myself.

"Don't be absurd, Elsie. I have no ghost—there are no spirits in this house. Now run along and finish your jobs before Mrs. Peterson awakes."

Elsie bobbed in an awkward curtsey and scurried away.

I left the parlour, intending to visit my library before I left for town. I stood at the head of the long, narrow corridor that led to the back of the house. Little light pervaded its pre-dawn gloom, and I shivered. I debated with myself for several moments about the importance of the papers for my business in town, before mentally shaking myself. I had allowed myself to become unnerved by an idle report, given by a maid, no less. No, it would not do. I plunged into the darkness in the direction of my library.

I opened the door and the sight almost stopped my heart.

My double stood in the centre of the library, the weak dawn rays falling through the figure onto the carpet. I looked closer and saw that it was not quite the double of myself—the right side of its face was horribly burned, contorted into an expression of the purest pain. My hand flew to my own face, my fingers exploring the skin, yet finding it marred by nothing but stubble.

The figure reached out a hand and opened its mouth, its lips forming silent words. I could not make them out, but felt perhaps they were a warning of some kind. The double took two steps toward me and vanished into the cold morning air. Before I could consider what the apparition might signify, I fell into a faint, and dropped to the floor.

I awoke some six hours later, with my brother in my room and the doctor scratching his illegible symbols in his notebook.

"Edgar! You return to us!" My brother strode to my bedside and peered into my face.

"Indeed I do. What time is it?" The memory of my intended meeting in town came to me before that of the figure in the library.

"It is eleven in the morning."

"I was supposed to meet with Fitzherbert three hours ago!"

"Well, you shan't be meeting with him at all now." My brother crossed himself and briefly bowed his head. The doctor, despite his scientific allegiances, did likewise.

"What has happened?"

"A fire claimed Fitzherbert's house in town this morning. His business associates were able to escape but Fitzherbert did not have their good fortune. God rest his soul."

I thought of the many other instances when I had avoided some misfortune or other by being somewhere other than where I was supposed to be at that moment, and I fell into a faint for the second time that day.

ICE

Click

Kristen awoke with a start, fumbling at her face to remove the sleeping mask. It had only taken a few seconds for her to realize that it was only the ice machine making the noise coming from the kitchen, but that didn't ease her mind. She'd once again made the stupid decision to stay in that evening and watch horror movies till 2:00 am on Netflix, which was a sure-fire recipe for two things -- an enjoyable (and cheap) night at home followed by a long unrestful night of interrupted sleep.

The movies didn't give her nightmares, but they somehow made her much more aware of every little sound and creak that occurred in her house. The ice machine, of course, was always one of the main culprits, jolting her awake at all hours of the night. Kristen sighed, frustrated more at her hypersensitivity than the noise emitted by a kitchen appliance. She tried to go back to sleep.

Click, Click, Click

Kristen shot up in bed again. The ice machine had been louder and more persistent this time. But it stopped. She started to lay her head back down on the pillow when the noise started again, this time at an even greater volume.

CLICK, CLICK, CLICK, CLICK

Kristen couldn't remember the ice machine ever being this loud, but guessed it was probably due to a jam. After swinging her legs over the bed and rubbing her eyes, she began stumbling toward the kitchen in the dark.

As Kristen got closer to the refrigerator, she noticed that the mechanized whir

JAM

by nick nafpliotis

that always accompanied the clicking was not there. Opening the freezer-side door, she peered at the ice receptacle. The kitchen was bathed in soft yellow light. Just as she'd expected, the ice had piled up and was shifting around with an energy that made it seem almost alive.

"Damn it," Kristen sighed as she gritted her teeth and dug into the small icy mountain to unclog the machine.

As she got near the opening, however, something strangely warm latched onto her first and third fingers. Its texture was like coarse hair, scraping against her skin in tiny rapid strokes. Before she could pull her hand back out, something punctured the nail of her thumb. She screamed.

Bright red blood oozed through the ice and around her wrist as she felt more punctures all over her palm and fingers. As she desperately tried to free herself, the sharp points inserted into her flesh held on even tighter. Whatever had a hold of her began writhing back and forth, its bristled fur shuddering with what appeared to be primal excitement. As more blood seeped out and her hand went further into the ice machine, the world became dark and blurry. The last thing Kristen heard before everything went black was the ravenous and excited-sounding clicking noise, which had never stopped since she'd put her hand inside the ice.

CLICK, CLICK, CLICK, CLICK

I KNOW WHAT I SAW

Once upon a time may be an apt beginning—
for non-believers.
Maybe I could say it was a dark and stormy night—
but it was not stormy.

The night was clear, a new moon night.
Darkness held our hands.
We were hunting for a campground—
after 9:00 pm.
Instead of toasting marshmallows,
or reading the best book ever,
or sleeping,
we were still in the car.
Sleeping would have been preferable to
Not Knowing.

A night search teases campers
with yawns, with grumbling stomachs,
with signs of campgrounds thirty miles back.
Oh yes, we saw that sign.
The billboard stood out when our headlights illuminated it,
and it was not a cheap, home-made sign with missedpellings.
The real sign told us of a campground up ahead,
and we heard that announcement because this was
a silent car full of family.

The Cascades loom over their prey,
waiting to pounce,
hungry for Wandering Travelers.
People get lost, disappear, die on dark nights in the Cascades.
Call me Miss Melodrama.
I know what I saw.

My brother no longer tells people about him:
    his dark hair and slim physique, his height—the size of him!
People look skeptical when they hear the story.
But this is not a story. No. And this account
cannot to be investigated or hunted down.
This happened fifty years ago—
An anniversary. A milestone.

When lost in the Cascades on a new moon night,
drive slowly.
Keep your eyes open.
Don't be afraid unless you stop but that won't matter
because you won't be able to see him if you turn back
it won't do any good to chorally whisper
"What was that?"
    It won't help to turn around in a group double-take
    he will be gone—
            swallowed by Dark's instincts.

—holly dunlea

DRY PLACES

by vic kerry

A few pictures hung on the walls of Arnie's office. Actually they were sayings that every addict and recovering addict should know. The one behind his desk chair read: Let go and let God. Arnie held close to that saying more than any of the rest. In his course of hard substance abuse and recovery, he'd gotten to the point that the only choice he had was to do just that.

Not a single day passed that Arnie didn't sit behind his desk and think about the day that his life changed for the positive. After years of wandering around from place to place abusing everything a human could, he found himself lying in an alley in Birmingham, Alabama. A needle he'd used several times before still stuck out of his arm. His breath left him, and he couldn't catch it. All the contents of his bowels and bladder emptied out and soaked through the pants that he'd been wearing for at least two months. The pavement underneath him burned from the midday heat of a July day, but he was so cold it didn't do anything for him.

Arnie was dying, and he knew it. That's when he let go and let God. Everything went black. At some point, days later, he woke up in St. Vincent's ICU—a new man.

Now as he sat at his desk, he looked over the appointment lines of his planner. He had an intake for this afternoon. The gentleman's name was Horace. Arnie looked forward to this opportunity to help another human being get off substances. After God saved him from death, he'd thrown all of himself into the work he thought he'd been called to do—helping people with rehab. It consumed his whole life.

There came a knock at his door. Arnie stood and walked to it. When he opened it, a thin man, mostly skin and bones, stood propped against the wall. His cheeks sank in as did his eyes. Yellow skin stretched over the man's skeletal features. He looked like walking jaundice. Arnie thought that he'd gotten to this guy just in time.

"Are you Horace?" he asked.

"That's me. I have an appointment."

"I've been expecting you. Come on in and sit down."

Arnie welcomed the man into his office. He patted the back of the old vinyl chair that clients sat in. The man dragged himself to it and sat. Arnie thought if he listened close enough he might hear the rattling of bones. The smell emanating from the man was something akin to a two-week-old corpse. Everything about him seemed unhealthy and necrotic.

"So how are you today?" Arnie walked around his desk and settled into his chair.

The man's eyes stared at him. From the deep recesses of his skull, they seemed full of life and emotion. "How do you think I feel?"

"I don't know. That's why I asked, but if you've come to me for help, I'm going to guess not so good."

"On the nose." Horace touched his nose with a long boney finger. "You ought to go on Jeopardy!"

Displeasure welled up in Arnie. He didn't care for sarcasm at any time -- not from addicts and especially not from this guy. It seemed to Arnie that someone in Horace's condition had no right to behave like he was better than a healthy recovering addict. He jotted down the response on the questionnaire that was part of the admission process. The emotion in the man's eyes was still there. Arnie realized that it was hate.

"Why are you so angry, Horace?"

"I'm not angry, Arnie. Why are you transferring your emotions onto me?"

"I'm not. You are being defensive, which is a sign of anger. Your eyes are also speaking volumes."

"So are yours."

"You chose to come for this intake. I didn't make you."

Horace's eyes brightened, and an eyebrow cocked upward. "Didn't you?"

Arnie decided that he was not going to accomplish anything by continuing this line of questioning. He turned back to his assessment. The words on the plaque above his head filled him up, and he took strength from them. The Serenity Prayer hung across the room from his desk. The words were large and in bold letters that made it easy to read.

God grant me the serenity to change the things I can, accept things I cannot change, and the wisdom to know the difference.

"Prayer is the last ditch effort of the hopeless," Horace said.

"What do you mean?"

"You were praying just then. Why are you hopeless? Am I an impossible case?"

"I was praying because that's what I do before all assessments." Arnie felt a knot in the pit of his stomach. It seemed that despite the fact that he looked half-dead, Horace was as perceptive as a healthy man.

"You can believe that lie if you want to."

Horace smiled. His teeth were little more than black rotten nubs right at the gum line. Arnie tried not to look at him. Everything about this intake made him uncomfortable, and he was positive that the man was reveling in that.

"What's your drug of choice?" Arnie asked.

"What's yours?" Horace asked back.

"When I was an active addict it was heroin."

The black nub teeth revealed themselves again. "How ironic. It's my drug of choice too. I would marry it if I could."

"I understand that. I felt the same way. She was quite a mistress." He wrote heroin on the form. "It almost killed me."

"I know."

The knot in his stomach tightened again. His mouth started to dry out. He wished he'd brought a cup of water in with him before he'd started Horace's interview. To go for one now would risk the man deciding that he didn't need help. Arnie felt a determination not to fail at his calling. He felt his salvation was balanced on how many addicts he could help.

"Why do you want to get off drugs?" Arnie said.

"I don't."

"So why are you here?"

"Because of you."

Horace reached across the table and grabbed Arnie's wrist. The addict's hand was hot and calloused. The heat radiated up Arnie's arm. It felt just like when he used to push the first syringe of smack in the morning. It was almost orgasmic. No wonder he'd fallen in love with the drug so long ago.

He remembered the first time he'd shot up. Sandra, a girl he'd met at a rave, took him into the bathroom. She pushed him up against the wall and started to work him over with her mouth. Before he could come, she stopped and smiled at him.

"Do you want to feel an organism like you've never had before?" she had asked.

"Yeah."

She had reached in her purse and brought out her junky prep kit. They cooked up a quick couple of ccs of smack, shot up, and went at it like rabbits on the nasty, damp bathroom floor. The experience was like no other before—except for this one right now.

Arnie came back to himself and jerked his arm away from Horace. His head swam. He didn't know if it was from the memory or the adrenaline pumping through his body.

"Please don't do that," he said.

"Sorry." The nub teeth smiled back at him.

"Do you have any medical problems?"

"Look at me. What do you think?"

Horace no longer smiled at him. His skin was still deep yellow, but the sunken cheeks seemed puffier. There was obviously something wrong with him, but Arnie had no idea what.

"I can tell you're not healthy, but do you have any diseases?"

"Hep C, genital herpes, hypertension, general malaise."

Arnie jotted down the diseases on the form. The letters were shaky and crooked as he did so. He tried to steady his hand, but the tremor continued. His hand hadn't shaken like that since he'd been riding the horse. Horace's sunken eyes studied the small quivering Arnie's hand made.

"Looks like you got a nasty case of the shakes," he said. "Maybe you should pray again."

"For what? They'll go away. Sometimes I get shaky if my blood sugar drops." Arnie reached into the drawer of his desk. He took out a soft peppermint ball. "This will fix it."

He popped the candy in his mouth. The sweet sugar started to melt. The flavor of peppermint exploded in his mouth like nothing he'd ever tasted. He smelled it and was pretty sure he heard it sizzle in his mouth. All his senses seemed to turn on full. The light in his office almost blinded him. The only time he could remember such an explosion of sensation was the first few times he'd shot up heroin. His hand no longer trembled.

"You shouldn't lie," Horace said. "God doesn't like it."

"What do you know about God? So far all you've done is make light of my faith and my God."

The anger inside of Arnie wouldn't stay away. It came out quick and fiery. He reached across the desk and knocked the other man's arms off of it.

"I am not making light of God, but I don't believe your faith," Horace said.

His hands trembled again, but it was the rage building up inside of him. All the extrasensory activity ceased, but the energy built up from it packed itself into the emotional rampage inside of him.

"What do you know about faith? If it hadn't been for mine, I'd look like you, on death's door. It's all I have."

"You have your memories."

"My faith helps me keep my memories at bay," Arnie said. "Those things can get me into trouble. They can get any addict into trouble. That's why you let go and let God."

"And he just takes care of everything?"

"You don't have faith in anything, do you?"

Horace shook his head. "No, I believe there is a God. I have faith that there is."

Arnie swallowed, and the brief time between that action and speaking again cleared his head. "That's a start. The first step we use here to gain recovery is to reach an understanding that there are greater things than ourselves."

"There are many things greater than me. I know that." Horace seemed to be showing some emotion.

The junkie's lip started to quiver. His eyes clouded with what must have been tears. Arnie felt empathy. He reached out for his box of tissue and passed it to Horace, but Horace grabbed hold of the counselor's hand again. Arnie fought the urge to jerk away like he had before. This time the addict was reaching out to a former addict. This was the breakthrough moment.

"Let go and let God," Arnie said. "When you do that the demon of addiction will leave you and go back to the hell where it came from."

Horace's grip moved up to Arnie's forearm. With a stiff tug, the junkie pulled the counselor to his feet. Arnie wanted to pull away but didn't. If Horace needed this kind of contact to give himself over to recovery and the Higher Power, then he would allow it. The stench of the man sickened Arnie as he was embraced. The hug crushed his arms to his sides, and he found himself in a painful bent position.

"Tell me—what do you fill your time with so that you don't go back on junk?"

The breath from the words burrowed into Arnie's ear. It felt like warm water dripping toward his brain. Everything changed. The junkie's words echoed through his skull as the world swirled in front of him.

Deep inside himself, Arnie searched for the answer. What had he filled his time with? Magnificent colors swirled around him as he saw himself falling down an impossible chasm. His mind snapped him back inside his body. He ached all over and felt spasms in his stomach. The roof of his mouth felt like sandpaper as he brushed his tongue across it. Parched and overwhelmed by oppressive heat, Arnie opened his eyes just a slit.

Harsh white light filled his vision. He blinked. The light took the form of sunlight. It beat down on him from high in a pale blue summer sky. A rock dug into his back. He wanted to move and get up but couldn't. His limbs wouldn't cooperate. The sunlight burned his eyes. He tried to close his lids, but they too wouldn't obey him either. Tightness ringed his arm. Although his eyes wouldn't move so that he could see what it was, he knew—an elastic band like what a phlebotomist used when drawing blood. Without seeing it, Arnie knew that a needle and syringe stuck out of his arm. His bladder and bowels let go.

As he lay in his own filth, he relived the worst and best day of his life. Arnie felt his life slipping away from him in that Birmingham alley. He prayed to God. The prayer was to not let him die. He wanted to let go and let God. It was in the Bible, was it not? Why else would so many of those programs use it? No sooner had he said amen in his head than he felt his life quit seeping away. Something else pushed its way out of him. Before he slipped into unconsciousness, he caught a glimpse of a shadowy creature escape into the air. It looked down at him from a skull-like face made up of what appeared to be smoke. It looked familiar.

Arnie came back to himself as Horace broke the embrace. He collapsed into his chair, partly due to the lack of support from the man and partly from the overwhelming power of the flashback he'd just had.

"Are you okay?" Horace asked.

Arnie looked at him. Everything seemed unreal. He felt that he was in a dream and what he'd just experienced was his reality. It couldn't be though. He'd lived out that episode two years ago. *What have I filled my time with since then?* He mulled over what the junkie had said. The answer was that he had done nothing to fill his time. All he had been able to do was to think about the time when he had stayed stoned. Even though he told himself he focused on getting others clean, he talked to them just so he could remember the thrill of use.

"Get out," he said.

"What?"

"I can't help you," Arnie said.

"What do you mean? I thought this was your calling from God."

He looked at Horace. The junkie didn't look like someone pleading for help. He looked lean and ravenous. His eyes had verve in them.

"I thought it was. I was wrong," Arnie said. "Get out."

"But you've already helped me so much."

"How?"

"I've let go and let God," Horace said.

"That's bullshit. Somebody just made it up. It's not even in the Bible." Arnie's words tore into his throat as he said them.

He'd never had true faith. Now it was clear. All he'd believed in was the twelve-step philosophy and some pseudo-religious stuff. The blue book had been his Bible, and he'd been a horrible disciple. Heroin hadn't coursed through his veins in a long time, but the horse had galloped through his memory several times every day.

"You are right about the Bible," Horace said. "Nowhere does it say that you should let go and let God—at least, not in those words."

Arnie watched Horace change from a solid figure into a smoky shadow of a man. The man's eyes caught and held Arnie's attention. They were the ones he'd seen as they left him in the alley two years prior.

"It does say that if you lose a demon you should fill your life with good things, or the demon will return," Horace said.

"What are you talking about?"

The shadowy figure rose and moved toward Arnie. He tried to get away, but the demon slipped down his throat. His whole body became warm just like it did when he used to do drugs. All his thoughts slowed down, and his mind numbed. He called out in his head for God's help. Instead the urge to shoot up became overwhelming. He was in bad need of the junk; he felt a need for it worse than any other need he had ever experienced.

Arnie sat with his back against the cold bricks of an abandoned building. Through gauzy eyes, he observed the world. A dreamy smile covered his lips. Heroin coursed through his body, warming him just like a thick blanket. Tiny dragons danced in front of him as three voices in his head discussed the Bible. One claimed to be God, but Arnie wasn't so sure. The voice kept telling him to kill people like the mayor and Roy Rogers. The other claimed to be Little Orphan Annie and sang about a hard-knock life. And then there was the third.

"Nothing like coming home," the voice called Horace said. "Home sweet home."

Split Asunder

by rivka jacobs

Lizbeth was irritated and restless. She flipped up the gold watch that hung from a pin attached to the blue satin of her bodice. It was after ten in the evening, and her husband was not yet home.

She gathered her skirt in one hand and turned away from the white front door flanked by glass sidelights. As she walked by the staircase, she put her free hand briefly on the handrail-turnout that began the banister that curved up to the second floor.

Lizbeth entered the sitting room and paused. Her full mouth drew together, then abruptly stretched into a grimace as she felt an overwhelming sense of hopelessness and pain. It was the same sitting room it had always been, with its cheap-looking dark carpet covered with pastel flowers. The wallpaper's busy floral design gave her a headache. The sparse furnishings were old-fashioned and uncomfortable. She glanced at the worn plush fabric of the only sofa in the room and the picture hanging on the wall above it. "I hate you," she said to everyone and everything.

Lizbeth continued into the kitchen. It was humid and gloomy. The out-of-date stove was cold. The place smelled of fresh scrubbing and stored onions and old meat. Their housekeeper, Bridget Sullivan, had tidied up for the night and gone up the back stairs to her attic room. There was an eerie silence now, a muffling pall that sank down and spread over Lizbeth's senses. She closed her eyes a moment, trying to steady herself, hoping her strenuous emotions wouldn't lead to another spell. She found an oil lamp sitting on top of the pie safe, retrieved a match, adjusted her wick, and lit it. A wavering glow leaped up around her, casting bent and peculiar shadows. Her husband thought it self-indulgent and wasteful to use lamps after nightfall in the summer, but he wasn't home, and Lizbeth didn't want to be alone in the dark.

She spun on her heels and walked back the way she had come, carrying the light by its wire handle. Past the wood-burning stove, through the oppressive sitting room,

into the parlor, she stopped in the hallway formed by the wall that supported the front stairway. She set the lamp on the floor and reached up, gripping a spindle baluster in each hand. *Like a prisoner I grasp the bars of my cell.*

She abruptly let go and lowered her arms. She adjusted her corset and brushed her fingers along the indigo silk braid that formed parallel lines running from her neckline to her waist. She lifted her chin and breathed deeply, trying to control herself.

Lizbeth picked up her light and calmly walked to the bottom step, hiked up her skirt in one fist, and began climbing. She hated being alone when one of her episodes hit; there was no telling where she would end up, and who she might see. She reached the landing and stopped. "I hate this house, I hate my life," she said out loud. Tears were pushing into the backs of her eyes and she stubbornly battled them into submission. *I won't cry. Father taught me that. Don't cry, don't move, don't say a word.*

As her mind formed the thought, an image of her father, Andrew Borden, flashed so suddenly it nearly made her lose her balance. "Lord help me," she said, sinking almost to her knees, seeming to see the back of Andrew Borden's black frock coat descend the steps below her, then dissipate like smoke.

Lizbeth shuddered, and rose to standing. She pulled herself up by the banister the rest of the way, stepping on her dress. Once she reached the second floor, she stumbled through what once was her old room, into the master bedroom that she now shared with her husband. She placed the lamp on top of the dresser.

The heat was smothering on the second floor. Lizbeth recognized the abdominal cramps that usually signaled the onset of her monthly pains. The back of her neck throbbed. She stood at the foot of the heavy and ornate, darkly stained double-bed, so neatly made up by "Maggie" hours before. The three windows were open, but the lace curtains veiling them hung limp and still in the stifling atmosphere. A growling sound escaped Lizbeth's throat, before she even realized it was coming from her.

She started screaming—a low, single note of despair that lasted several minutes. She quieted; panting, she listened. As always, there was no sound, no reaction. The house didn't even settle—it was like a tomb. The perspiration rolled down her temples from her masses of auburn curls bunched around her hairline. She felt like running to one of the windows that looked out on the Kelly house next door, and yelling, "You heard me, I know you heard me! It's that crazy Lizzie again, isn't it?" But she didn't.

She began removing her sash and overskirt, then unfastening her blouse. She walked over to the full-length floor mirror that stood on the other side of the bed, tilted slightly in a way that made her look compact and squared. She had become too thin, she thought, as she inspected her reflection now clad only in a chemise, corset, and stockings. She had once been robust and assertive; now she was a man's property, a wife, childless and barren. Her face once again contorted, twisted with pain, as she thought of her husband touching her, forcing her. "It's a woman's lot," her sister Emma told her over and over. Emma, who was a forty-year-old spinster living on her own in New Bedford—what did she know about marriage?

Lizbeth ground her teeth together to keep from screaming again. "It's the same house, the same room, the same God-forsaken room. I've never left, I'll never leave. I was my father's—thing—and then he passed me along to a man of his choice, a man made in his image, twice my age. An old, evil man . . ." She threw up her hands to cover her face as it mutated into something agonized and unrecognizable.

"I'm only thirty-two years old, God help me," she cried. Again, she sucked in her breath, clamped down on her emotions, dropped her arms and straightened. "Stop," she told the image of the woman in the mirror. "Stop it now." She reached around with both hands and deftly began unlacing the corset, moving from the small of her back upward. She averted her face from the mirror as she removed the last of her clothing and found her cotton nightgown and slipped that over her head.

She looked once more into the depths of the looking glass as she picked out the pins in her hair, shook the mass of it loose so that it fell in bumpy waves covering her breasts. *At least my father is gone now.*

Andrew Borden had died after contracting diphtheria two years before. He had never remarried after Lizbeth and Emma's mother died in 1863. "Oh he wanted to," Lizbeth whispered like a hiss in the air. "He wanted that big oaf of a woman Abby Gray, but Emma put a stop to that." She had been five years old at the time, and Emma twelve. The Great War was over, and Mr. Lincoln was dead, and Andrew Borden, undertaker, landlord, hated by the entire town of Fall River, had wanted another wife. But Emma, sister Emma, pubescent and her father's pet until little Lizzie should be old enough, convinced the old man that his two daughters were enough to satisfy him.

Lizbeth wanted to spit at the mirror, wanted to run into Emma's old room and tear it apart as she'd done many times before. Stomping, screeching, her face a mask of wretchedness as she threw bed linens and coverlets, ripped apart pillows and smashed the ceramic water pitcher and basin. In the past, such incidents had inspired her father, then her husband, to hit her and lock her in a closet to make her calm down. Eventually specialists were consulted. The men got together and concluded that these episodes were Lizzie's "spells" brought on by her monthly burden.

She turned to glance through the master bedroom doorway that led to her old room. "How convenient," she said. She gazed back at the Lizbeth in the mirror. "How nice of you, father, to choose an old friend of yours to be my husband, to let him live in our old house, to give us your old bed. You at least had the courtesy to move to the guest bedroom." Her stomach roiled, her abdomen felt heavy and contracted, as if it were an overripe fruit about to burst. "I was only twenty years old when you married me off," she said to a shadow she saw before her. Or was it behind her—a man with a hard face and a white beard? "And all I ever wanted was to be free, free of you, of all men, of everyone. Free to do whatever I please."

She leaned slightly forward. Was there something moving beyond her duplicate self that seemed to bend toward an internal light, as if the polished surface had its own source of illumination? A single eyeball suddenly appeared blinking from the middle of her forehead. Lizbeth, shocked, leaped backwards. But while her form moved when she did and her reflection disappeared from the mirror, the single blinking eye hovered in the same place.

Lizbeth jerked her head to the left, to the right. She spun in a circle, searching for who was in the room. There was no one else present. She angrily flung herself around to confront the mirror once more. Now there were two eyes, floating disembodied in the depths. "Who are you?" she asked aloud. "What is this?" The irises were a brilliant aquamarine color framed by brown-gold lashes. Brows, cheekbones, the faint smudge of a nose were almost visible. Lizbeth felt a chill. *Her* eyes were aquamarine framed by golden brown lashes. She felt some kind of enormous pressure, as if she were under water. She managed to shuffle a step closer. The face looking back at her, intermingled with her reflection, appeared frightened. The woman in the mirror, growing more and more solid, looked very familiar.

Suddenly the other broke through. Solidifying, emerging with a crackling sound, the woman tumbled forward while praying rapidly in a high-pitched, terrified voice. Lizbeth scrambled back to get out of the apparition's way.

The sounds of gasping and rapid breathing and a rattling stream of barely audible words "Oh God oh God oh God oh God" echoed in the stagnant air. Lizbeth was the first to pull herself together. She stood sentinel-like, her arms slightly raised, as she studied the trembling woman huddled on the rug at her feet.

"Who are you?" Lizbeth asked.

The other took a few more deep gulps of air, and then looked up into Lizbeth's face.

She felt as if she'd been struck by lightning, as if electricity had nailed her to the floor. The other gradually stood, weaving and swaying. She appeared to be amazed. They stared at each other for several minutes.

"Are you . . . Lizbeth?" Lizbeth asked.

"I'm Lizzie, Lizzie Borden. Are you . . ."

"I'm Lizbeth, Lizbeth Borden Beaumont. You came through my mirror."

"I . . ." She tilted her head as if this would help her understand. "I broke into my father's room, while he was out late. I was using his mirror."

They were both dressed in the same nightgown, their hair an identical length. But the other, Lizzie, was chubbier, with an attitude of entitlement about her. "How old are you?" Lizbeth asked, no longer frightened.

Lizzie leaned to the left, then to the right, her gaze running up and down Lizbeth's body. "I'm thirty-two. What day is this? What year is this?"

"It's August 3, 1892," Lizbeth said, adjusting her position as the other Lizzie orbited around her, studying her. "What do you mean you 'broke into' father's room?"

Lizzie stopped and recoiled somewhat. She turned her head slightly, watching Lizbeth from the side, from the corner of her eye, like a wary animal. "He keeps everything locked now. He keeps all the keys."

"He's still alive, then? Andrew Borden?"

"Yes, yes he is. Where's Emma?"

"My sister Emma lives in New Bedford. Father is dead. I live here with my husband, Charles Beaumont. Or I should say, my husband keeps me here like a pet, to do with as he pleases. I only exist to please him."

Lizzie's round cheeks reddened, her brows lifted, her lips parted as if to say something, but no words came out. They peered at each other for a time. Finally, the other, Lizzie, said, "You are not me. I wouldn't let that happen to me. It's not going to happen to me. I'm going to find a way to get out of this house."

"You'll never escape," Lizbeth said, and shook her head slowly.

"If I had the strength, if I had a way, I'd kill them both, Abby and Father. He's giving all his money to her, to her relatives. Emma and I will be destitute. If I could find someone I could trust, to help me ..." She stopped, suspicion and fear flickering in her eyes. "I shouldn't have told you that," she muttered.

Lizbeth felt light-headed. A surge of understanding coursed through her mind, a kind of fire filled her veins. "You can trust me," she said with an icy calm. "You are me. I am you—I will be you. Stay here for twenty-four hours. Let me take your place. I can give you the life I will never have."

Lizzie's color darkened. Her skin glistened. Her eyes gleamed. "You will kill them for me?" she ventured, her voice like that of a little girl. "You would do that for me?"

"I will go through that mirror. I will take your place. I will take care of your problem, yes. And then I shall return and you will resume your life. You might be accused, you might have to endure some hardship, but in the end the authorities will not be able to convict you. Because the evidence, the perpetrator, will be somewhere else, somewhere they can't find her."

Lizzie furrowed her brows, frowned slightly. "But I'm afraid. I don't want to stay here. I don't want to meet your husband. Do you promise you'll come back and get me?"

"Of course I will," Lizbeth said, grinning. "You're innocent, a virgin, with the rest of your life ahead of you. Why would I condemn you to my hell? Now tell me, did father kill your pet pigeons with a stout ax like he killed mine?"

Lizzie nodded, tears in her eyes.

"And is the hatchet still in the cellar where he left it?"

[short story]

The Hillside

by a. a. garrison

The hillside tradition was without a proper name, despite the fear and pride it inspired.

The village lay in the dusty vastness of southern India, the only region that possessed this particular rite. All locals observed the event, which required participation by every man of age. Unfair? Perhaps. But to decline the hillside was to be ostracized. The same punishment went for speaking of what transpired there, even among the other villagers.

Ram Chaknah was born and raised in the village, a stout, handsome lad who stood a head taller than his peers. Though a peasant of low caste, the boy was not immune to the hillside and its demands. So when he turned sixteen, he at last went with the men on that special day, rather than staying home with the women and children. The mystery would soon be revealed, and Ram wasn't quite sure how to feel about it.

He left with his father and older brother, the three departing in the hot mists of morning. Mother stayed in bed, feigning sleep, as did most other village women. Ram wore the attire characteristic of his caste: a muslin shirt atop a white, dress-like lungi, mirroring his father and brother. The teenager's uncommon height raised him above his elders, and he wondered if this would prove an advantage or a handicap. He would ask were he allowed to speak of these things.

Outside in the street, Ram and company joined an assembly of the village men. They wore varied dress, from modern-day western trappings to Gandhi's classic white cottons, with all manner of turban and skullcaps and more Indian headdresses still. All the men were silent and solemn. They walked with intimate closeness, regardless of caste or condition, in a rare show of equanimity. The village's rutted dirt thoroughfare hosted a river of these hard-faced mutes, flowing intransigently beneath the burgeoning morning sun. The group was led by the oldest man in the village, identified at once by his magnificent red beard and the Brahmin's ornate orange robe. Also, he wore a goat horn from the shoulder.

When Ram's father and brother fell in step, so did Ram, without a thought in his mind.

And so they went, this hundred-strong congregation of farmers and tradesmen and their sons. Down the parched roadway, past humble fields and scattered wells, across a cobble bridge where a stray bull grazed. Just beyond the village proper, the throng encountered a pickup truck, and it was the truck that yielded. The driver, an outsider unfortunate enough to have business here today, could only stare and wait. The villagers flowed around the obstruction like water around a rock.

They made for the hills to the east, moving as one. All knew their destination.

Ram filed along like the rest of his brethren, now relaxed enough to remember his lifelong questions. What secrets did the hills harbor? The lush, grassy landscape had been his haven as a child, where he and the other village children would congregate and conspire. The place had a certain reputation, the same as a city park. Several shepherds employed the area for their sheep, but not today. The shepherds were marching with the rest.

New gravity befell the men as the scenery changed, disputing the surrounding idyll in a perverse contrast. Ram watched his fellows harden further—brows sharpening, gaits lengthening, frowns deepening—and the change slowly translated to him. He searched for clues about what was to come, but the villagers showed only the dark reverence Ram had seen on this day since birth. Even his father and brother returned only empty, distant gazes, those of foreigners. Ram couldn't help but feel that they took a sick, self-important pleasure in his ignorance, perhaps along with all the hillside's veterans.

The men wove through the hills' narrow little pass—until the old man in front reached a sudden stop. Silently, austerely, he turned to the men and raised a terrible fist. Then the men began climbing a hillside.

The elder's funereal brown eyes touched every passing man, including Ram. He shrunk from the arresting gaze; it made him feel alone and unclothed.

And so they were at their destination.

The chosen hillside was, not surprisingly, the tallest of them all, a centerpiece of the subtle cleavage that comprised the series of hills. The incline rose proudly above everything in sight, with a smooth, even arch that would catch the sun the day long. It resembled the forehead of a bald head, Ram had always thought—or, alternately, that of a skull.

Up this slow, unbroken hillside the men went. The climb was easy enough, but to Ram it felt to be a sheer cliff.

Halfway up, the elder stood in wait, preceding the men as they crested the hill's little horizon—but hadn't the elder been down below, directing his stare? Ram had time to think this a fakir's magic trick, before he concluded that the elder had simply taken a shortcut, presumably for this very effect. Still, the illusion had its impact.

Again the men stopped at the urging of the elder's raised fist. Automatically, they fanned out in a rough line, obeying the script to which Ram remained ignorant.

And then, as fluidly, single men were parting from the group—one left, one right, going respectively down or up the hillside. They departed at the elder's prompting, that same fist directing them to their stations. Ram watched fathers and their sons separate in this fashion, and he couldn't help but wonder if it was intentional.

When the elder reached Ram, the fist pumped left, assigning him back down the hillside. He did as he was directed, even though his father and brother were sent the other way.

Once returned to the foot of the hill, there was a moment's wait. Ram looked uphill, but the rest of the villagers were invisible, shrouded by the sloped geography and the mysterious morning mists. The men here remained a sizable mass despite the split, and were as disciplined in their stern silence. Ram's fear lifted just enough for him to notice that, for all his youth, he was the tallest, burliest man among them.

Before he could consider this, however, a noise erupted from above—a goat horn's baritone blow, recognized as that of the village elder. Chaos followed.

Immediately, the contingent of villagers cried out in a primal, savage chorus, raising the same violent fists of the elder. The men simultaneously shed their grave demeanor for this bloodthirsty show, now as crazed as they'd been subdued. As spontaneously, they charged up the hill.

Ram felt only the slightest surprise. The change felt wholly natural, as will anything performed by enough peers. After only a lull, he was right there with them, as loud and animated as anyone. Why they were charging, he didn't know, and in the moment, he didn't care.

The explosive energy propelled the men back up the incline. They moved faster than before, legs pumping above sandals and sneakers and bare feet, screaming all the while. As they gained altitude, another, equal roar could be heard—coming at them, from up the hill. Ram caught the first note of it just as the rest of the men broke from the mists, as spirited and unleashed. They barreled down the hillside at speed, on a collision course for those below.

It broke Ram's trance, and he stumbled to a stop, immediately abandoned by the others. He watched as the two bodies converged at the hillside's median—and at once attacked each other. Neighbor on neighbor, brother on brother, sons and fathers—the fighting was merciless and indiscriminate, with the willingness of an unlearned act. Fists flew into stomachs and faces, sending out sprays of sweat and noise. In seconds, there were men on the ground.

Ram remained at a distance from the melee, stunned.

Then an impact—a foot in his side, from some flanking attacker. It sent Ram reeling, and for a prolonged second the blow only deepened his confusion and inhibition. Clumsily he turned to see a wiry, middle-aged man named Raj Batra, a cotton farmer of Ram's own caste. Ram had never heard Batra so much as curse, but now the man was scowling and livid, and telegraphing a punch.

Something inside Ram changed; it felt like an opening hand or a discarded garment.

He dodged Raj Batra's swing and instantly retaliated with one of his own. Ram's oversized fist connected with the edge of the man's slender jaw, at once changing Raj Batra's course and sending him reeling as Ram had just seconds ago. Ram followed up with a brutal shove into the man's ribs, knocking him flat. Batra rolled some feet down the hillside, tried to get up, and failed.

Without a second thought, Ram entered the surrounding maelstrom. It felt right.

The assault had heightened, with sweat and blood soaking every combatant. A hot odor had established itself, like none Ram had ever smelled. The sides were no longer being observed; the fighting become general. Ram punched. Ram kicked. Ram bit. Ram used his abnormally large body in new ways. The recipients of his attacks were all faces he'd known for years or life, from friends to patriarchs. He lost some duels, but won far more. He did not exchange blows with his father or brother, but only because they did not present themselves.

Suddenly, Ram was seized about the torso.

He staggered, studying that which was wrapped around his waist and shoulders: It was Kumar Das, a smooth-faced boy a year older, and a caste higher, than Ram. Kumar, small and diminished, was attached bodily to Ram in a lame attempt at attack, his aim unclear. Ram reacted with a shrug and a twist, but Kumar did not let go, his shrill battle cries blaring in Ram's ears. Ram swung harder, twirling about in a sharp arc, but still Kumar held on. The boy neither wanted to attack nor be freed; he was clinging to Ram out of fear, it would seem. The two looked to be dancing.

Ram swung around again, this time getting leverage and accentuating his spin. But instead of separating, the two plowed into a faceless third party. Kumar held fast, but the other man went down hard. The combined velocity of Ram and Kumar was deadly.

So Ram went with it, again spinning, now using the boy's weight instead of fighting it. Kumar, perhaps sensing this strange symbiosis, moved with Ram similarly, enhancing their attack further still. They barreled into others three at a go, as a conjoined, misshapen One, whirling about like a Siamese top. The scheme was devilishly effective, and Ram exploited it to its fullest. He couldn't see Kumar's face, but the boy's screaming changed note, shifting from fearful to victorious. Ram and Kumar both suffered blows, but their combined power kept them standing.

They remained whirling about as the horn blew a second time. Everyone stopped.

The effect was instantaneous and profound, ceasing the event as if by a switch. The noise was gone. Punches halted mid-swing. Wrestlers detached in sync, letting go of one another like videos played in reverse. Likewise, Kumar was at last uncoupled from the pillar of Ram's body. Then the two exchanged a single conversant look, knowledge passing between them—and that was all.

Freed from the battle's rapture, Ram was struck with the belated, repeating question—Why? Why? Why? Head spinning, he found himself amidst a patchwork of concussed and bleeding men. Only a scattered few were left standing, and he was one of them. Seeing this, Ram felt a surge of power, strong and curious, washing over him with the warmth of a blanket.

At once, all questions left Ram's mind. He understood. To stand tall and look down on those laid low was the prize of this weird pageant. The realization brought a momentary shock. Was this feeling of power not absurd and illusionary? But the intoxication of the effect was quick to push away such thoughts. Ram might feel differently were he one of those on the ground—but he was not on the ground.

The whole day clicked into place as seamlessly as a solved puzzle.

Ram understood very well.

As Ram stood percolating in his newfound status, the elder reappeared, the goat horn hung from his shoulder. With another mournful blow, the men began gathering up the fallen, dusting them off and nursing injuries. Those who couldn't rise were carried off. Ram had no idea how much time had passed, all linearity having ceased the moment he heard that first horn. And still not a word was exchanged, or so much as a gesture. The men reassembled and left as they'd come. Back in the village, they remained silent, as did the wives and daughters and boys.

In the days to follow, Ram's ego stayed inflated, with those of the others who had been left standing on the hillside. It was seen in the postures and heard in the voices, and reflected in the regard of their fellow villagers. These men banded together as elites, like soldiers returned from war, enjoying the license of their victory. And Ram was counted as one of them. He had more doubts of this perceived superiority, but he continued pushing them away. He had been one of those standing. Didn't that mean something? Did it perhaps mean everything?

This notion sustained his high until there was no question of his merit.

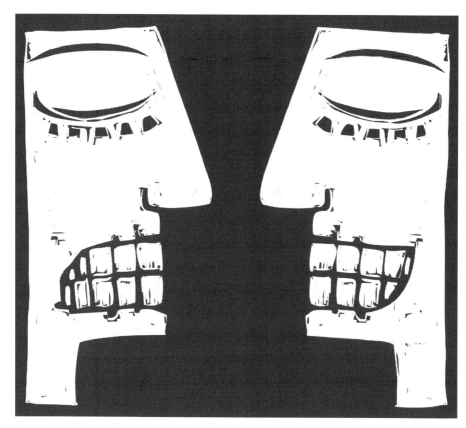

NIGHT CHANNEL

The dark tunnels, the under passes.
They all stare at me.
There all dark, they see me, they know me.

Darkest dark, blackest black. No touch separates
us, still stagnant.

In the muted greasy hides a suicide.
Perfection. Death is a boulder on our flesh, never stopping
never sleeping.

This destination is despair.

We have choices….tickets
hope or misery?

I am not afraid of heights nor falling,
because what lies in the middle is peace.

I may not see a rose bloom again
or a sparrow care for her baby but
at least I can see an end, the only thing I can't judge.

Pills are tucked deep inside of me,
trying to make up for the damage.

My ribs itch for comfort or a soothing coat
of cyanide.

A thrashing whisper tells all of us to end it.
Arise and shine I've met the sweet sky,
the stars made me believe that life was
not so bad after all.

—brittney wright

PICTURE TAKER

by george lee

There's a picture on Maria's cell phone.

In it she's sleeping. Dreaming, maybe.

Maria lives alone.

And Maria doesn't have a boyfriend, or anyone who would take a picture of her sleeping.

There's another picture on Maria's cell phone.

It's of a figure, gender anonymous, holding up the cell phone in front of Maria's full-length mirror. The mirror hangs on the back of her closet door, which she always keeps closed, because she feels that open doors are chaotic and disorderly. The flash from the phone bounces off the mirror and blocks the figure's face, and obscures the rest of the body in abstract light.

Maria can be seen in the background of this photo too, sleeping.

Dreaming, hopefully.

Maria didn't notice these photos until this morning. She was sipping coffee. It was six am and she was bored, waiting for time to pass. So she decided to look through old photos on her phone, hoping to entertain herself.

Now she's afraid to sleep, and is even more afraid of her closet.

She calls her mother, but ends the call on the second ring. What is she going to say exactly? A scary something is taking photos of her while she sleeps? That she has monsters in her closet? No, even to her it sounds ridiculous.

She leaves for work, shaking at the fact that the dress she is wearing for work came from her closet.

At work Maria can't concentrate. She thinks about the photos, keeping her cell phone in her purse and her purse in her locker in the back room. She's afraid to be alone, afraid to go home, afraid to fall asleep and dream.

But work ends and she has to take some action. So she leaves work slowly, sitting in her car for a good while, listening to the radio and trying no to think.

Maria's cell phone dings. It's a text from an unknown number. She considers ignoring it but her curiosity is stronger than her fear. Flipping open the phone a picture pops up.

It's a picture of Maria in her car.

It's a picture of Maria in her car at this moment.

Maria doesn't look around for the photographer. Instead she starts her car and drives. She drives all night, reaching her parent's house in the early morning. She would have called them and warned them she was coming but as she was crossing over a bridge she tossed her cell phone out the window, uncertain if it was the right thing to do or not.

At home Maria tells her parents of the stalker. They worry and talk about calling the police, which at this point Maria doesn't argue with. However, now she doesn't have any proof, having thrown her phone away several hundred miles back. She clings to her parents like a small child, not wanting to be alone and making sure they check that every door in the house is closed. When night comes she refuses to sleep in her old room, preferring the safety and closet-less living room where she can watch the television all night long.

But it's the second night of her not sleeping, and her eyelids grow heavy around 2:30 am. She falls asleep. And dreams. In the dream she is having dinner with several people she is certain she knows, but can't name or see clearly. The table they are sitting at is long, nearly reaching from one end of the room to the other and is a dark, rich colored wood, perhaps mahogany. Prestigious in appearance with matching chairs padded in red velvet. Rich foods -- turkey, ham, assorted vegetables and trimmings adorn the table, a fantasy Thanksgiving dinner. The heavily laden table and guests are the only decorations in the otherwise white and windowless room. Everyone appears to be having a decent time, laughing and talking loudly, telling stories and jokes Maria is sure she has heard before, but the sounds are fuzzy and indiscernible. No one is actually eating the food though, and suddenly the dinner is over and everyone has gone. Maria is left alone in the room, helplessly searching every wall for the door, yet there is no exit to be found.

She wakes up in a cold sweat. The television is still on, playing re-runs of a sitcom that only the canned laugh track finds entertaining. She wipes the sweat from her forehead with one hand while clearing out the gunk from her eyes with the other.

She sees beside her a picture frame, silver and glistening under the lamplight. She doesn't remember seeing it before. She leans in closer, and sees it is a photo of her sleeping on the couch, except she is a child of nine or ten in the picture.

And in it she is dreaming, maybe.

This picture itself is no cause for alarm. She is uncertain if she should create a fuss over it. Probably an old picture of her that her parents really liked. Perhaps she didn't notice it before when she fell asleep. She deeply wishes this to be the truth.

The clock above the fireplace reads 9:00 am. There is no noise to indicate that the house is awake. She rises and searches for a note on the kitchen counter, the usual place her parents would leave a note about their whereabouts, but there is no note.

Her heart begins to pump faster and drops from her chest to her stomach. Quietly she walks down the hallway to her parents' room. The walls are full of family pictures, which usually would bring her comfort but now she avoids looking at them. The door to the room is cracked open. She pushes it back, the creaking echoing in the stillness. Underneath the covers lies two bodies, and she sighs relief. They must have slept in. It's unusual, but it happens.

She walks toward the bed, the closer she comes to it the more something appears missing. Two bodies lie beneath the covers, yet no heads lay in the pillows. There are two silver frames instead, each containing a picture of the appropriate heads, severed cleanly across the neck, eyes open and mouths posed into a smile.

No scream comes from Maria's throat. Her feet cannot move. It takes several moments before she can bend her knees and run, flying out the front door and into her car. Now she needs the police. Now there is proof.

Now she is really alone.

There are plenty of police cars and yellow tape outside Maria's childhood home. Maria is sitting on the couch, a policewoman beside her offering comfort as she's asked by many others the same questions over and over again in slightly different ways. The crime scene photographer takes several photos and she flinches at every flash.

Maria eventually feels strong enough to move from the couch to the kitchen. To get some water, she says. No, thank you, she can get it herself. The policewoman and others give her some space – but not too much. The photos in silver frames have been confiscated and thankfully removed from sight. She leans against the kitchen counter, staring into nothingness. From the silverware drawer there is a ringing noise.

It's a cellphone.

She opens the drawer.

It's her mother's cell phone.

The ID reads "Martin."

It's a message from her father's phone to her mother.

She could call the police in to check it out.

Her curiosity is stronger than her fear.

Flipping open the phone she finds it is a picture of the scary thing from her closet. It is the same as before except the thing is posing in front of her dresser mirror, the closet door open behind it.

The thing is in her childhood room. It is in her room NOW.

She screams this at the investigators who run to her. They turn and rush to her room and open her door, finding nothing. Maria rejects this and pushes into her room. She opens the closet door and enters it, no longer able to feel much of anything anymore.

The door slams shut behind her, encasing her in the darkness. From outside she hears banging and yelling. She cannot open the door. No one outside can open the door. She is trapped with no exit.

As she bangs against the inside of the door, she feels a hot breath blow a few wisps of her hair against her cheek. The policemen and detectives and anyone else on the outside of the closet hear a muffled scream, and then hear nothing. The door opens easily now, and when they look in the closet there are only clothes.

They are alone now.

A funeral is held. Family members cry over the deaths. No body is in Maria's casket. Her parents coffins have bodies, but no heads. All of the coffins are closed. It's a very popular story in the news for several weeks. Then it passes, and though it is never forgotten, it becomes something of an urban legend not really believed anymore. It's the natural order of things, a way to continue living normally after such a strange series of events.

In Maria's coffin, just before it is closed for good, someone, or something, places a photo on the white satin pillow. A picture of Maria, her head severed much like her parent's, except her eyes are closed and her mouth as well. She looks peaceful, like she is sleeping.

Dreaming, hopefully.

A Crone's Glory

by rita hooks

Like old souls, mid-October shadows passed by the window. As Dot folded the laundry, the long strands of gray hair clinging to the clothes took her by surprise. At first she denied ownership, but the coarse iron-gray hairs could only have come from her head. Her husband Roger's much shorter, silkier hair still retained its youthful color. As she folded her husband's underwear, Dot noticed how the static electricity from the dryer attracted her stray hairs to his Calvin's. She picked the hairs off one by one, each steel wire clearly visible against the black cotton knit. But as she pulled them off, they would jump right back on as if magnetized. It was tedious work, but she didn't want Roger to find the defiling hair. She had had a similar experience long ago when nursing her infant son. She had found with dismay that one of her dark coarse hairs had fallen among the soft golden curls of her baby's head and, seeing it as a violation of his purity, quickly got rid of the offending hair.

Roger and Dot shared a quiet life. But he often became impatient with her, calling her his old ball and chain. She lamented that he had expected more out of life and was disappointed. They were sitting in the living room leaning back in their matching recliners, when Roger said, "The blue jays and mockingbirds are at it again." Dot laughed. Then she saw how even in thick woolen socks, his ankles looked thin. She felt pity, and then a sad dread rose in her chest.

Upon getting out of bed the next morning, Roger groaned.

"What is it?" Dot asked.

"Look," he said, pointing his finger.

She saw it. A long gray hair on her pillow.

"Just like in Faulkner. Dot, you've become a character straight out of a Gothic horror story."

Dot knew the story well. Not only had Miss Emily killed her lover, but for forty years she lay beside his body until she herself had become an old woman. On the day of Emily's funeral the townspeople found a long strand of iron-gray hair in the indentation of a head on a second pillow placed next to her lover's corpse. Dot remembered the revulsion she had felt as a young student reading the end of the story and how more disturbing than the man's rotting body was the old woman's gray hair.

Dot, although hurt by Roger, understood. They were both aging.

"Why don't you dye your hair?" Roger asked. "You look like a crone."

"I like the natural look."

"You and your natural shit. Like breastfeeding the kids. All you got out of that was saggy tits."

"Roger, how can you say that?" she asked.

"Your milk was probably full of DDT. So much for natural. I'm warning you. Someone's been coming on to me."

"Roger, you wouldn't," she said.

He responded, "You should be happy for me. It's natural."

Not long after threatening her, Roger told Dot that he had fallen in love with a new worker at the pharmacy. Her name was Estelle. He had reassured his wife that they weren't having sex. He just loved the girl. The next time Dot folded his clothes, she found a dark hair that she didn't recognize. She tried not to dwell on it. Having believed that she was the love of Roger's life, Dot found herself lost and frightened. Of course, Roger couldn't just have casual sex like some other men; he had to fall in love. Dot was curious about the girl, who probably cast a spell on him with her sexy tattoos and body piercings. Dot imagined the dark luster of the girl's hair next to the pallor of her young skin.

But old women have their own kind of magic. Unbraiding her hair, Dot collected the long crinkly strands that had fallen out; then she took Roger's briefs from his dresser drawer. Laying each hair out to its full length, she ritualistically selected a single hair, placed it on the inside of the fly of each pair of his Calvin's, and chanted,

Pity and dread, pity and dread
With an old hair from this crone's head
Binding and binding until red
Pity and dread, pity and dread

As was their wont, Roger and Dot enjoyed a couple of drinks at the end of the day, but Roger was drinking more and more. During the winter holiday, he was often drunk and began to drink away from home, stumbling in late at night. Dot would let him sleep it off. She guessed that he had been with Estelle. She imagined that he couldn't face her right after being with another woman, so instead of coming home afterwards, he would stay out and get wasted.

Dot continued to keep their home; she always had a big pot of soup bubbling on the stove. And she was meticulous about washing and folding the clothes, pulling off any of her stray hairs, only to place a single hair inside the front of her husband's underpants. Before long, her jealous suspicion spiraled into jealous rage, and Dot, like a banshee, prophesied:

Pity and dread, pity and dread
With an old hair from this crone's head
Binding and binding until red
Pity and dread, pity and dread

As the days slowly passed, Dot had less and less laundry to do because Roger had begun to wear the same clothes for days at a time and had even ceased bathing for long stretches. When Roger was home, he was usually asleep, and it seemed to Dot as if he would sleep forever.

One night Roger came in with several bottles of whiskey and went on a binge. At the end of the third day, Dot heard an agonized scream coming from their bedroom. The unearthly howl caused the hairs on her arms to stand erect. She froze at first, and then proceeded almost eagerly down the hall in the direction of the cry that had morphed into the pitiful yelping of an injured dog.

When she entered the room, Roger was out of bed, swaying on his feet. With unfocused eyes, he stared into the dresser mirror.

"Help me," he pleaded.

"Now what have you done to yourself?"

"I didn't do this," he said, pointing to his crotch.

Like a red balloon, it had swollen to four times its natural size.

Dot gloried in the fact that a long gray hair had wrapped itself tightly around the base of her husband's penis, causing it to swell enormously.

"It'll be okay," she said. "I'll just get the shears."

A
Sane
Fellow

Today my cat spoke to me.
I don't think it's the start of a
break down as he asked for a
mouse. A very sensible thing.

If he had asked for a wardrobe,
then I would have phoned the men
in white coats to drag me away.
But a mouse is as resonable a

thing as a dog asking for a bone.
I have wanted many things, but
who will get them for me? To
show me his devotion, the cat

brings me little mutilated things on
the mat when I come home. Though
how he managed to leave those dead
women in my bed; I really can't say.

—matthew wilson

[short story]

The Sentinel of Beaumont Avenue

by santos vargas

The climb to the summit was laden with the smell of urine. Crack vials and used condoms seem like weeds on a manicured lawn. My plateau was dark stained with gooey tar, and weird protrusions rise upwards like steel trees that bare no fruit but the metal branches continue their attempt at redemption. I listen to the mid-afternoon sounds, as they slowly rise, climbing the smog-stained bricks like ivy with tentacled fingers.

The women folk gather clothes from small caves they call clothing stores. They don't sccm to travel in packs but for some reason find themselves in a pack. Music drowns out some of the voices, men folk sitting in front of what they call a bodega playing with some tiles and drinking from cans. They scream at one another from across the street.

My nemesis, I hear it approaching, the metal centipede. It snakes it way around the seared path it has created. It never deviates, and it screams at it approaches as if warning the sacrificial victims that wait for it. It swallows those self-sacrificial ones and defecates others. Yet it always feeds in the same place. One day I will slay the beast.

I see other predators in the corner. These predators are the vampires I loathe; they stand and wait for their victims to come to them. I see them hand over money, and they receive a packet. Some come in cars, and others walk; even some are defecated from the centipede and head straight to that corner. I hear a small animal crying to be fed. I hear a woman folk crying not to be beaten by the man folk. I hear two dogs barking things, honking, and somewhere in the distance a flying bird made of metal beaks through the clouds. My nostrils are filled with the smell of overcooked beans and other mouth-watering scents. Pigeons fly over my head waiting for me to leave so they can have the privacy of being alone on the roof. There is a gargoyle that sits on his own ledge and he too is impatient. I feel I have overstayed my welcome. Yet I am the sentinel of 2350 Beaumont Avenue at least till my mom calls.

Black Sail Veils

Black sails were all I had.
I cast them high, lilac clad.
Shearing sounds tore through my skin
Jeering shrieks came tumbling in
Marrow deep did we seek to go
Toward heavy hearts did the cruel wind blow
Then still against the sharp, cream shale
We threw on heads our black sail veils
Hollow whispers brought sounds from home
The waves were white, like sprung from bone
And with those waves I rose and fell
Up toward heaven and down to hell

—navo banerjee

[*short story*]

Bella

by rie sheridan rose

The rain fell in sheets of silver bullets hard enough to sting the skin. The concrete buildings on either side of the street funneled the storm into a howling torrent of water and wind. Peter Milton tried to open his umbrella against the storm until it offered its belly to the beast and turned inside out.

"Dammit." He tossed the useless umbrella into a corner rubbish bin and turned his collar up in a vain attempt to keep the ice-cold rain from sluicing down his back. *Great. Just what I needed.*

Hunching his shoulders, he began fighting his way through the city night toward his car—and ultimately to the brand new suburban home where his new wife waited—bucking the aggressive wind that clawed at his coat as if begging him to stay with it. He'd had practice ignoring tears and importuning, so it was easy to disregard the storm's complaints.

As he passed the mouth of an alleyway, he heard a muffled sobbing barely audible over the storm. He cocked his head.

"Hello? Is someone there?"

No answer … but the sobbing continued unabated. The heartbreaking loneliness of the sound aroused his curiosity. There was a world of loss in that sobbing. He felt an impulse to console the source.

He forgot all about his bride who was waiting at that white-picket-fence home her father had bought them. She was no doubt worried by his tardiness. But he felt a need to know who made that pitiful crying.

"I'm not going to hurt you," he promised, stepping into a grimy alleyway thick with the smells of garbage and sex. "Are you in pain? Do you need something?" He walked slowly into the dimly lit alleyway, cautious that someone might be waiting to ambush him.

As his eyes adjusted to the poor lighting, he saw a naked figure crouched against a rough brick wall.

"Shit!" he cried involuntarily, tugging loose the belt of his trench coat and shrugging out of it. He no longer cared if the rain completely soaked his shirt. He bent beside the hunched female and wrapped her in his coat.

"Jesus, lady. It's freezing out here. Why don't you have any clothes on? Did someone attack you? Are you hurt? Need a doctor?"

The woman looked up at him—tears standing in her beautiful violet eyes, rain mixing with their tracks on her cheeks—and he was lost. She had a drowned-rat appearance—her black hair twisted in ribbons and plastered to her skull. He had never seen a more delicate face.

His eyes drifted lower and he glimpsed the lean musculature of an athlete or dancer topped by high firm breasts before she pulled the coat tighter around herself.

"Thank you," she whispered. Her voice was husky, yet musical.

"Can you stand? My car is just around the corner. Let's get you out of the rain."

She slipped her arms through the sleeves of the coat, and belted it around herself as she stood. A nod was his only answer.

Peter forgot Catherine would be waiting for him at home—Catherine, his bride of six weeks; Catherine, still in the Happy Homemaker phase of marriage; Catherine, who drove him bat-shit crazy with her billing and cooing and "will you be late for dinner?" With her tears, her demands to know every single thing he did every single moment of every day.

The girl in the trench coat was much more immediate—and a damn sight prettier—than his married-because-it-was-expected bride. His boss's daughter. The cereal-box prize. Every bachelor in the building was jealous that he got the nod. What a joke! They didn't have to live with her.

He led the way to his nondescript mud-colored Sedan, wishing he'd bought the BMW he dreamed about instead of paying for furniture and landscaping for the house he'd never wanted and wouldn't have bought on his own. Yet another hand-out from his most magnanimous father-in-law. *Damn interfering old SOB.*

Peter was doing okay, but he wasn't rich enough that he could keep up the appearances Catherine required of him and still drive his dream car. He had nothing to offer this naked nymph to prove he was worth more than a cup of coffee and a hot meal.

Still, you never could tell. Rescue from the rain might be enough for her when all she had to offer was her looks. She might just be ever so grateful.

He shook his head to clear it.

What the hell was he thinking? He couldn't take advantage of this woman. That wouldn't do at all. Catherine was waiting at home. She was his wife, and this woman was a stranger in need. She didn't need any problems added to the ones she already had.

His mama raised him better. He forced himself to look away from the flash of bare thigh offered as she sat in the passenger seat. Then he shut the door behind her and trotted to the driver's side of the car.

He got in and slammed the door shut. He grabbed for his seatbelt. "You'd better buckle up there, miss," he told his shell-shocked passenger. "Wouldn't want us to get stopped. It might be a bit awkward."

She looked at him vacantly then slowly drew the belt across her body, only to stare at the latching mechanism as if she had never seen one before.

With an impatient sigh, he took the buckle out of her hand and latched it securely. "There you go—what should I call you? I can't just keep saying 'miss' or 'hey, you.'" He smiled to take any sting from the words.

She looked up at him with those startling violet eyes. "Bella," she breathed.

"Bella...I like that. It suits you. Now, where should I take you?"

"I have nowhere to go." Her voice was a whisper.

"Well, I can't just leave you in the middle of this rainstorm. It's coming down like ice bullets. You'll catch your death of cold. There's a nice motel about a mile from here. I'll get you a room for the night, and that will give you a chance to rest and contact someone to come get you if you want. How does that sound?"

"I appreciate the offer, but there is no one to call."

"You don't have any friends or family?"

"No." She lowered her head to her chest. Her ebony hair curtained her delicate features. "There is no one left."

"That's terrible! You poor thing."

Improper thoughts raced through his head. Maybe she really would be grateful. The girl was so damn hot. She made Catherine look like a crone.

The lights of the motel glimmered through the rain, the neon splashing pink and blue trails in the water on the windshield as he pulled into the parking lot near the rear of the complex. He killed the ignition. "I'll go in and get your key. You wait here, and we won't have to answer any awkward questions."

"Anything you say," she answered in her soft breathless voice. Her violet eyes were vivid—almost glowing—in the motel lights.

Peter smiled at her. "I'll be right back."

He dashed through the storm and yanked open the lobby door. "Whew, it's really coming down out there!" he commented to the young man behind the counter. "You have a room I can get for the night?"

"Got one left. Single do?"

"If that's what you've got."

"That'll be $40 for the night."

Peter pulled his wallet out of his pocket and laid two twenties on the counter. He took the key from the clerk and headed back through the rain.

He had a second's fear the car would be empty when he got back to it, but Bella still huddled in the passenger seat.

"Hey, there," he said, opening the car door. "The room is right over here." He pointed behind him. "Let's get you inside."

He helped her out of the car and walked her over to the room with a hand in the small of her back. He could feel the heat of her through the fabric of the coat. The contact sent an electric current coursing through him. He felt stirrings in places that had no business stirring--not since he became a married man.

The room was small and smelled of cleanser and chlorine. The décor featured crushed velvet and shag carpet. It was a vile place, but at least it was dry.

Now that they were inside, Peter found himself at a loss for what to do or say. He knew he should go home to Catherine. Catherine was a sweet girl and deserved his love and respect. And they were married now, after all. He had no business being here with this strange woman. But she was so beautiful …

"I should go," he murmured, his hand on the doorknob.

He willed her to ask him to stay.

"Do you have to go?" she said.

The whisper was so soft he doubted his ears at first, thinking he had conjured it from his longing.

But when he turned, she was standing right before him, the coat discarded to reveal the lithe body so very different from Catherine's. Her startling violet eyes radiated an incandescence that dazed Peter's senses.

She stepped closer, and Peter found himself with his back against the door. She was everything his heart desired—the fantasy figure of a thousand adolescent stroke-fests. Full-figured Catherine, with her plump blond curls, plump little hands, and plump complacent mind—Catherine was no match for this lean, leonine lady. *I'll bet Bella is an animal in bed too.* He was aching to find out. His cock pressed painfully against the fly of his work slacks.

Bella reached out and took his hand, drawing him to the bed with a smoldering glance over her shoulder.

Peter tore at the tie around his neck with his free hand, jerking it free, and then scattering buttons to the four corners as he yanked on his dress shirt.

Bella laughed, the sound guttural and deep for someone her size. It was incongruous coming from such a dainty beauty.

Peter no longer cared. His entire focus was on the bed, and what they were about to do there. Thoughts of Catherine had flown. His world began and ended with Bella.

She got on the bed with catlike grace, dropping his hand long enough for him to complete his disrobing. Freed of its restraints, his cock jutted like a lightning rod.

Languidly draping herself across the pillows, Bella smiled a secretive smile and beckoned him.

Peter crawled up beside her and began to nuzzle her damp hair. She smelled of lavender and other more exotic flowers. But underneath the floral scents were notes of less savory odors.

Of course, what should he expect? He'd found her naked on the street, after all. She'd probably had a rough time of it.

Bella trailed a line of kisses from his chin to his groin, and the sensation was overpowering.

He gasped and said, "I shouldn't."

"But you want to," she answered, her voice throaty and full of need. Then she took him in her mouth, and he was lost.

The sensations crashed through him in waves of pleasure, cresting higher and higher until he could take no more. The pleasure began to edge toward pain. Something was piercing the flesh of his manhood.

"Stop. That's enough," he protested, pushing at the crown of her head.

She pulled back long enough to show him two eyes of violet fire and a mouth filled with rows of needle-like teeth. "Oh, I've just started," she replied, her voice thick and distorted.

Peter screamed.

And Bella fed.

[*short story*]

Cookies from Mother

by david greske

The car pulled into the garage and Melanie stepped from the passenger door, bright-colored bags dangling from each hand. Sam hurried around the front of the car and took the parcels from his wife. He kissed her on her cheek. Arm in arm they strolled up the sidewalk.

"Glad to be home?" He opened the front door and stepped to one side to let Melanie enter the kitchen first.

Melanie shrugged. "I suppose, but I'm gonna miss all the fun we had."

Sam set the bags on the table and wrapped his arms around his wife's petite, tanned waist. "Are you saying that I'm no fun? What about those nights on the beach?"

Those nights on the beach—how could she forget? "Mmmmmm. Those nights certainly were delicious."

It had been nice to get away, disconnecting from the world of cell phones, computers, and Facebook. The abandonment of these daily distractions renewed their attraction to each other. And by the way her husband was acting, Melanie thought this newly charged affection could stick around for a while.

Sam winked and kissed his wife. "Listen, why don't I run to the post office and pick up our mail?"

"Okay," Melanie said, "but don't be long. I have a little treat for you when you get back." Melanie lifted her blouse. She wasn't wearing a bra.

"How can I refuse an offer like that?"

By the time Sam returned from town, Melanie had everything from their Bahamas vacation put away. She even managed to hang the oil painting she'd bought from a street vendor.

"So, did anyone send us money?" she asked when Sam walked into the kitchen.

"No," he said, "but everyone seems to want some." He tossed a handful of bills on the table. "But you got a couple of things."

"Really?" Melanie said, walking into the kitchen. She had changed from the lacey blouse into an oversized Chicago Cubs T-shirt. Sam knew by the way her nipples poked at the fabric she was still braless.

Melanie took the two parcels from her husband and examined them. One was short and round; the other tall and rectangular. Both were wrapped in brown paper. Both were missing return addresses. Melanie examined the packages, turning them upside-down and right-side up several times. She shook the bigger one.

"I wonder what's inside?" Sam said.

"Let's open them and find out."

Melanie opened the round package first, ripping the wrapping like a child tears into a Christmas gift. Under the paper was a red, tin canister. She removed the top and found the tin filled with cookies. On top of the treats was a small, white envelope. She set the tin on the table and opened the envelope. She read the note aloud:

"Dear Melanie, I know how much you like my cookies so I decided to send you a batch. I also know how much you want the recipe and how I tell you it's my secret. Well, I must be getting soft in my old age because I've finally decided to let you have it. The ingredients that make up my special flour, however, will still be my secret—at least for the time being. Since you really can't bake the cookies without it, I'll be sending some of it to you. Happy baking! Love, Mom."

"Cookies," Sam said. "You're mother sent you cookies."

"Well, that's mom." Melanie plucked one of the treats from the wax paper nest. "Want one?"

"No thanks. You know how much I like sweets."

"Suit yourself." Melanie popped the cookie in her mouth and winkled her nose. "Tastes a little stale."

"Well, what did you expect? We've been gone for three weeks and there's no telling how long they sat on the dirty post office shelf."

Melanie ignored her husband, picked up the second package, and worked at the wrapping. Underneath the paper was a cardboard box held closed by heavy strapping tape. Melanie slid her fingernails under the tape and tore it off. She opened the flaps and lifted out a simple brass canister. She popped open the top. Inside was a powdery substance.

"This must be the flour," Melanie said, showing it to Sam.

Sam peered inside the canister. "Ah-ha."

Melanie pulled a bowl from the cupboard above her.

"What are you doing?" Sam asked.

"I'm going to bake cookies."

"Now?" He had other things in mind and they didn't involve baking cookies. "You're mother just sent you a bunch of them."

"I know. But they're so much better when they're fresh."

"Okay. Then you won't mind if I go have a couple of beers with the boys."

"No, not at all. Go have fun."

As Sam walked out the front door, Melanie turned her attention to the recipe. She pooled all the ingredients into the bowl, stirring them briskly with a wire whip just as the recipe read. Then she folded in two cups of the special flour.

When Sam returned several hours later, the kitchen smelled of sugar and cinnamon. Despite the fact he'd never developed a taste for sweets, he had to admit the place smelled delicious.

At the counter, cookies were stacked on cooling racks. Melanie had a smudge of flour on her thigh and a smear of it on her cheek. Sam thought *she* looked good enough to eat.

"So, how's my little cookie monster?" Sam said.

Startled, Melanie spun around, her Cubs T-shirt speckled with cookie ingredients, her cheeks puffed like a gopher's.

"Okay," she managed to mutter between chews, "but I'm a little disappointed. These really don't taste the same as mom's." She shook the cookie at Sam. "They taste kind of chalky."

"Well nothing ever tastes as good as your mom makes it." Sam picked up the brass flour container and turned it over. A bit of flour dropped onto the counter. He wiped it into the sink with his palm and rinsed his hand under the tap. He waved the canister in front of his wife. "Whatcha gonna do with this thing?"

"I don't know," she said, popping another cookie in her mouth and taking the container from her husband. "Maybe I'll wash it and turn it into a vase. It'd be cute, don't you think?"

Sam wrapped his arm around her waist. "I don't know how cute a vase it would make, but I know how cute you'd be naked." He cupped his right hand around her breast and squeezed. "I bet Betty Crocker never baked cookies like these."

Sam scooped his wife into his arms, crossed the kitchen, and carried her into the bedroom. But while they made love, Melanie kept thinking about the cookies cooling on the kitchen counter.

Melanie walked in the front door, stomped the dirt from her shoes, and turned the letter over in her hands. Sam, sitting on the sofa watching the 49er's pound the daylights out of the Minnesota Vikings, looked up when Melanie entered the room.

"So, did any one send us money?" he said.

"No, but my sister sent me a letter," Melanie said. "But the postmark reads Albuquerque."

"Must've gotten lost. That's our postal service for you. Raise the prices and provide poor service. Could you imagine if the rest of the world ran that way? I just don't understand why your sister doesn't call or e-mail. It'd make things so much simpler."

"I know, but you know Dana. The world is one big conspiracy to her and the phone companies and computers are a big part of it."

"She always was a bit of a radical."

"She never has much to say anyways."

"Uh-huh," Sam only half listened to his wife now. He was intent on the football game.

Melanie walked into the kitchen, grabbed the last cookie from the jar, and took a butter knife from the drawer. Holding the cookie between her teeth, she slipped the blade of the knife beneath the envelope flap and slit it open. She unfolded the letter and scanned her sister's tight, close handwriting.

The cookie dropped from her mouth and broke into a dozen sugary pieces when it hit the floor. Her hands trembled and her legs turned to rubber. She dropped into one of the kitchen chairs. The letter slipped from her fingers and fluttered to the air like a wounded butterfly. Something in her head snapped when her sanity collapsed.

Sam, hearing the commotion in the kitchen, rushed into the room. He looked at his wife with dumbfounded bewilderment.

Melanie was sprawled on a chair, her legs spread out in front of her. A string of drool, like nylon thread, streamed from the corner of her mouth and gathered on the swell of her left breast. Cookie crumbs speckled her lap. Her unblinking eyes stared endlessly forward.

"What is it, Melanie? Did something happen to Dana?"

Melanie struggled to speak. Though her lips moved, no sound emerged from them.

Sam leaned closer, putting his ear next to his wife's lips. Her voice was faint, nothing more than a whisper.

"Cannonball. Cannonball."

"Cannonball?" Sam said, grasping his wife's shoulder. "I don't understand?"

"Cannonball. Cannonball."

Sam shook his head. What happened to his wife? Why was she behaving like this? Did something happen to Dana?

Spying the letter, Sam leaned over and plucked it from the floor. He read it once . . . then again . . . and again.

Dear Sis,

News like this is never easy to share, so I guess it's best I just tell it like it is. While you and Sam were gone mother passed away. I tried to reach you and tell you the sad news, but was unable. (I guess you must've left those cell phones of yours home.) The mortician, Pastor Clarke, and I agreed we couldn't wait for your return before mom's funeral so that has already been taken care of. (I hope you forgive me for that, but I didn't know what else to do and you were going to be gone for such a long time.)

As you know, Mother's last request was she be cremated. (Remember the fight we had with her trying to convince her cremation was better for the environment than burial.) Because you couldn't be at the funeral and knowing that you were much closer to her than I, I thought it was only right you should have her remains.

In a few days you'll receive a package. Inside you'll find a simple brass urn. I remember how much mom loved that old maple tree in your backyard. Maybe you'd like to lay mom to rest there. I'd have delivered her remains myself, but I fell down a flight of stairs and am out of commission for at least six months. (When it rains, it pours, I guess.)

Again, I'm sorry having to drop this on you this way, but I didn't know what else to do.

> *Love Always,*
> *Dana*

Sam stared at the brass container on the dining table. It was filled with an arrangement of dried flowers—*dead* flowers. He remembered when he turned the canister over and a small amount of flour spilled onto the counter. He remembered wiping the powder into the sink and flushing it down the drain with a blast of water. After all, it was just flour—wasn't it?

"Cannonball," Melanie whispered. "Cannonball. Cannonball. Cannonball."

"Oh my God," Sam said. "That's impossible."

At last, Sam realized the word his wife muttered was not *Cannonball*, but *Cannibal*.

"The Diary of Sophronia Winters":
Tension, Terror, and a Fire Axe

a review by denise noe

First broadcast on the radio on April 27, 1943 on the anthology program *Suspense!*, "The Diary of Sophronia Winters" is a tense audio drama. Agnes Moorehead stars as Sophronia Winters and Ray Collins as Hirum Johnson and both play their parts perfectly.

At the start of the story, Sophronia says, "For forty years, I've never had what could really be called a thrilling experience." (Later we learn that she was born in 1892 which means these events are set in 1932.) She has used her inheritance from her father's death to travel to St. Petersburg, Florida. On the beach, she meets handsome, friendly Hiram Johnson. The two feel an immediate connection, partly because of her name.

"My sister-in-law's name was Sophronia," Hiram cheerfully comments. He also says they look quite alike.

When Hiram and Sophronia find a nine-point starfish, he remarks, "My sister-in-law Sophronia used to collect nine-point starfishes."

Hiram proposes marriage. He runs a hotel in Maine and would love to have Sophronia's help.

They marry and the next scene finds them entering the hotel. It is without visitors at this time of year. As Hiram brings her inside, we hear a pained Sophronia complain that he is hurting her arm.

Then he forces her to look at a wall portrait of sister-in-law Sophronia.

He says, "She was murderess. She was hanged in Portland twenty-five years ago

for the murder of my brother Ephraim." She murdered Ephraim in the hotel lobby. The weapon she used was a fire axe that still hangs on the wall in the hallway on the way to that lobby.

Our narrator Sophronia is understandably horrified.

After midnight, Hiram insists Sophronia visit his sister-in-law's grave that is on the grounds. Ominously Hiram says he knew she "was one of those restless sleepers who wouldn't stay quiet" in the grave but would find a way to roam around.

Most horrifyingly, Hiram elaborates that he has found her three times in different guises. There are three graves of women he murdered because he believed them incarnations of homicidal sister-in-law Sophronia! There is a fourth grave dug but not yet filled.

Naturally, our narrator Sophronia is terrified that the fourth grave is meant for her. Her fear for her fate also draws her attention to that fire axe on the wall.

Good audio drama depends not only on the story and acting but on the sound effects which are top-of-the-line in "The Diary of Sophronia Winters." The sounds of waves, of footsteps, of keys in locks and doors opening and shutting all help to paint the scenes in the mind's eye.

"The Diary of Sophronia Winters" is an excellent audio drama that should be heard and savored by anyone who appreciates the best in suspense.

Dark Shadows:
The Soap Opera,
the Horror Show

a review by denise noe

The original *Dark Shadows* was a unique TV phenomenon. A horror show in a soap opera format, the program was a marriage of as seemingly disparate genres as could be imagined. This bizarre show succeeded as a mixture of the supernatural and the soap opera format, expanding the horizons of both. The result created innovative relationships among characters human and those with supernatural powers—not to mention convoluted, fascinating plot points that in such enchanting detail are not to be found elsewhere, either in literature or experimental television.

Dark Shadows was originally planned as a "Gothic" soap opera. It utilized the tried-and-true formula of Gothic fiction: a foundling searching for her roots, a secluded mansion, and an eccentric, wealthy recluse. Dark secrets and memories of past transgressions haunted its tormented characters.

A similar experiment had been attempted on *The Guiding Light* TV series a few years previously but failed. The Gothic elements were discarded, the Mrs. Danvers-type housekeeper returned to her native Scotland, and the show was absorbed into the normal florescent-lit soap opera world.

The suggestive Gothicism of *Dark Shadows* also failed, as originally attempted. Since the show's ratings were poor, Dan Curtis, the show's creator, along with the scriptwriters, floundered desperately for a gimmick to save it. Several ghosts of the "maybe they really are, maybe they are imagined" variety appeared. Then the show "crossed-over" into the "real" supernatural with the appearance of a ghost in a scene that featured the ghost alone.

When it went completely supernatural, it was through the discovery of a chained vampire, Barnabas, in the family mausoleum; this event was quickly followed by the introduction of the child ghost, Sarah, who had been the vampire's little sister in life nearly two hundred years ago. A doctor appeared on the scene and made an effort to cure the vampire of his vampirism, and not only that—the female doctor, Julia Hoffman, fell in love with the vampire Barnabas. These innovative developments revolutionized the show's stories, and Dark Shadows became very ambitious. The witch responsible for the curse, Angelique, continued to hound him through the ages. Black magic, warlocks, the Frankenstein monster, werewolves, various curses, one character taking possession of another, time travel mostly backward, twice parallel, and, in one case, forward—they all had turns at shaping this television phenomenon. Unlike the typical soap operas, there were special effects always pushing the available resources of the show. And perhaps most memorable was the truly eerie music by composer Robert Cobert with his orchestra. Atmosphere and dreams were also important in establishing mood.

Dark Shadows left behind the grown-ups' reality of pesky logic and cumbersome physical laws for the children's universe—a place where time is endlessly fluid, identity in flux, and the miracle is the everyday. Thus, it was appropriate that the child actors played their characters not as learners stumbling uncertainly through a world new to them, but rather as miniature adults: mature, wise, and confident.

Dark Shadows demonstrated that the two genres could be made to fit together surprisingly well, probably because they had more in common than anyone had previously suspected. For example, death on *Dark Shadows* was a way station, not an endpoint. We wait for the character to come back as ghost, vampire, phoenix, or to be reincarnated. We may miss the deceased for a few episodes or we may find them with us the next day in a different time zone, i.e., past, present, future, or "parallel."

A form of this development is actually quite conventional within the soap opera genre. After all, any soap opera fan worth his/her salt knows what to expect when a character is believed dead but the body is not found or is destroyed beyond identification. Our erstwhile hero/heroine will be declared dead. Then we may see his/her funeral and watch as the heirs feud over the will. But it's only a matter of time before we meet the "deceased" again. Usually he/she will have amnesia, a most peculiar form of amnesia in which all faculties are retained but no life history is remembered. (This Soap Opera Amnesia has a questionable medical basis.)

In the web of character relationships that make up a soap opera world, the personalities of *Dark Shadows* had all the possibilities given to the traditional soaps' inhabitants—plus one. As Robert C. Allen comments in "A Reader-Oriented Poetics of the Soap Opera," there are three major types of relationships between soap opera characters: kinship, romantic, and social. Much of the appeal of soap opera resides in the complexity and overlap among these categories of actual and potential relationships for any particular character. Mistaken parentage has been a stock device in soap operas for decades. Enemies can become brothers; sisters, merely close friends; fathers, foster-fathers; and so on—all at the drop of a discovered birth certificate. On *Dark Shadows*, such character development can take on an even more complex character – such as when two enemies find it necessary to become at least temporary friends working together to destroy a greater, mutual enemy.

Soap operas have traditionally shown that the role is more important than the actor who plays it by their habit of frequently replacing the actor and carrying on with the story line. *Dark Shadows* demonstrated the primary importance of role over performer by reversing this time-honored soap practice of the same actors being cast as different characters. Thus, as Kathryn Leigh Scott, a *Dark Shadows* actress until the last year, observed in *My Scrapbook Memories of Dark Shadows*, the program's actors functioned like a stock company with a repertoire of characters. Perhaps this innovation was successful with the public for much the same reason that the rare illness of Multiple Personality Disorder is an epidemic throughout TV and popular literature. The actor is able to explore multiple facets of his/her talent and actually deepen the appeal of the character.

In one way, the soap opera format meshed with horror as a fortuitous accident. Jonathan Frid, who became the show's biggest star, had been a Shakespearean stage actor. He was what is known, by his own admission, as a slow study. The unedited, virtually live format of *Dark Shadows* required him to memorize his lines in the morning and say them the same afternoon. His distress was ironically the show's gain. The look of controlled panic on Frid's face as he tried to recall his lines became the sexy vampire's signature gaze of enigmatic mystery.

The original *Dark Shadows* did not eschew the standard soap opera themes of romantic passion and unrequited love—in fact, far from it. Much of the series centered around witch Angelique's unrequited love for vampire Barnabas as well as his never-ending attempts to re-unite with his beloved Josette or one of her many incarnations.

In the primary love story of *Dark Shadows*, the soap opera format joined with horror's imaginative freedom to yield a special poignancy. Robert C. Allen discusses two relevant types of fictional "duration: story-duration (the days, months, years depicted in the narrative) and reading-duration: the actual time it takes to read the text." In both senses the romantic passions of Angelique and Barnabas were long-lasting. The "reading-duration" lasted through four years on the air. But, of course, the "story-duration" was far more impressive, lasting through centuries. The long, drawn-out plot(s) following Angelique and Barnabas through so many bizarre travails contributed mightily to making their amorous frustrations sympathetic and popular with the audience.

The writers of *Dark Shadows* have acknowledged borrowing scenarios liberally from a variety of classic works. *The Picture of Dorian Gray*, *Frankenstein*, *The Turn of the Screw*, *Wuthering Heights*, *Dr. Jekyll and Mr. Hyde*, and some lesser-known horror stories by H.P. Lovecraft, are only a few of the works they drew upon. How they used these influences in the *Dark Shadows* stories was exceptionally creative.

But no source that I have read has commented on the strong resemblance of the central love affair in *Dark Shadows* to that of the major romance in America's cultural psyche: Angelique-loves-Barnabas-loves-Josette echoed the Rhett-loves-Scarlett-loves-Ashley scenario of *Gone With The Wind*. In both triangles, there is a gut feeling that the first two characters—the acrimonious couplings—really belong together.

The denouement of the Angelique-Barnabas tale is ultimately tragic and bitter—yet also lingering with hope—as is the fabled ending of *GWTW*. As the soap opera wound toward cancellation, Angelique performed an unexpected act of generosity that led Barnabas to the startling realization that she is indeed his "one true love." But before he can tell her, she dies in his arms. Like Scarlett O'Hara, Barnabas has been blind to his true love. Like Scarlett, he realizes the truth when it is too late.

Or is it? The ambiguity of *GWTW*'s ending has surely helped immortalize the love story. Rhett Butler's "Frankly, my dear, I don't give a damn!" and his disappearance in the mists is followed by the intrepid Scarlett's vow that she will win him back since, after all, "Tomorrow is another day." And millions of fans have been left to fantasize over the possibilities.

Similarly, no death on *Dark Shadows* is ever truly final—though Angelique's was about as final as it could be since the original series was discontinued shortly after her demise. But the viewer is left with the tantalizing possibility of a resurrection (ghost, vampire, reincarnation) that will unite Angelique with her Barnabas.

Perhaps it is more than coincidence that a new (though short-lived) *Dark Shadows* returned to television at approximately the same time Scarlett, Alexandra Ripley's ill-reviewed but best-selling sequel to *Gone With The Wind*, was published. I don't want to suggest anything supernatural (?!) at work here. However, *Dark Shadows* and *Gone With The Wind* are akin in that both stories reflect the Western tradition placing romantic love at the center of life, and both are part of our evolving American cultural mythos.

End Notes:

Allen, Robert C. "A Reader-Oriented Poetics of the Soap Opera." *Imitations of Life: A Reader on Film and Television Melodrama*, ed. by Landy, Marcia. Detroit. Wayne State University Press. 1991.
Scott, Kathryn Leigh. *My Scrapbook Memories of Dark Shadows*. Pomegranate Press. 1986.

A previous version of this essay was published in "World of "World of Dark Shadows"" and has appeared online at "Men's News Daily."

The Innocents:
A Victorian Terror Tale

a review by denise noe

Released in 1961 and filmed in black and white, *The Innocents* is a subtle re-working of Henry James' classic *The Turn of the Screw*. It is directed with a sure hand by Jack Clayton and boasts an excellent screenplay co-authored by Truman Capote and William Archibald.

Deborah Kerr plays governess Miss Giddens, Megs Jenkins housekeeper Mrs. Grose, and Michael Redgrave the Uncle of orphans Flora (Pamela Franklin) and Miles (Martin Stephens).

The film opens with Uncle engaging Miss Giddens to care for the orphans at a country estate called Bly. He says their previous governess died but advises Giddens to avoid the subject with the children because they were extremely fond of Miss Jessel.

Giddens appears happy at the sprawling estate as she cares for Flora. The governess is distressed to find Miles has been expelled from school for reasons that the officials do not make clear. When she meets him, he seems like a good boy.

However, from the start of her life at the estate, Giddens is unsure about things she hears and sees. She becomes convinced that ghosts haunt Bly. When Mrs. Grose tells of its history, the violent love of the deceased valet Quince and Miss Jessel, Giddens is certain of the identities of those "horrors." Giddens believes they threaten the children. But the film leaves open the possibility that it is Giddens herself who threatens them.

Perhaps the most unsettling parts of the film are Giddens' ambiguous reactions to Miles. There is a hint that a forbidden desire creeps over her when she kisses the ten-year-old child. That hint is given special force when he innocently states, "You can't say there's not a man here because I'm here."

In his single scene, Michael Redgrave is credible as the relative saddled with children in whom he takes no real interest. Megs Jenkins gives us a Mrs. Grose who is appropriately responsible, caring and earnest. Both Martin Stephens and Pamela Franklin are credible as charming children who could be keeping secrets.

However, the film really belongs to Deborah Kerr. Her nuanced and many-layered portrait of the governess who may or may not be hallucinating catapults the film into greatness.

The Innocents is free from the blood and guts that modern horror so often features. Yet it tantalizes and terrorizes more than many graphic films. It also marvelously lingers in the mind. *The Innocents* shows the power wielded by suggestion. This review is meant to suggest that anyone who appreciates the finest in restrained horror see *The Innocents*.

The Andy Griffith Show: "The Haunted House"

a review by denise noe

The Andy Griffith Show is one of television's most famous situation comedies and, in this writer's opinion, one of its best programs ever. Interestingly, one episode, "The Haunted House," should have a special appeal to Borden buffs.

Little Opie Taylor (Ronny Howard) and pal Arnold Winkler (Ronnie Dapo) are playing when Opie bats a baseball through the window (crash!) of what appears to be an abandoned house. The boys run up to the place and hear an eerie noise. The rumors that this house, known as the haunted Rimshaw House, seem to be true!

Cut to the Mayberry jail: Sheriff Andy Taylor, Deputy Barney Fife, and perennial inmate, town drunk Otis Campbell. Of course, Otis is a drunk in a "dry" county so Andy and Barney suspect he's getting his booze from a bootlegger's still but get no information about his source from him.

Opie tells Andy, his Dad, as well as Barney, about the baseball lost in the forbidding House.

Andy, Barney, and slow-witted filling station employee Gomer Pyle (Jim Nabors) all make treks to the Rimshaw House. Fife and Nabors give especially humorous performances as grown men utterly terrified by the abode in which a hatchet appears to float in the air, eyes in a painting move, and mysterious knocks are heard.

Gazing at a painted portrait, Gomer says, "That's old man Rimshaw who put chains on his hired man—and then done away with him!"

Barney adds, "With an axe!"

"With an axe!" Gomer exclaims. "Shazaam!"

This reviewer cannot help but wonder if the Lizzie Borden case and spooky stories about the scene of the crime were not somewhere in the back of the mind of the writer of this episode, Harvey Bullock, when he crafted this storyline.

As one might expect, there are reasonable explanations for the seemingly supernatural occurrences. This is *The Andy Griffith Show* after all. The revelation about a distillery hidden in a reputed haunted house is clever and funny. Andy Griffith is the level-headed one, of course, while his sidekicks Barney and Gomer get the chance to demonstrate their comedic reactions to what is actually a set-up of phony supernatural trickery.

As one might expect, there are reasonable explanations for the seemingly supernatural occurrences—after all, this is *The Andy Griffith Show*!—and those "reasonable explanations" are satisfyingly clever. To anyone who might be viewing "The Haunted House" episode of *The Andy Griffith Show* for the first time, and to anyone who looks forward to re-watching this superb episode of a classic sitcom, this writer says a hearty and heartfelt, "Have fun!"

[advertisement]

Lizzie Borden: Resurrections

A history of the people surrounding the Borden case before, during, and after the trial

by Sherry Chapman

$21.95

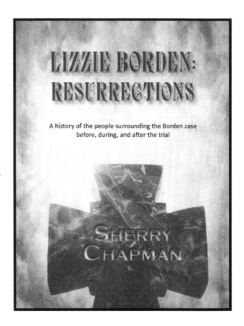

Whatever happened to Lizzie Borden after the trial that accused her of bludgeoning her father and stepmother with a hatchet in 1892 Fall River, Massachusetts? It's all in here, and it doesn't stop with Lizzie. A plethora of persons were involved around her in some way. From her friends to her foes, from the doctors to the policemen; from her Manse to The Nance, at last comes the first book of its kind that tells what caused Officer Philip Harrington (who greatly disliked Lizzie) to die suddenly in 1893. What happened to neighbor and friend Dr. Bowen after the crime and trial? Why doesn't Edwin Porter, who covered the trial then wrote the first contemporary book on the murders, *The Fall River Tragedy*, have a gravestone – and who is buried with him? Not by him. Actually with him.

From original source documents, photos of the graves, obituaries and death certificates each on whom records could be found has their story told in details unknown until now. What were they doing before anyone much had heard of Lizzie Borden? What was their role in the case? When did they die and how?

Some of the results may surprise you, whether you read this book for pleasure or research. There are no legends here, but a factual telling of the stories of these persons who are today all gone but need not be forgotten. And with this book they may be hard to forget.

Available *NOW* through createspace.com/4876021

FOR WHOLESALE INQUIRIES, PLEASE WRITE TO:
PearTree Press, P.O. Box 9585
Fall River, MA 02720
peartreepress@mac.com

[*advertisement*]

Lizzie Borden:
The Girl with the Pansy Pin

a novel by Michael Thomas Brimbau

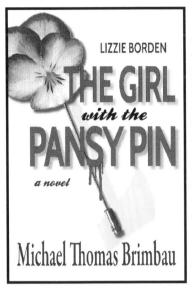

Lizzie Borden and her sister Emma lived a life of privilege and entitlement, with wealth and social status far greater than their neighbors. But it was not enough. In time, Lizzie and Emma grew restless, aching for a more opulent life—to reside on the Hill in a big house amongst their peers and Fall River's finest families.

But Father's riches were window dressing, dangling just beyond their reach—quarantined by a frugal patriarch who was unable or unwilling to change his scrimping ways. Andrew Jackson Borden had no intention of moving to the Hill and abandoning the home he had purchased for his second wife, or spending the money he had worked so hard for all his life. Now he was planning to give it all away—to his wife, their stepmother.

In time, discord in the family began to ferment and fester—and there were signs that things were not as they should be.

On a sultry August morning, in the naked light of day, someone entered 92 Second Street and brutally hacked and murdered Andrew and Abby Borden. Soon the finger of guilt pointed to Lizzie. But she loved her father. He meant everything to her. The gold ring she had lovingly given him and that he always wore said as much. She would never have harmed him. Or would she?

The Girl with the Pansy Pin tells the gripping story of a desirable and vivacious young Victorian woman desperately longing for adventure and a lavish life. Instead, she was condemned to waste away in a stale, modest existence, in a father's foregone reality, with little chance of ever discovering love, happiness, or fulfillment. Now they have charged poor Lizzie with double murder.

Available *NOW* through createspace.com/4343650
$22.95

FOR WHOLESALE INQUIRIES, PLEASE WRITE TO:
PearTree Press, P.O. Box 9585
Fall River, MA 02720
peartreepress@mac.com

Get the latest news at
girlwiththepansypin.com

[advertisement]

A River and Its City

The influence of the Quequechan River on the Development of Fall River, Massachusetts

Second Edition

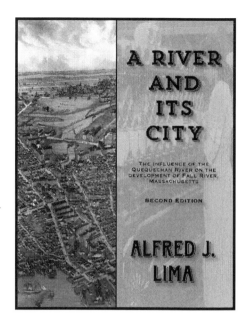

by Alfred J. Lima

with contributions by Kenneth M. Champlin and Everett J. Castro

For such a relatively small stream, the history and impact of the Quequechan River on the Southeast region of Massachusetts, the United States, and the world is rather remarkable.

No other river can boast all of the following: it has unique geologic characteristics; native tribes have used it for thousands of years; it has been the location of the full gamut of Colonial industries; it was the site of one of the significant battles of King Philip's War; it is the backdrop of a poem by Henry Wadsworth Longfellow; it has its own witch legend; and it was the site of a battle with the British during the Revolutionary War.

In addition, it provided the power that initiated the textile industry in Fall River, and it later provided the process water for cooling the steam engines for textile mills, making the city the largest cotton textile manufacturing center in the country at the time and the largest in the world after Manchester, England.

Available *NOW* through https://www.createspace.com/4380290

$20.00

FOR WHOLESALE INQUIRIES, PLEASE WRITE TO:
PearTree Press
P.O. Box 9585
Fall River, MA 02720
peartreepress@mac.com

Fall River Revisited

[*advertisement*]

by Stefani Koorey and the Fall River History Club

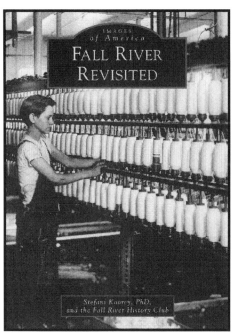

Founded in 1803, Fall River changed its name the following year to Troy, after a resident visiting Troy, New York, enjoyed the city. In 1834, the name was officially changed back to Fall River.

The city's motto, "We'll Try," originates from the determination of its residents to rebuild the city following a devastating fire in 1843. The fire resulted in 20 acres in the center of the village being destroyed, including 196 buildings, and 1,334 people were displaced from their homes.

Once the capital of cotton textile manufacturing in the United States, by 1910, Fall River boasted 43 corporations, 222 mills, and 3.8 million spindles, producing two miles of cloth every minute of every working day in the year. The workforce was comprised of immigrants from Ireland, England, Scotland, Canada, the Azores, and, to a lesser extent, Poland, Italy, Greece, Russia, and Lebanon.

Available *NOW*
$22.00

Now Available!

The Sadness I Take to Sea and Other Poems

by Michael Thomas Brimbau

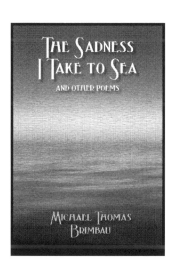

[*advertisement*]

Do Come In
and Other Lizzie Borden Poems

by Larry W. Allen

with a new Lizzie Borden sketch cover by Rick Geary, famed author and illustrator of *The Borden Tragedy*.

Lizzie Borden. For some, the name conjures an innocent young woman who bravely faced her trial with strength and fortitude. To others, she has become the icon of all things gruesome because of the bloody nature of the crimes for which she was charged. And yet others see Lizzie Borden as a woman who got away with murder.

These 50 poems trace the life of this enigmatic woman—from the 19th through the 20th century. We meet her as a young adult and watch her develop into an old woman living alone on "the Hill."

Do Come In is a remarkable collection of poems entirely devoted to the Lizzie Borden story.

So *Do Come In*, and meet Lizzie Borden and other characters as diverse as Jack the Ripper, Bob and Charlie Ford, and Rachael Ray, in poems that range from humorous to horrific.

Available *NOW* through https://www.createspace.com/3354462.

$14.00

FOR WHOLESALE INQUIRIES, PLEASE WRITE TO:
PearTree Press
P.O. Box 9585
Fall River, MA 02720
peartreepress@mac.com

Lizzie Borden: Girl Detective

by Richard Behrens

Introducing Miss Lizzie Borden of Fall River, Massachusetts, a most excellent girl detective and the most remarkable young woman ever to take on the criminal underworld in late 19th century New England.

Many years before her infamous arrest and trial for the murders of her father and stepmother, Lizzie Borden pursued a career as a private consulting detective and wrestled unflinchingly with a crooked spiritualist, a corrupt and murderous textile tycoon, a secret society of anarchist assassins, rowdy and deadly sporting boys, a crazed and vengeful mutineer, an industrial saboteur, and a dangerously unhinged math professor—none of whom are exactly what they seem to be.

In these five early tales of mystery and adventure, Lizzie Borden is joined by her stubborn and stingy father Andrew; her jealous and weak-chinned sister Emma; her trusted companion Homer Thesinger the Boy Inventor; and the melancholy French scion Andre De Camp. Together, they explore Fall River's dark side through a landscape that is industrial, Victorian, and distinctly American.

You have met Lizzie Borden before— but never like this!

Available **NOW** through https://www.createspace. com/3441135.
$14.95

FOR WHOLESALE INQUIRIES, PLEASE WRITE TO:
PearTree Press
P.O. Box 9585
Fall River, MA 02720
peartreepress@mac.com

Get the latest news at
LizzieBordenGirlDetective.com

Contributors

Alex Johnston is a paleontology student and aspiring author.

Phillip Jones is a senior in high school and lives in rural Tennessee.

Nicholas Larche is native to New York and is currently attending the University of Detroit Mercy School of Law. While an adept researcher, Nicholas prefers to write flash fiction and poetry. His work has been published and is forthcoming in the *Seton Hall Legislative Journal*.

Darrell Lindsey is the author of *Edge Of The Pond* (Popcorn Press, 2012) and has been nominated for a Pushcart Prize (2007) and a Rhysling Award (2014). He won the 2012 Science Fiction Poetry Association Contest (Long Form category), as well as the 2014 Balticon Poetry Contest.

Amanda Rioux is an amateur writer, professional daydreamer, avid pizza enthusiast and hater of the Oxford Comma. She watches entirely too much television, considers Liz Lemon her spirit animal, and has an admitted problem with procrastina....

Francis J. Kelly was born in Dungannon, County Tyrone, on the 2nd of April 1933. He received the gold medal for his primary school teacher training at St. Patrick's College Drumcondra and later studied Irish, English, and Economics at University College Dublin where he met his wife Olive. He also studied for the HDip in University College Dublin and taught Latin and English at Saint Michael's College for over 30 years. He passed away in January 2014.

Bruce Boston's poetry has received the Bram Stoker Award, the Asimov's Readers Award, the Gothic Readers Choice Award, the Rhysling Award, and the Grandmaster Award of the Science Fiction Poetry Association.

Mark Patrick Lynch lives and writes in the UK. His short fiction, mainstream and genre, has appeared in print anthologies and journals ranging from *Alfred Hitchcock's Mystery Magazine* to *Zahir*. His book, HOUR OF THE BLACK WOLF, is published by Robert Hale Ltd. An e-book original novella, *What I Wouldn't Give*, is available for ereaders. You can find him online at markpatricklynch.blogspot.com and @markplynch on Twitter.

Wayne Scheer has been nominated for four Pushcart Prizes and a Best of the Net. He's published hundred of stories, poems and essays in print and online, including *Revealing Moments*, a collection of flash stories, available at http://issuu.com/pearnoir/docs/revealing_moments. A short film has also been produced based on his short story, "Zen and the Art of House Painting." Wayne lives in Atlanta with his wife.

Rick McQuiston is a forty-five-year-old father of two who loves anything horror-related. His work has appeared in over 300 publications. He has written three novels, six anthology books, one book of novellas, and edited an anthology of Michigan authors. Currently, he is hard at work on his fifth novel.

Fabiyas M V. was born in Orumanayur village in Kerala, India. He won the Poetry Soup International Award, USA, in 2011 and 2012, a prize by the British Council in 2011, the Whistle Press Poetry Contest, India, in 2012, and the RSPCA Pet Poetry Contest, UK, 2012. *Moonlight and Solitude* is his first book, published by Raspberry Books, Calicut, Kerala, India. His poems have been broadcast on All India Radio.

Gary Pierluigi is a Canadian poet.

Vic Kerry lives and writes in Alabama. He is married with six dogs and one cat. His novel, *The Children of Lot*, and novella, *Decoration Day*, are available at multiple online bookstores.

Angela Ash has, as she states, "experienced many odd and interesting things in my travels, but my current muse is my niece, who most decidedly emerged from the rabbit hole five years ago." Angela lives in Louisville, Kentucky "with my ever understanding husband and our two beautiful girls ... often referred to as "cats" by some terribly uncreative people."

Nick Nafpliotis is a music teacher and writer from Charleston, South Carolina. During the day, he instructs students from the ages of 11-14 on how to play band instruments. At night, he writes about weird crime, bizarre history, pop culture, and humorous classroom experiences on his blog, RamblingBeachCat.com. He is also a television, novel, and comic book reviewer for AdventuresinPoorTaste.com.

James B. Nicola is the winner of three poetry awards and recipient of one Rhysling and two Pushcart nominations, has published over 400 poems in *Atlanta Review, Tar River, Texas Review, &c.* A Yale grad and stage director by profession, his book *Playing the Audience* won a Choice Award. First full-length collection: "Manhattan Plaza" scheduled for 2014.

Phil Richardson is retired and lives in Athens, Ohio, where he writes fiction and memoirs. His wife, whom he met in a creative writing class at Ohio University, is a poet and a mystery writer. Two of Phil's stories were nominated for the Pushcart Prize in Fiction and he has won or placed in several writing contests including *The Starving Writer, Five Stop Story, Wild Violet, Writers Digest Contest, Green River Writers*, and *ELF: Eclectic Literary Forum*.His publications include over seventy stories in on-line publications and in print, including such magazines as *Five Stop Story* (UK), *Big Pulp, Greensilk Journal, Danse Macabre, The Starving Writer*, and *The Storyteller*. Phil's website with links to some published stories is philrichardsonstories.com

Holly Dunlea is a veteran teacher at Pembroke Academy in Pembroke, New Hampshire. "I lead a quiet country life, but when I travel, I love adventure. I have traveled through all of the lower 48 states and have observed a myriad of American behavior that demonstrates the diversity of our country. Wherever I find myself, I keep writing, and I have maintained that love of writing with the help of inspirational teachers and kind friends." Holly lives in Loudon, New Hampshire, with her husband, Pat.

Meg Eden has been published in various magazines, including *B O D Y*, *Drunken Boat*, *Mudfish*, and *Rock & Sling*. Her work received second place in the 2014 Ian MacMillan Fiction contest. Her collections include "Your Son" (The Florence Kahn Memorial Award), "Rotary Phones and Facebook" (Dancing Girl Press) and "The Girl Who Came Back" (Red Bird Chapbooks). She teaches at the University of Maryland, and will be a visiting writer at AACC in 2014. Check out her work on FaceBook at megedenwritespoems

Kevin Holton is the author of seventeen short stories and several dozen newspaper articles under various names. His book review "On Aimee Bender's The Color Master" will be featured in the coming issue of *Pleiades*, and he is a member in good standing of both Mensa and Sigma Tau Delta. Kevin is also a junior editor with an independent publication company.

Santos Vargas was born in NYC in 1962. He has been dabbling in poetry for years. He enjoys his hobby of writing and performing on his spare time. He currently lives in Pennsylvania.

Chantal Boudreau is the author of ten novels, seven of them published by May December Publications, and dozens of short stories with a variety of publishers, primarily fantasy and horror, the most recent in *The Grotesquerie*, an all-female horror anthology from Mocha Memoirs Press, and *Chimerical World: Tale of the Seelie Court* from Seventh Star Press. She is a member of the Horror Writers Association in good standing.

Adrian Brooks currently lives in the Dallas-Fort Worth area and works as an ad copywriter. "I am much more passionate about creative writing. I've been writing in a variety of styles for several years."

Eugene Hosey holds an MFA from Georgia State University. He has written articles, film and book reviews for *The Hatchet: A Journal of Lizzie Borden & Victorian Studies*. Also he has done editorial work for research documents, books, and personal journals. But he is primarily a short story writer, a regular contributor to *The Literary Hatchet*, and a fiction editor.

Rita Hooks lives in Florida where she works as a writing tutor at a community college. She has published on *East of the Web* and *Haibun Today*. She also has a blog at ritadalyhooks.wordpress.com.

A.A. Garrison is a thirty-year-old man living in the mountains of North Carolina. His short fiction has appeared in dozens of zines and anthologies, and he is the author of *The End of Jack Cruz*, a post-apocalyptic horror novel from Montag Press. He blogs at synchroshock.blogspot.com.

John Hayes is a sculptor who once appeared as a scurvy-looking corpse on *Homicide*. Now he gives poetry readings, acts, and directs in community theatre. *Flesh and Blood, The Literary Hatchet, Night To Dawn, Thema, BareBone, Wily Writers, Modern Haiku, Writers Journal, Champagne Shivers, Premonitions*, and *From the Asylum*, are some of the magazines that have published his work.

Erik Hofstatter is a dark fiction writer, who dwells in a beauteous and serenading Garden of England, where he can be frequently encountered consuming reckless amounts of mead and tyrannizing local peasantry. At a young age, he built a Viking ship and journeyed myriad sea miles away from native land in search of plunder and pillage. His work appeared in various magazines and anthologies around the world such as *Schlock, The Strange and The Curious, Inner Sins, Sanitarium* and *Psychopomp*. *Moribund Tales*, his first collection of short dark fiction was published by Creativia and became Amazon's Top 10 best-selling horror anthology in UK, USA, and Canada.

Walter Dinjos resides in Nigeria where he is writing his first fantasy novel. He blogs about silly story ideas at sillystoryideas.blogspot.com.

Denise Noe lives in Atlanta and writes regularly for The *Caribbean Star* of which she is Community Editor. Her work has been published in *The Humanist, Georgia Journal, Lizzie Borden Quarterly, Exquisite Corpse, The Gulf War Anthology, Light*, and *Gauntlet*.

David Greske is the author of five novels and over twenty short stories that have appeared in several magazines and anthologies including *Black Ink Horror, Thirteen, Bones, Ugly Babies*, and *Barnyard Horror*. He co-wrote the screenplay to his novel, BLOOD RIVER, which has been made into a feature film by ForbesFilm. David currently lives in Minneapolis, Minnesota, where he is busy writing the screenplay for *Blood River 2* and pulling together a collection of his short stories. For further information go to davidgreske.com

Rivka Jacobs has been published in *The Magazine of Fantasy and Science Fiction*, and in the anthology *Women of Darkness*. More recently her stories have appeared in The *Sirens Call* eZine, the "Women in Horror" issues for 2013 and 2014, the "Monster" issue from summer 2013, and the "Revenge" issue from 2013. Another ghost story will appear in the upcoming spring 2014 "Traditional Horror" issue.

Rie Sheridan Rose is a short story writer whose work currently appears in numerous anthologies including *Reloaded: Both Barrels; Nightmare Walkers and Dream Stalkers; In the Bloodstream*; and *The Grotesquerie*. Individual short stories "Drink My Soul...Please," "Bloody Rain," and "Hope's Chest" are available as e-downloads.

Icy Sedgwick was born in the North East of England and lives and works in Newcastle. She has been writing with a view to doing so professionally for over ten years, and has had several stories included in anthologies, including *Short Stack and Bloody Parchment: The Root Cellar & Other Stories*. She spends her non-writing time working on a PhD in Film Studies, considering the use of set design in contemporary horror. Icy had her first book, a pulp Western named *The Guns of Retribution*, published through Pulp Press in September 2011, and re-published through Beat to a Pulp in May 2013. Her novella, a horror fantasy called *The Necromancer's Apprentice*, was published by Dark Continents Publishing in March 2014.

Lee Glantz, Batik artist and poet, was born in Kingman, Arizona, and now lives in Barrington, Rhode Island. Her poems have appeared in *Rhode Island Roads, Crones Nest, Newport Review, Traveling Poets Society, Literary Hatchet, Evening Street Review*, and the anthology, *Regrets Only* (Little Pear Press). Her book, *A House on Her Back*, was published by Premiere Poets Chapbook Series.

David Schultz has been writing poetry and short stories for about five decades. "My subjects haven't always reflected topics in vogue, but I've found that there are people with an appreciation for good things that aren't necessarily in the popularity limelight."

Peter Damien has published short stories in a range of places. Recent ones include "Ghost Love Score," published by South Africa's *Something Wicked* magazine, "The Haunting House" in an anthology called *No Rest For The Wicked*. His day job is as a writer for BookRiot.com, "where I professionally Have Opinions About Books. I live in Seattle, Washington, with my two kids, my parrot, and one gazillion books."

Deborah Walker grew up in the most English town in the country, but she soon high-tailed it down to London, where she now lives with her partner, Chris, and her two young children. Find Deborah in the British Museum trawling the past for future inspiration or on her blog: http://deborahwalkersbibliography.blogspot.com/ Her stories have appeared in *Nature's Futures, Cosmos,* and *Daily Science Fiction* and *The Year's Best SF 18*.

Georgie Lee took the leap from living on top of a mountain to a small apartment in the city. She writes now under the city lights.

Eric Dean lives in Tulsa, Oklahoma, and has loved to write since he was a child—"I still love to write, and I am still a child." Please visit him at his website at ericwrites.com.

Michael Lizarraga was immersed in monster books before he could read and studied Journalism and English Literature at California State University, Northridge. He is a Los Angeles-based horror/fantasy author, a freelance magazine writer, and an old school gothic-thriller/comic book/kung-fu flicks junkie. His work has appeared in anthologies *Tales of the Undead - Suffer Eternal:Vol. III* (Horrified Press), *The Pulpateers* (Schlock!) and *Timeless Worlds* (Schlock!), and in magazines *Bete Noire*, *Blood Moon Rising*, and *Dark Gothic Resurrected*.

Daniel Bulone lives in the rural part of Monterey County, California, where he teaches middle school English.

Brittney Wright has been writing for nine years. She enjoys poetry, short stories & novels. Her inspirations are Jim Morrison & Yves Saint-Laurent. "I believe in writing about emotions and struggle. I think those moments in our life sometimes define us."

Robert Wilson was born and raised in Morgantown, West Virginia. Always controversial, his writings tend to veer towards the darker side of life that most other writers fear to tread and he uses surrealism and dark humor to convey his views. His influences include Chuck Palahniuk, Charles Bukowski, Henry Rollins, and D. Harlan Wilson. You can find more of his writing at robertjw4688. tumblr.com

Paul Magnan has had stories published in *Kazka Press*, *Every Day Fiction*, *The Horror Zine*, *eFiction*, and several other venues.

Matthew Wilson, 30, has had over 100 appearances in such places as *Horror Zine*, *Star*Line*, *Spellbound*, *Illumen*, *Apokrupha Press*, *Hazardous Press*, *Gaslight Press*, *Sorcerers Signal* and many more. He is currently editing his first novel and can be contacted on twitter @ matthew94544267.

Navo Banerjee is a researcher from Berkeley, California. "I aim not only to create, but reveal something about nature with every piece of my own poetry and fiction."

Literary
THE Hatchet

34593050R00116

Made in the USA
Charleston, SC
12 October 2014